Llyfrgelloedd Caerdydd
www.caerdydd
Cardiff Lik
www.cardiff.gc

D1142833

The Cornerstone

A fast-paced fantasy adventure from Nick Spalding, the bestselling author of the smash hit romantic comedy *Love... From Both Sides* and its sequels *Love... And Sleepless Nights* & *Love... Under Different Skies*.

A great book will transport you to another world...
literally, **if you're not careful.**

On a gloomy Thursday afternoon, Max Bloom enters his local library in a last ditch attempt to stave off an epic case of teenage boredom. Among the hushed stacks he discovers The Cornerstone, an ancient book tucked away on a dusty, forgotten shelf. Opening the cover, Max is instantly transported to an alternate dimension full of things intent on killing him - thus avoiding boredom with *remarkable* success.

He meets a beautiful girl called Merelie (brilliant), who tells him he could be a Wordsmith, a sorcerer able to craft magic from the written word itself, one strong enough to save both their worlds from the Dwellers - hideous monsters from beyond the universe (not so brilliant).

This all sounds completely unbelievable. The kind of thing you'd read in a fantasy novel. But The Cornerstone doesn't lie... and the danger is very real.

In a world threatened by monsters, where books are worshipped and powerful magic exists, Max Bloom must make a choice: close The Cornerstone and run home - or trust Merelie, become a Wordsmith, and save two worlds from certain destruction...

WITHDRAWN FROM STOCK

ACC. No: 02929999

By Nick Spalding:

Love... From Both Sides
Love... And Sleepless Nights
Love... Under Different Skies

Life… With No Breaks
Life… On A High

The Cornerstone
Wordsmith: The Cornerstone Book 2

Copyright © Nick Spalding 2011

First published in Great Britain in 2011

This second edition published 2013 by Racket Publishing

The rights of Nick Spalding to be identified as the author of this
work have been asserted in accordance with the Copyright, Designs
and Patents Act 1988.

All rights reserved. No part of this publication may be
reproduced, stored in a retrieval system, or transmitted in any form
or by any means, electronic, mechanical, photocopying, recording
or otherwise, without the prior permission of the publisher.

The Cornerstone

Nick Spalding

Racket Publishing

Contents

Part One

It was, for all intents and purposes, the perfect day to visit the library.

A sullen, overcast October afternoon, it was the kind of day the word listless seemed invented to describe – until you remembered somebody had also thought up charmless, which was even more appropriate.

It was drizzling. The constant, *sticky* kind that's good at getting under the collar and giving anyone foolish enough to venture outside a wet neck for their trouble. You'd think all hope and joy had been banished from the world on a grey afternoon like this – if you were in a melodramatic frame of mind.

Max Bloom was just plain bored as he reached the town centre, having been forced out of the house by his irate mother.

The town was Farefield, which nestled on the south coast of England between two major cities - and suffered from something of an inferiority complex because of it.

It was a Thursday. This doesn't have any bearing on the events about to unfold, but the devil is always in the details, if you look hard enough.

Max trudged along, a boy with less sense of purpose than an ambivalent sloth. He meandered through the shopping precinct like a miniature rain cloud. The shoppers gave him a wide berth, trying to avoid the aura of teenage misery he emanated from every pore. On this overcast day, Max had turned moping about into an art form. If it was an Olympic event he'd win. Or rather he wouldn't, as the effort of taking part would be too much of a bother.

You could tell how morose he was just from his body language.

His hands were plunged into the pockets of the black hoodie he wore, the hood up to protect his sandy hair from the incessant drizzle. His shoulders were slumped, and his feet scuffed along the ground in a slow, hypnotic rhythm. There was a mournful expression on his face, like a puppy chucked out in the rain for leaving a present on the new Persian rug.

Max hadn't wanted to leave the house.

He would've been more than content to stay indoors, spending his time in the valuable pursuit of lying on the bed staring at the ceiling, or engaged in the thrilling pastime of looking out the window at the rain and clouds until his brain imploded.

It wasn't like he was bereft of things to keep him occupied. He had an X Box 360, an iPod, and a selection of DVDs from all genres under the sun - but none of them seemed worth the effort of plugging in, turning on, or sticking in the DVD player.

Therefore Max had decided to spend the afternoon sighing. Leaving enough time for some tuneless whistling before tea. His mother had put up with this for precisely twenty three minutes before ordering him out of the house, citing the need to carry out rigorous vacuuming in his bedroom. So he'd ridden his bike into town, where his sole purpose in life had become to get in the way of people trying to spend their money.

He had no plans, other than to hang around WH Smiths and flick through magazines until the spotty shop girl told him to go away.

Going into the local library was the furthest thing from Max Bloom's mind as he strolled past Boots.

Max certainly wasn't much of a reader. He might flick through a Batman comic or movie magazine now and again, but that was about it, and he'd reached the grand old age of seventeen having read precisely *three* books.

The first was Lolita by Vladimir Nabokov, as he'd heard it had dirty stuff in it. It did, but not the kind he was looking for – treating the whole thing far too seriously in his opinion.

The second book had been Harry Potter and the Philosopher's Stone, which he'd read under duress. About halfway through he'd decided the whole thing was a bit silly and abandoned it for a four hour session of Grand Theft Auto.

And the third?

Ah, now the third was something *different*.

For the first and only time in his life, Max Bloom had been captivated by a story.

His grandfather had given him this book at Christmas three years ago. On one crisp day in the lull between the Christmas festivities and New Year, Max had devoured the entire novel in one sitting.

It was Jack London's Call of the Wild – about a dog called Buck, ripped from his comfortable domestic existence and plunged into a life of hardship as a sled dog in the Canadian Yukon.

Max loved dogs – especially his grandfather's massive black Labrador Nugget. The dog in London's novel may have been a Saint Bernard / German Sheppard cross, but he still looked like Nugget in Max's imagination, making the story feel more personal and real to him. No other tale had ever captured him like it, before or since.

Nobody knew how much he loved that book… and he meant to keep it that way. Being a seventeen year old boy was hard enough on the self-esteem without people knowing you cried every time you read a story about a stupid dog.

Having said all that, if Max was being completely honest about it, he had read *one* more book. But it had been the Haynes Manual for the Austin Montego, so really didn't count, all things considered.

Regardless, not being any kind of bookworm, the notion of spending time in a library would usually be met with a sneer, a groan and a two fingered salute. However, Max was *astronomically* bored today and the same devil that likes all those details also makes work for idle hands.

- 2 -

Farefield library was stuck at the back of the shopping centre, tucked out of the way as if the town was embarrassed by it.

A monument to the folly of early eighties architecture, it was built of grey concrete and had about as much personality as… well, anything made of grey concrete, really. On a dismal day like this, it was hard to tell where the library stopped and the sky began. Birds had to be careful flying over it, if they didn't want to end up getting their beaks bent.

Most of the library's ground floor was visible through large plate-glass windows. Behind these were a collection of sad looking displays, staring out at the passers-by through the curtain of persistent rain.

A majority promoted books, of course. Popular authors like J.K Rowling and Stephen King dwarfed the displays of lesser known writers, but a few managed to poke through here and there.

There was also a window full of cardboard stands advertising movies, because the library also prided itself as a purveyor of fine quality DVDs. Spider-man vied for centre stage with Transformers, and Buzz Lightyear tried to outshine Harry Potter – who was getting more than his fair share of window space.

All the displays were getting limp, having been subjected to the library's antiquated air conditioning system for far too long. It wasn't quite as humid as a rain forest in there, but an Amazon tree frog would have felt quite comfortable. Potter's wand had flopped, Optimus Prime's head had fallen off and Spider-man looked like he was nursing a nasty case of rickets.

Another window featured hand-made pictures by local school children, celebrating the upcoming Halloween festivities. Pumpkins, witchy-woos and bandy legged skellingtons were pinned with care to a series of rickety display boards, giving the locals a good eyeful as they sauntered past.

It was only when Max noticed the entrance that he realised where his bored feet had taken him. He looked at the building with one slightly raised eyebrow, amazed he'd happened upon this strange and alien place.

Libraries were the domain of the socially inadequate. Certainly not the type of place a cool, rebellious seventeen year old should consider frequenting.

A brief internal conflict took place in his head:

'Hi Max. It's your brain here. I'm bored and in need of stimulation. Yonder library offers the best chance of this, so I suggest we go in and have a look.'

'Really? I was thinking of going into Game and watching the Call of Duty trailer eight times in a row.'

'No Max! That isn't good enough. I have to suffer with you destroying my cells when you play those games all the time. I'm asking that just once we do something I like!'

'Um... okay. I suppose it could waste half an hour.'

'Exactly! It's a new experience and we should be all for them!'

'Alright... but I'm killing you with six hours of Halo when we get home.'

'Deal!'

With a decision made, Max heaved a leaden sigh and walked in, hoping against hope that something inside might keep him occupied for a while.

A tall middle-aged woman, wearing a dark green power suit and her hair in a tight grey bun, was sat behind the main desk reading a paperback. She looked at Max with a suspicion born of many years dealing with teenagers who ran rampant throughout the otherwise hushed aisles of the library, breaking the tranquil atmosphere and being far too enthusiastic about themselves.

'Do you belong?' she said as he walked past.

'What?' Max hadn't expected to be challenged like this.

'Do you belong? To the library?'

'Er... no,' he replied, worried she was about to suggest some kind of painful initiation ceremony.

'You'll have to give me your details for the computer, then,' she told him, touching the keyboard beside her.

The ancient cream coloured PC wheezed into life and they both waited for an uncomfortable few moments while the tiny processor inside tried its best to clear the screensaver. Everything was going relatively well until the librarian tried to use the mouse. The second she touched it, the blue screen of death appeared, along with that dissonant *gank* noise Windows makes when it decides the stress of existence has become too much and commits electronic suicide.

'Blast!'

'Happens to my laptop all the time,' Max pointed out.

'You'll have to fill out your details on a card. I'll upload them later, once this thing is working again.'

The librarian rifled in a desk drawer, produced a piece of card and a pen, and handed it to Max with a look of slight impatience.

Max quickly scribbled down his name and address and handed both back with an ingratiating smile. 'There you go.'

She examined the card and popped it in a nearby rolodex. 'Thank you, young man. Once I've logged your details into the computer, I'll print up a membership card and have it posted to you.'

'Ok.'

'In the meantime, you're free to browse the shelves. I can check books out for you, should you find any to your liking.' The librarian looked down her nose at him. 'Please do not speak loudly, and try not to disturb other library patrons during your visit.'

Her task complete, the librarian returned to the Danielle Steele she'd lifted from the romance section earlier that day.

Max took this as his cue to leave and ambled off towards general fiction feeling like he'd done something wrong – though not entirely sure what.

Unfortunately, the movie section was between Max and the books, so his attention was immediately diverted by DVD covers featuring explosions and big guns.

The books didn't stand a chance.

The British library is a fine old institution, offering people the chance to broaden their horizons with a vast selection of fact and fiction to suit all tastes. An ocean of knowledge is waiting to be set sail upon by the lucky reader.

At least that's the idea of what a library *should* be. It's a view that hasn't trickled down to Farefield Borough Council just yet.

In this library, you'll find books by Stephen King, Danielle Steele and Tom Clancy. It just won't be any of the *good ones.*

You'll also find parts two, four and seven of any fantasy or science fiction series of your choice. You've got no chance of finding part one however, rendering the whole thing pointless unless you like guesswork.

Décor wise, you'll be unsurprised to learn the library walls are painted beige and the carpet is that thin, green corduroy stuff that only comes in squares.

The tall librarian with the stern gaze and abrupt customer service manner is Imelda Warrington.

Imelda has been head librarian here for twenty years and is passionate about the place, even if nobody at the council and few people in the community share that passion. She's in a constant battle with the bean counters, and is always trying to improve the selection of books on offer - on more than one occasion dipping into her own pocket. She recently bought Catcher in the Rye on Amazon for a fiver.

To Max she'd seemed like a right evil old bat, but you should never judge a book by its cover, or a librarian by her hair bun.

Max put down the Rambo DVD, having seen it would cost £2 to hire, which he didn't have.

With reluctance, he scuffed his way over to the first section of books, the ones in big print. Moving past these with the confidence of one born with 20-20 vision, he arrived at the main stacks, the A section greeting him with open arms.

The task of searching a library's shelves can be daunting. There are so many books it's easy to lose focus unless you know what you're after. The title of the specific volume is ideal. Knowing the name of an author is also excellent. Having an idea of genre is a serviceable method of reducing your choices.

It's certainly not a good idea to hunt for a book if you have absolutely *no idea* what you're looking for.

Enter Max Bloom then, a boy of little literary experience and even less patience. He made it to the B section before giving up – which all things considered, wasn't a bad effort on his part.

Max stared at the bookshelf a while longer, before he gave the whole thing up as a bad idea, and flopped down in the nearest chair in melodramatic fashion, sending up a cloud of dust. The black leatherette armchair, not used to this kind of treatment, buckled under one leg and the backrest hit the shelf behind, causing one book to fall out and drop onto Max's head.

Rubbing the spot where it'd hit him, Max bent down and picked the book up. It had a plain white cover, and the title on the spine in a basic black font was: 'Read Me If You're Bored by Clive Bonnet'.

It sounded *perfect*.

Max examined the cover more closely. It featured the cartoon of a man in a shirt and tie sat at a desk, head propped up with one arm. The expression on his face was one of utter misery.

Below the picture it said: 'A collection of short stories for the hard of thinking!'

Aah… this is a comedy book.

Max was well aware this type of thing existed, but he could never get his head round the idea that something full of just words could ever be considered *funny*. He was of the absolute belief that anything worth a laugh involved people getting hurt in a variety of interesting and unexpected ways. Hours spent on You Tube had only confirmed this.

Other patrons of the library seemed to agree. When he looked inside the front cover, he saw that the book had only ever been taken out once – six years ago.

Another communication with his brain took place:

'Come on brain, this is silly. I know we're bored, but we must be able to find something better to do than read this stupid thing.'

'I know it doesn't look like the best book in the world, but if it isn't a heavy read and the words aren't too long, let's give it a pop for ten minutes, eh?'

'Oh, alright… I'll give it a go. But the first time I read anything *remotely* romantic or even *slightly* historic, it goes back on the shelf and you're getting Halo-ed good and proper.'

Max flicked through the first few pages. There was a lot of white space, the print looked quite large and no horrific long words were in evidence, so he sat in the dusty chair and started reading.

Clive Bonnet favoured short, punchy titles for his stories like 'Cat Pause', 'Potty Problems' and 'Juggling Hot Coals'.

All of which sounded terrible.

In fact, there was only one story that looked worth a punt called 'I, Zombie'.

Max *loved* zombies.

He loved killing them in video games, watching them in movies and dressing up as them at Halloween. There was a half finished costume hanging in his wardrobe back home for just such a purpose. It was the third iteration of the same get-up he'd been wearing for five years now. The smell alone was terrifying. You couldn't go wrong with zombies, as far as Max Bloom was concerned.

With a mild glint of hope in his eye, he started to read.

It was pretty standard fare. Written in the first person, it told the tale of a deceased teacher who wakes up in the morgue as a zombie with his mind still intact – which was an original spin on the idea, if nothing else.

The story was quite graphic and Max enjoyed the descriptions of the bodily functions the title character still experienced despite being dead. Bonnet went into these at some length. This suited Max down to the ground, as there's nothing funnier than a farting zombie when you get right down to it.

Things took a turn for the worse about halfway in though, when the zombie storyteller started to talk about his wife; moaning on about how she wouldn't love him anymore because he was a monster, and he'd never be able to hold her in his arms again.

Blergh.

Max feared there was a sappy moral of some kind homing into view and didn't like the prospect one bit. However, it was zombies, so he persevered.

He reached the end of the first chapter – the rapidly rotting teacher lurching up the driveway to his house, deathly afraid his wife had been eaten by the undead. Max felt the story would benefit from the discovery of her mangled corpse and turned the page, eager to see if Bonnet felt the same way.

- 3 -

Between the next two pages was a piece of paper, folded in half. Max picked it up. The paper was stained brown with age and felt odd between his fingers. The texture was almost silky to the touch.

He'd once been on a hideously dull school trip to Westminster Abbey to see the Magna Carta. It had been sealed in a glass case and the teacher had impressed upon his pupils how delicate it was.

The pages of that old book had looked a lot like this.

With great care, Max unfolded the paper to see if anything was written on it. He fully expected to find lots of ancient words, written in complicated serif handwriting. The kind that's so old they use the letter F instead of S - like thif.

There was indeed writing on the scrap of paper, but it was in a plain, modern hand:

Hello.
I need your help.
They're coming... and I'm terrified, but I know you can stop them.
Books can be doorways. Find The Cornerstone book. You'll know it by its sound. It's there somewhere.
I'll wait for as long as I can.
Please help me. Please help us.
I'm so scared.
M.

A shiver ran down Max's spine. All thoughts of zombies were forgotten.

He read and re-read the odd message, trying to figure out its meaning.

It could be some kind of weird prank... but it'd be a pretty terrible joke, wouldn't it? You'd have to wait for someone to open this one book in particular, which could take months, or even years. Max had a cursory look around, half expecting to see some cobweb covered pensioner pointing at him, a look of crazed glee on his face.

That was just silly.

Still, it didn't make much sense, did it? Books as doorways?

What the hell was a 'Cornerstone' book and how could it make a sound?

He re-read the last lines of the note:

Please help me. Please help us. I'm so scared.

Max felt another shiver run down his back.

It occurred to him that if this actually was a practical joke, then the instigator may have added copies of the message to other books, raising the chances of some poor sap finding it and falling for the gag. He stood up and pulled out novels closest to where Clive Bonnet's had been, holding the books by the cover and flapping them around in the air.

He gave up after five, when no other notes had fluttered out.

The idea of going through every book in the library was crazy – it'd take him all day – so he decided to treat the message as a one-off, until evidence came to light suggesting otherwise. Having settled that, it was now a question of what to do next.

He could just tuck the paper back into Read Me If You're Bored, put the book back, leave the library and forget this weird episode ever happened. That would just plunge him back into the depths of abject boredom though, which was to be avoided at all costs.

The next choice was to take the note to the librarian at the front counter. Max could imagine handing it over and the sour look she'd give him. He could further imagine the note being torn up, as she told him it was a silly joke – a prank perpetrated by one of his fellow enthusiastic teenagers, no doubt.

A part of Max spoke up to point out that the librarian was probably right and this was indeed a silly joke.

Another part of him couldn't stop turning the message over in his head however, convinced it was a genuine cry for help.

He was determined to get to the bottom of it.

Wherever the bottom of it was. Or the top for that matter.

The best place to start would be with this Cornerstone thing. As far as Max was aware, a cornerstone was a foundation block in a building and not a book... so no help there, then.

Also, what did the message writer mean by the sound it made?

The sound a book made when you dropped it on the floor?

That was just *thud*, wasn't it?

Last birthday, Max had received one of those novelty cards from his best mate Steve Figson. It played a tune when you opened it: a tinny version of Baby Got Back by Sir Mix-a-Lot. Figgy had loved it.

Maybe that's what the cryptic message meant? You opened the book and it warbled a tune at you.

Opening countless library books, listening for one playing a melody, was as ridiculous as hunting for non-existent notes, so he dismissed the idea immediately.

Therefore, with no other clues to follow, Max had this:

There's a book somewhere in this library that makes a noise and it might be a doorway of some kind.

The cogs were whirring in his head so loud you could almost hear them.

Maybe the book isn't a doorway itself, just close *to one...*

He looked around.

There were two doors in sight. One was a fire exit to his right. The other was a door to the left with big black letters printed on it saying: Private – Staff Only. Max listened to what the door had to say and walked over to the fire exit instead to get a better look.

It was flanked by bookcases on both sides. These looked normal, with no discernible cornerstone-ish quality to either.

Feeling foolish, he put his right ear to one shelf, straining to hear something over the low rattle of the air conditioning. This yielded nothing other than slight neck strain.

The fire exit stood at the end of an L shape, created by the aisle Max was in and another at right angles to it. An elderly lady was sat halfway down the other, giving Max a strange look. He offered her a sheepish smile, backed out of her line of sight and went back to the library chair, the de facto base camp for his investigations.

The staff door was now the only other option, so he walked over to it, praying nobody would come out while he stood there like an idiot with his ear to the bookshelf. This proved just as fruitless an experiment here as it had at the fire exit.

His door options were now severely limited to the front entrance – no books there – and the one leading to the second floor, which housed the local branch of the Citizens Advice Bureau.

Max thought he could use a bit of advice right now, but doubted the earnest volunteers upstairs would be up to speed on mysterious messages left in random books that gave you the creeping heebie-jeebies.

So what now, genius?

He looked at the crumpled note again, hoping new instructions had magically appeared on it.

They hadn't.

Standing there in the humid library, Max finally realised what he was doing and his brain piped up:

'You do realise you've become obsessed about a scribbled note you found in a stupid book, don't you?'

At this point, the futility of the whole exercise hit him like a sack of bricks and all at once he felt like a prize berk. Here he was, wasting perfectly good video gaming time in a library, trying to decipher a message that could have been written years ago, and looking like a right idiot listening to bookcases.

With an angry grunt, he screwed the note up, stuffed it in his pocket and walked off in the direction of the exit.

- 4 -

Max Bloom wasn't the type of boy who scared easily, but the sudden loud noise that shattered the library's silence would have been enough to make anyone recoil in terror and worry for the condition of their underwear. The sound was *incredible* - like a billion people in an enormous celestial choir shouting *aaaahhh* at an absurdly high volume.

Max made a strange high pitched *eeeep* noise at the back of his throat. His knees buckled and he dropped to the floor. The noise vibrated through his whole body and seemed to shake the library to its very foundations.

Tears streamed from Max's eyes as the choir's song enveloped him, driving out all coherent thought. It struck his nerve centres in such a profound way that every fibre of his being was paralysed. It was like drowning in an ocean of sound.

Mercifully, the choir stopped as abruptly as it had started.

Max let out a whimper and sat down heavily on the floor, biting his tongue in the process. With the unpleasant coppery taste of blood in his mouth, he groped his way to the chair and sat, putting his head in his hands.

After a few minutes of recovery time he looked up, searching for the source of the crippling sound. He felt drained and incredibly tired, but needed to know where it'd come from, so forced his way to his feet in order to search.

On wobbly legs, Max made his way along the aisle, holding the shelves for support, wondering how everyone else had been affected by the bombardment.

He reached the fire exit and looked down the other aisle. Sure enough, the old woman who'd given him the funny look was still there. Max supposed she might be quite deaf – being in her seventies at least – but thought even she would have noticed a million people shouting *aaaahhh* at a volume usually reserved for thrash metal concerts.

The pensioner looked quite serene however, sitting in her chair munching a scone. She'd obviously heard and felt nothing.

Great. I've gone mad… or had a seizure of some kind.

That sounded plausible.

Just like Pete Schlitz, the German exchange student he'd known at school. Pete was epileptic and they'd all been told about the condition by their tutor, in case he threw a fit and needed help. Schlit-head – as he was affectionately known – had never done this in front of Max, but he could imagine what had just happened was similar to the type of thing Schlit-head experienced.

Despite the idea of suffering something as serious as a seizure, Max actually felt a little better. The enormous noise was otherwise inexplicable – and he liked his world to be nice and *explicable*, thank you very much. Resolving to tell his mother and pay a visit to the doctors at the first opportunity, Max hobbled towards the exit.

The noise started again. Only this time it wasn't loud enough to melt concrete.

Instead it was now a soft, quiet sound that retained its unearthly quality, despite the drop in volume.

Max didn't know where his hackles were, but was sure they were now raised. He stopped in his tracks and listened, able to analyse the song now it wasn't pounding his nervous system to a pulp.

It was, in actual fact, quite beautiful.

The million voices came from men and women of all ages. There were definite vocal ranges he could make out, from a low male bass to a high female soprano. He moved forward and the choir grew louder, indicating he was moving closer to its source.

So much for it being a seizure… maybe I am going mad.

If he was, it didn't feel that unpleasant. The choir's song filled him with a sense of drowsy well-being as he walked – or rather floated – along the aisles with an awestruck expression on his face. The library was pretty much empty, so nobody noticed the spaced-out seventeen year old boy wafting through the stacks like a dope fiend in a pair of helium trousers.

The choir grew louder and Max's hackles rose even higher. As did his testicles, which retreated as far up as they could go, knowing a potentially dangerous situation when they saw one.

The volume continued to escalate and pressure mounted across his chest. The sense of well-being faded, replaced with considerable discomfort. He was being pulled along now, unable to break free of this strange siren song.

Gasping for breath and going an alarming shade of blue, Max stumbled towards the saddest, oldest and tattiest looking bookshelf in the whole library.

It was about four feet high and sulked in one corner near the children's section, against a wall covered in brown hessian.

A sign was hung above it on a drawing pin. In Imelda Warrington's careful hand-writing it said:

Books for sale. 50p each. All money donated to local hospice.

On the shelf sat a collection of second hand books, filed in no discernible order. Among the treats on offer was a book about carp fishing circa 1976, a copy of The Complete Works of Shakespeare - which looked anything but, two boys own World War 2 novels featuring hyperbolic titles and scant attention to historical accuracy, and a beginners guide to taxidermy called 'Stuff It'. All these took a back seat to the book three quarters of the way along the bottom shelf, next to a biography of racing driver Jackie Stewart.

- 5 -

At first glance it looked like a perfectly ordinary book.

It was old and looked worn around the edges. About ten inches high, an inch thick and with no dust jacket, the book was a rich dark green colour that still retained its lustre, despite the apparent age. Picked out in silver writing down the spine was the title.

The Cornerstone.

All fairly standard stuff, though this book did depart from its fellows in one major respect. It was singing.

The Cornerstone was the source of the choral sound that currently held Max in its firm embrace. He knelt in front of the bookshelf as the choir ratcheted up the volume even higher. The small part of his brain that was able to function screamed at Max to get away from the horrible singing book and this awful bloody library. He couldn't move a muscle though, totally transfixed as he was by the powerful song.

A glorious silver light began to emanate from the book, pulsing with the rising and falling cadence of the choir.

It started to flash like a beacon, causing a dark after-image to swim across his field of vision every time it faded. Max wasn't sure if it was really there, or if oxygen starvation was making him hallucinate, but it was beautiful and terrible all the same.

In a final desperate bid for survival, Max's brain piped up:

'Oi! We're going to die here! Do something!'

He wiped dribble from his slack mouth and reached out an arm that weighed a ton towards The Cornerstone. The effort was monumental. His head pounded, his chest heaved and his entire body shook, as if the temperature had plunged thirty degrees.

Max's finger tips brushed the C of Cornerstone and the spell was instantly broken. The choir, silver light and intense pressure on his body disappeared. He groaned and fell forward, reaching out a hand to steady himself against the bookshelf, breathing in long, deep gasps of air.

Max looked around to see if anyone had noticed what had happened, but nobody was paying any attention. In fact, he could only see one tall man in a raincoat, standing in the fantasy section reading the back cover of a thick novel - part two of a five part series. This guy didn't look like he'd just been put through the wringer, so Max supposed the phenomenon must have once again affected only him.

He turned back to The Cornerstone, which now contrived to look no different to the other books it sat on the shelf with. Reaching out a tentative hand, Max shut his eyes and grimaced as his fingers came into contact with the book once more.

Nothing happened.

Max poked the book a couple of times, but this didn't provoke a response.

This is where I pull it out and the universe explodes.

Max pulled out The Cornerstone. The universe remained resolutely unexploded.

Holding it his hand, he couldn't believe this thing had nearly sucked the life out of him.

Max's grandfather Charlie was a prodigious reader and had a book collection in the thousands; some bought in shops, others picked up second-hand from numerous car boot sales. His entire house was taken over by sturdy chestnut bookcases crammed full of hardbacks and paperbacks. One amazing find at a jumble sale had been an entire series of classic novels - including a few Jane Austens and a smattering of Charles Dickens - printed in the early part of the 20th century. The set had been priced at £10, which Max's grandfather had thought obscenely cheap. He'd bought them all with barely concealed glee and made them pride of place on one of his enormous bookcases back home.

Max had been bored out of his brains many times in Charlie's house while his mum made small talk with her father. He'd always end up idly scanning the bookshelves and had looked at the novels in the collection a number of times, very glad nobody was forcing him to read one.

The Cornerstone looked similar. Plain, dusty and about as exciting as a wet weekend in Bognor.

The title was embossed in silver on the front cover, but there were no pictures or illustrations, so nothing gave away what was inside. The spine was broken, worn and covered in scuff marks, as if the book had been kicked around and treated in a careless fashion. It looked rather unremarkable on the whole. It wasn't glowing or singing, for instance.

Very carefully, Max cracked open The Cornerstone, holding it like a bomb about to go off.

The pages felt similar to the crumpled note in his pocket. They had that same silky quality and felt equally odd to the touch.

The actual contents were strange as well. There was no library insert to be stamped when the book was borrowed. In fact, there was no indication this was a library book at all.

Flipping the page, there were no publishing details to be seen either. Nothing about copyright, reprint dates, or what other excellent titles may be available from the same author.

This book had none of that, just:

House of Carvallen

…written at the top of the page.

There was no information about the author either. Not even a name. Max thought it strange that The Cornerstone gave no indication who'd written it. He guessed they'd wanted to remain anonymous in an attempt to create an air of mystery.

The title was printed again on the third page, and at the top of the fifth it said:

- 1 -

Max started to read, eager to see what this strange book was about:

It was, for all intents and purposes, the perfect day to visit the library.

A sullen, overcast October afternoon, it was the kind of day the word listless seemed invented to describe – until you remembered somebody had also thought up charmless, which was even more appropriate.

It was drizzling. The constant, sticky kind that's good at getting under the collar and giving anyone foolish enough to venture outside a wet neck for their trouble. You'd think all hope and joy had been banished from the world on a grey afternoon like this – if you were in a melodramatic frame of mind.

That's weird.

How big a coincidence was it that the book started on a day similar to this one and featured a library?

He continued:

Max Bloom was just plain bored as he reached the town centre, having been forced out of the house by his irate mother.

The town was Farefield, which nestled on the south coast of England between two major cities - and suffered from something of an inferiority complex because of it.

It was a Thursday. This doesn't have any bearing on the events about to unfold, but the devil is always in the details, if you look hard enough.

Max had heard of books where the reader identified with the main character, but this was ridiculous. He read down the page, getting more and more freaked out as he did.

It was about him. It was about *today*.

Everything was in here: going into the library, finding the note in Clive Bonnet's book, collapsing when the choir broke into song.

More disturbing, there were private things about him written here that nobody else could know. Even what he was *thinking* was laid out in front of him on the page, as if somebody was reading his mind at every turn. All that had occurred in the last hour or so was captured in detail.

Whoever the author was, Max didn't like the way they handled the story. The whole thing was done in a cheerful, flippant tone that Max didn't think took the situation anywhere seriously enough.

This was his life being turned upside down on this increasingly weird Thursday afternoon and it should be treated with a bit more respect, damn it.

With mounting terror, he got to a paragraph that read:

Max looked around to see if anyone had noticed what had happened, but nobody was paying any attention. In fact, he could only see one tall man in a raincoat, standing in the fantasy section reading the back cover of a thick novel - part two of a five part series. This guy didn't look like he'd just been put through the wringer, so Max supposed the phenomenon must have once again affected only him.

He turned back to The Cornerstone, which now contrived to look no different to the other books it sat on the shelf with. Reaching out a tentative hand, Max shut his eyes and grimaced as his fingers came into contact with the book once more.

Nothing happened.

Max poked the book a couple of times, but this didn't provoke a response.

This is where I pull it out and the universe explodes.

This was describing what he'd done mere moments ago. He was reading a book that was describing itself being picked up and read by Max Bloom, who was reading a book that was describing itself being picked up and read by Max Bloom...

A wave of vertigo washed over him and he slammed The Cornerstone shut, sitting back with his eyes closed.

Was that written down as well?

What had just happened? Did it outline Max reading a passage from the book, being overcome by vertigo, shutting the cover and sitting back with his eyes closed?

He bet it did.

What would happen if he read to where *now* was being described? Could he carry on and see his own future?

He opened The Cornerstone where he'd left off and read down the page, eventually getting to this sentence:

He opened The Cornerstone where he'd left off, and read down the page, eventually getting to this sentence:

He opened The Cornerstone where he'd left off, and read down the page, eventually getting to this sentence:

At this point, the universe exploded.

Max was engulfed by a blinding silver light and heard an enormous rushing sound - as if the ethereal choir had collectively realised they'd left the gas on at home and were hurrying out of the church to go check. He felt an unpleasant fluttering sensation in his stomach and was pulled violently forward from the centre of his chest, as if some cosmic angler had hooked him and was reeling in.

Max threw his arms out to cushion himself from the impact with the bookshelf. No collision came however. He felt himself propelled further forward, way beyond the confines of the library and out into some unfathomably large space.

After a few moments of disorientation, the blinding light faded and Max's rapid forward movement slowed, giving him the chance to catch his breath, recover his shattered wits and look around.

The dark space he floated in wasn't black like the night sky, but a deep, loathsome shade of purple, like a fresh, painful bruise. Around him, the atmosphere writhed and boiled, making him feel sick. It was like being surrounded by some vast living organism that twisted and turned in this nightmarish void.

The word *digestion* drifted through Max's head, which didn't help matters one bit.

The silence was oppressive. The only sound he could hear was his own shallow breathing.

'Hello?' he ventured.

There was no response, but he could have sworn the purple stuff started to squirm around a bit quicker.

'Is there anybody there?'

The writhing mass definitely reacted to this.

Max wasn't a genius, but was smart enough to know that if you found yourself thrust out of reality into a strange alien environment, it probably wasn't a good idea to go around shouting your mouth off. You had no idea who, or what, might be listening. This led to the uncomfortable feeling that he was being watched.

As if on cue, the boiling mass around him started to coalesce into heads and bodies. Not human ones, either.

There were definitely eyes in there, though.

And worse - *teeth*.

Abject terror was now the order of the day and Max - by nature an agnostic sort - started to pray like mad. These hastily prepared pleas were thankfully answered and he was pushed further on into the purple sea, away from the amorphous creatures. His speed increased again and purple space quickly gave way to total darkness.

The choir returned and began a deep, rumbling note that would have rattled the fillings in Max's teeth if he'd had any.

I'm really not sure how much more of this I can take…

The blinding silver light engulfed him again and Max was thrust forward at an incredible rate. Lacking anything more constructive to do, he decided screaming might be a good idea.

As he gave his lungs a good workout, the sound and light show came to a sudden end, indicating the journey was over. This was just as well, because Max was approaching the point of projectile vomiting and was about to end up very far from the nearest washing machine.

Vision and hearing returned. Max found himself sat with The Cornerstone open in front of him, just as he had been.

He wasn't in Farefield public library anymore though, that was for certain.

- 6 -

It was *a* library, but other than the fact it contained books, it had nothing in common with the place he'd just left. This library had never felt the sting of council cutbacks and was never used by the elderly to kill time before picking up the pension. It didn't feature any hand drawn children's pictures, and most certainly did not have a Citizens Advice Bureau.

What it did have were monstrous, gothic shelves containing a countless number of impressive books.

They looked extremely old. Bound in a selection of exotic looking materials, the spines were covered in languages Max didn't have a chance of understanding. Some books also bore symbols. Max could recognise a few of these, but rather wished he didn't as none of them looked pleasant - reminding him of some of the more lurid nightmares he'd had recently. The nightmare he was in right now was a lot worse though, as it appeared to be happening while he was awake.

'Hello!? Is there anybody here?!' he shouted.

Much like in the purple void, there was no response. Max looked at the colossal oak bookshelves rearing up on both sides and saw that some twenty feet above his head they became lost in a thick, swirling mist.

Behind and ahead, the shelves marched away in a straight line, creating a long corridor with no apparent end.

Feeling the onset of claustrophobia *and* agoraphobia, Max looked down, trying to settle himself.

He noticed a space in the bookshelf to his left. It was the same size as The Cornerstone.

Books can be doorways.

That's what the message had said and he'd found one that evidently was. It'd sucked him out of his mundane, drizzly little world and brought him to this strange, gigantic library.

Panic blossomed in his chest. Max ripped open The Cornerstone, hoping it would catapult him back the same way it had brought him here.

Nothing happened.

In fact, the book's pages were now completely clean and unmarked. The writing had disappeared.

Great, what do I do now?

For want of a better idea, he stood up and started to walk down the long aisle. Having no idea what might be lurking in this strange place, this was conducted at a very slow, sensible pace.

The mist hanging above was a particular source of concern.

It looked designed to hide hideous monstrosities until the last second, when they would reach down an enormous suckered tentacle and pluck unwary souls to their doom. There would be big, sharp teeth involved and large, nebulous eyeballs.

This line of thought accomplished nothing - other than causing testicle shrinkage of epic proportions - so Max tried to put the mist and its potentially lethal denizens out of his head. He looked down and noticed that the floor was made of smooth, grey granite and was, as far as he could tell, totally devoid of any dust or grit.

Mum would love how clean this place is.

This brought on a pang of scared homesickness and he increased his pace, a new sense of urgency propelling him forward.

After twenty minutes - roughly the attention span of most seventeen year old boys, if left devoid of mental stimulation - his pace had slowed back to the legendary trudge and Max found himself inexplicably bored. It shouldn't be possible to be yanked through a doorway into another universe and become bored after less than half an hour, but Max had achieved it.

He stopped in front of a random shelf and looked at the closest books. They were still incomprehensible, but the symbols on their spines were less nightmare-like, leading Max to deduce he'd walked out of the section containing really evil books and into the part of the library that held just mildly evil ones.

With everything quiet and Max calmed down, this was the perfect time for something loud to go *bang*. It came from back down the aisle some distance away - an echoing, loud crash like something large had been dropped on the ground.

A heavy book covered in nasty symbols, for instance.

Max's heart leapt into his mouth. It leapt even further when there was a second bang, this one much closer.

Running.

That's always a good idea in a situation like this, isn't it? Max took to his heels.

To start with, he didn't waste time looking round. If some hideous creature of the night was hunting him down, he had no intention of getting a good look at the bugger before it swallowed him whole. When the banging sounded right behind him however, he had to glance over his shoulder.

Books were flying off the shelves, as if some huge, invisible creature were running along the aisle with both arms out, scooping them onto the ground.

Max tried to run faster - visions of sharp teeth and tentacles flashing through his head - but it was no good, the thing was gaining on him. He could feel its cold breath on the back of his neck.

Then, in apparent defiance of all the laws of physics, he went sideways. Something had pulled him out of the path of the invisible horror, just in the nick of time. He was yanked into an alcove along the right hand side of the stacks and swung around, the back of his head smacking into a bookcase.

Max couldn't quite see his assailant / saviour, but got the impression of a moving wall with arms, such was its size.

The world went blurry and he dropped to the ground in a daze.

'Whaa?' he said.

'Oh no, you've hurt him!'

It was a girl's voice, full of concern. Max heard a grunt coming from the moving wall. He could also hear the sound of the invisible monster's progress as it carried on down the aisle.

'Get out of the way. Let me see if he's ok.'

The wall moved to one side. Max's vision was still blurred and his head spun in a sickening whirl, but he could just about see the girl as she leant forward. She was blonde and beautiful, with the deepest blue eyes he'd ever seen.

'You don't look too bad,' she said. 'Just a bit discombobulated, I expect.'

'Whaa?' Max tried again.

'You've hit your head quite hard. That's better than being caught by the guardian though.'

'Mnhnm,' he agreed.

'I'm sorry. This must be all very confusing for you.'

He felt her hand grasp his.

'I hope you'll be able to help us,' she continued. 'It was a bit of a shot in the dark, sending the message like that, but I had to take the chance. It was the only way of getting through to your world without anyone here noticing.'

'Mnhnm.'

'You really shouldn't be in this part of the Library though, it's far too dangerous. You came through before we could get The Cornerstone out.' Her brow furrowed. 'Quite why the custodians had it down here baffles me. You could have been killed!'

Max could wholeheartedly agree with that last statement and tried to tell her so.

'Hmnmn.'

'I could fight the guardian with Wordcraft, but you're no way near ready yet,' she said, which was perplexing to say the least.

'Mnhnmn.'

'We'll have to get you back before it returns. Here, hold The Cornerstone up.'

He did as he was told.

Nothing happened, what with the pages being blank and everything.

'Book blank,' he mumbled.

The girl frowned. 'Oh, blast. It's lost power,' she said, biting a fingernail. 'One crossing shouldn't have drained it that much though... never mind, we can fix it.' She took The Cornerstone and shoved into the nearest shelf between two thin hardbacks.

The girl waited a few moments, an impatient look on her face.

She really was *extraordinarily* pretty. Max wished he'd met her under better circumstances - when he wasn't scared out of his wits and dribbling.

'That should be enough,' she said, plucking the book out and thrusting it back into his hands.

'Read!' she commanded.

Max opened it and peered at the page:

'That should be enough,' she said, plucking the book out and thrusting it back into his hands.

'Read!' she commanded.

Max opened it and peered at the page:

The universe exploded again.

On a day full of shocks, surprises and horrors, Max was delighted to open his eyes and see the now familiar shape of Imelda Warrington standing over him, a look of deep concern on her face.

He was back in Farefield, sat up against the ratty old bookshelf. The gigantic mist-filled library had gone.

'I have just two questions for you, young man,' Imelda said. 'How exactly did you find The Cornerstone and where did it take you?'

Part Two

'You know about this thing?' Max said, waving The Cornerstone at her.

'Of course I do, you silly boy. I'm the librarian.'

She grabbed his hand and hoisted him to his feet.

Max wobbled on the spot. 'I think I need to sit down somewhere comfortable,' he said, offering Imelda a sickly look.

The librarian studied him for a second. 'Yes, that'd probably be a good idea.' She held out a hand. 'But first, I'll take The Cornerstone, thank you'.

Max was too drained to argue and handed the book over.

'Come on,' she ordered, and marched off in the direction of the staff room.

The staff room was brown. Brown chairs, brown sofa, brown walls, brown carpet, brown coffee table, brown sideboard, brown cabinets.

Max sat with a grateful sigh in one of the chairs, while Imelda fixed him a strong cup of tea. She said nothing while the tea brewed, just stared at the book lying on the table, a thoughtful expression on her face.

Max looked around the room, wondering if the person who'd decorated it had been inspired by the local sewage works.

'Here,' Imelda said, handing him a steaming mug.

He thanked her and took a sip. It was warm, sweet and just what he needed.

Imelda sat in a chair opposite and studied him. 'What's your name, young man?'

She'd obviously forgotten about the hastily completed library card.

Max thought of giving her a false identity, then decided it wouldn't be a good idea. This woman looked the type to weed out lies easily.

'Max. My name's Max. Max Bloom,' he said in his best James Bond. 'You took my name down earlier, remember?'

'Oh yes... I recall,' Imelda replied. 'Got yourself into a spot of bother, haven't you?' She pointed at The Cornerstone.

'Yeah, you could say that.'

'Well?' Imelda demanded.

'Well what?'

'How do you know about The Cornerstone... and where did it take you?'

'I could ask you the same questions!' he said, pointing a finger. 'The first one anyway.'

'You could, but you're not getting anything out of me until I know why you're involved in this.'

Max sipped his tea, eyes narrowing as he looked at her over the mug.

'How long have you known about The Cornerstone?' Imelda said.

He glanced up at the clock on the wall. 'About an hour... more or less,' he guessed.

'An *hour*?'

'Yep.'

'You mean you had no idea about it before you walked into this library?'

'Nope.'

Imelda sat back in her chair with disbelief. 'Well, you're either very special Mr Bloom, or just very unlucky.'

'Oh, it's the second one, definitely.'

He told her about coming into the library in an attempt to stave off boredom. Imelda nodded in a resigned fashion – she knew damn well most teenagers would only see the library as the absolute last resort for entertainment these days.

He then went on to describe finding the note.

'May I see it?' she asked.

Max fished around in his jeans, pulled out the crumpled piece of paper and handed it to her. She read the message several times before looking up.

'You shouldn't have seen this, Max. Whoever wrote it should never have sent it across. This world is off-limits to anyone not authorised to be here.' Imelda looked at the note. 'They must be clever though... powerful too. It must have been someone in the Chapter House.'

Max didn't have a clue what she was on about, but he wasn't a complete idiot.

'It was a girl. She had blue eyes.'

'Who was?'

'The girl who wrote the note.'

He continued his story, to the point where the strange girl and her protector had saved him from the library guardian - sending him back before he got flattened.

Max took another sip of lukewarm tea, wondering what the librarian's reaction would be. It wasn't good.

'You were in extreme danger, Max. This girl has got you caught up in something you had no business being involved with. It was stupid and careless.' Imelda tucked the note away in a pocket of her suit jacket. 'There are wiser people than her who make sure the doorway between worlds is off limits to anyone not powerful, skilled or old enough to use it.'

'They the ones that made The Cornerstone?'

'Well done,' Imelda approved. 'Yes they are. It was created to allow passage - but only when necessary. It's designed to allow safe and easy transport for anyone it deems fit.'

'What, like me?'

'That's what troubles me. Why it would let you across is a mystery.'

'Will the blonde girl get in trouble?'

'All other forms of contact are banned and the doorway is closely monitored by The Cornerstone to prevent it.'

'Looks like it wasn't doing its job then.'

'No, it wasn't. It's only meant to be used by certain people.'

'Like you?'

Imelda nodded. 'Yes. It's the only contact I have.' The sadness in her voice was unmistakable.

'If it's so important to you, why leave it lying around on that crappy shelf? Somebody could nick it.'

'I have to leave it out in the library where it can be close to the other books. Nobody's going to steal it, it won't allow it. The Cornerstone can take care of itself.'

Max remembered something. 'So that's why the girl shoved it into the bookcase when it didn't work. What do other books do? Charge it or something?'

'It's not the books. It's what's written in them. The knowledge they contain.'

That was about as cryptic as you could get. 'The knowledge?'

'Yes. Haven't you heard the phrase knowledge is power?'

'I have, but it doesn't help. I've still got no idea what you're talking about,' Max replied with absolute sincerity.

'I'm sure you don't... and you don't need to know either. In fact, I've said way too much already. There was a reason he put me here all those years ago and it wasn't to spill all our secrets to teenage boys.'

'So what am I supposed to do?'

'Go home. Pretend none of this happened.'

Max slammed the mug down onto the table, spilling the remnants of the tea. 'That's it, is it? I get sucked into the library from Hell because some blonde magically punted a bit of paper across dimensions, and you're telling me to forget it and bugger off home?'

'That's about the size of it, yes.'

Max leapt to his feet, pointy finger at the ready. Imelda stared at him with her arms crossed.

'Well... well... I'm going to tell everyone about this you know! I'm... I'm going to tell my mum!' he blustered, realising how embarrassing that sounded as soon as it was out of his mouth.

'Really?' Imelda said, amused. 'Do you think your mother will believe you?'

This deflated Max's anger even further. 'Good point,' he conceded.

'It is, isn't it?'

He came to the realisation she had him over a barrel on this one. 'So you're not going to tell me anything else then?'

'No.'

'And you don't need my help?'

'No. I can deal with it, thank you.'

'But what about... you know... *her*? Will she be ok?' he asked, feeling quite awkward.

Imelda had been round the block a few times and recognised an instant crush when she saw one. 'The girl will be ok, Max. I'll make sure she's taken care of. By the sounds of things, she has an Arma with her anyway, so I'm sure she's fine.'

'What the hell's an Arma? You mean that big hairy sod?'

'Enough!' Imelda said, putting an end to the conversation by getting up and going to the door. 'I suggest you make your way home, young man. It's getting late.'

She held the door open and Max knew damn well he wouldn't get anything else out of this harridan today. There was something extremely weird going on here though, and he wasn't about to let it go in a hurry.

He stalked out of the staff room, avoiding eye contact.

'Max!' Imelda called after him.

He turned and favoured her with a look of withering contempt. 'What?'

'The book, Max,' she said, holding out her hand.

Max became aware that he was holding The Cornerstone, his only tangible proof that any of this had happened. He couldn't remember picking it up. The idea of relinquishing it to this woman didn't hold much appeal.

'I don't suppose you'd let me take it out on loan, then?' he chanced.

'No. I wouldn't. Hand it over.'

Max frowned and gave it back to her.

'I'm not forgetting about this, you know,' he promised and marched off in a huff.

Imelda stood at the staff room entrance and watched him go, The Cornerstone grasped tightly in her hand, a very worried expression on her face.

- 2 -

All the way home, Max Bloom's brain was on fire. He'd never heard stories of people being sucked into other worlds by magic books, but intended to spend a constructive couple of hours on Google making sure.

He also decided he hadn't gone completely mad and dreamt the whole thing up. The brief conversation with the librarian had proved that. If he had gone crackers and created a fantasy in his head, it wouldn't have included a bossy middle aged librarian and a room decorated by Armitage Shanks.

Also, if it had been a fantasy, the librarian would have surely looked more like a bikini model.

His thought process was then diverted by the image of a gorgeous bikini-clad babe, holding a library card in a suggestive manner - and remained so until he was sat in his dad's study at the computer googling: *supernatural, books, doorways, vortex, library, Cornerstone.*

The results that popped up were numerous but unhelpful, so he googled bikini models for a while, which while equally unhelpful, was a lot more enjoyable.

Max considered telling his mother what had happened today despite Imelda's warnings, but dismissed the idea. Amanda Bloom was the type of woman the phrase *highly-strung* described perfectly. She was wound tighter than a crossbow and survived on a combination of nervous energy and caffeine.

Max could just see her reaction if he told her a story as unbelievable as this one. She'd have him down the hospital for a check up faster than you could say attention deficit disorder.

He couldn't talk to his dad Peter either, as he was currently away in Malaysia, doing whatever it was he did for a living. Max knew computer components were involved in some way, but his eyes always glazed over whenever his dad tried to explain further.

That left his sister Monica. Or Moan-ica, as he preferred to call her. Max could almost hear the howls of derisory laughter and see the impressions she'd do of him running away from an invisible library monster. *Decades* would pass before Monica would let it go. Telling her was a definite no-no.

With his options dried up, Max resolved to sleep on the issue. Tomorrow might bring some inspiration.

Sleep was a long time coming though.

His mind refused to stop turning over the events of the day. Images of strange notes, glowing books, thick mist and a boiling purple sea played through the projector in his mind on a constant loop. The one image that wormed its way into his thoughts more than any other was that of the beautiful girl he'd met. As he finally started to slide towards sleep, Max promised himself he was going to see her again whatever it took - grumpy librarians be damned.

Imelda Warrington wasn't getting much sleep either. Unlike Max, she wasn't at home. Instead, she was still sat in her brown staff room, The Cornerstone back on the coffee table.

She'd stayed after the rest of her staff had gone home for the night, citing the need to catch up on some admin, and had spent the next few hours in a frustrating and fruitless attempt to make contact with the world The Cornerstone opened a doorway to.

Her problem was the book had a high level of sentience and could be very temperamental. It would work when it wanted to, not when commanded. It wasn't supposed to act this way, but it's hard to design an object that powers itself on words conjured up by the conscious mind without a certain level of awareness *rubbing off*, as it were.

The Cornerstone had leeched knowledge, emotion and personality from the countless books it had been kept alongside for years and had developed a discernible character of its own because of it.

In short, it was bloody stubborn and point blank refused to let Imelda do anything with it tonight.

Speaking to those on the other side was something that annoyed her anyway. Usually, she'd just send a written report, like a travel correspondent sending back stories for a newspaper. Tonight though, she was the one that needed information, so there was nothing for it but a trip back through the book to speak directly to them.

If The Cornerstone would co-operate, of course.

The pages remained resolutely blank and there wasn't a flicker of power, no matter how long she left it stuck in the shelf next to the other books. She'd even put it in the classics section for an hour, hoping the high brow literature might please it and make it more tractable.

It hadn't.

The book sat in front of her doing nothing.

This was the boy's fault... and possibly the girl's. From the description Max had given, Imelda knew damn well that Merelie Carvallen had written the note and sent it, like an angler fishing for a bite.

The girl certainly had the skill, but no matter how desperate she was, Merelie should have known better than to break the rules like this.

She isn't stupid though. There must be something pretty catastrophic going on for her to take a risk like this.

But that was ridiculous, wasn't it?

Imelda felt sure she would have been contacted if anything untoward was happening.

No doubt about it... none at all.

She gave The Cornerstone a harsh look. 'You're really not helping matters, you know that?' she said, feeling a bit silly talking to a book - even if it probably could understand her.

- 3 -

The next day dawned as drizzly and dull as the last.

Max woke with a start from a dream about a giant book with pointy teeth chasing him through a shopping precinct. The thing had cornered him by Waterstones and was about to bite him on the ankles when he snapped out of it.

He got up, dressed in yesterday's clothes and yawned his way out of the bedroom. The morning then took an immediate turn for the worse when Monica confronted him on the landing.

'Morning crap face,' she said. 'What's a horror bone, then?'

'What?' he replied, rubbing sleep dust from his eyes and cursing the invention of the little sister.

'What's a horror bone? You kept shouting it in your sleep last night, you big weirdo.'

'*Cornerstone?*' he ventured.

'Cornerstone, horror bone... whatever. What is it, then?'

'Nothing to do with you, dog breath.'

Monica gave her brother the most contemptuous stare she could muster for eight fifteen in the morning and stormed into the bathroom, slamming the door in his face. Max took this as some kind of victory and went downstairs to the kitchen.

His mother was in good spirits as she was due to spend the day with her friend Georgina on a hardcore shopping trip in the city. She didn't even lecture him about wearing the same faded hoodie again as he rummaged around for breakfast cereal.

She did ask him how his day was yesterday and he made something up about going to Figgy's house.

'You spend way too much time with him, you know. He's got a foul mouth, and his dad's on the dole,' Amanda said, in a tone that implied this was tantamount to being a raving psychopath.

'Mum, he got made redundant by the Honda dealership. It's not his fault. And Figgy only swears when he knows somebody like you is around to hear it.'

'Whatever Max, I just don't like him.' Amanda's tone changed and she smirked at her son. 'So, who is she?'

'What?'

'Who is she? The girl?'

'What girl?'

'The one you kept talking about in your sleep.'

This could be awkward.

'Er… what was I saying?'

'You were mumbling about how much you liked her blonde hair, and something about selling her a door for 50p, which didn't make much sense. Someone you know?'

'No.' Max thought for a second, '…er, I mean yes. I met her in the library yesterday.'

'What's her name?'

'Not a clue.'

'Well go back! She could be there again, eh? If she is, get her name and ask her out. You obviously like her if you're having dreams like that!'

Dreaming was about right when it came to his chances of going out with that kind of girl. Besides, the ability to ask somebody out on a date is somewhat hampered when they're in a different reality to you.

'Leave it out, mum. She was just some girl I met, nothing else.'

'Alright, alright, I'll drop it,' Amanda said, disappointed. 'So what are my firstborn's plans for the day?'

'Um... well, I thought I'd go back to the library.' Max replied, which was the absolute truth. He did intend to go back, just not for the reasons his mother suspected.

'Ah ha!' Amanda waggled her eyebrows up and down.

'Not because of her! There's... there's a book I'm interested in.'

'Please. Pull the other one, son of mine. You're not the type to be sticking your head in a book, I know you too well.'

'You'd be surprised, mum.'

'Well, whatever your reasons, it's better than being sat in front of that bloody X Box all day. It's not good for you.'

Nor is being eaten by an invisible library monster.

'It's something to do,' he agreed, turning his full attention to the bowl of Sugar Puffs he'd made.

Amanda went upstairs to decide on what outfit to wear.

Max munched his way through breakfast, wondering what the best strategy to employ would be when he saw Imelda Warrington again.

Strategies of any kind were quite unnecessary as it turned out. Max simply strolled in to the library an hour later and Imelda Warrington came bustling up to him with a look of tired concern on her face.

'You've got to use the book again, boy. It won't let me do anything!' she snapped.

He was taken off guard and had to re-orient himself. Max had been prepared for a lengthy argument with Imelda before learning any more about The Cornerstone and the blonde girl, so this was a bit of a surprise.

'Um... okay. Why?' he asked.

Imelda grabbed Max's arm and frog-marched him toward the staff room. She didn't say another thing until they were inside with the door locked.

'The Cornerstone isn't working for me for some reason. I've been trying all night with no success. How am I supposed to find out anything if I can't make contact?' Imelda wasn't quite wringing her hands, but it wouldn't have gone amiss.

'Gotcha,' Max nodded. 'Any ideas why it's not working?'

She looked away, embarrassed. 'It seems to be in a mood with me,' she mumbled.

'The book... is *in a mood with you?*' Max said, resisting the temptation to unlock the door and run.

She gave him an exasperated look. 'It's not just a book. I thought you'd worked that out by now! It has more power than you can possibly imagine. It also has a distinct... personality.'

'Okay...' Max was dubious about a book having a personality, but was willing to go along with the idea if it got him answers. 'Why do you think I can help?'

'You were the last person to use it. Maybe it... it likes you. I've never known it work for a random stranger before, so there must be something special about you.'

Max thought for a second. 'Not me. Nothing special about me. It's her. The blonde girl. I just found her message, that's all.'

'Well, that does make sense. Merelie has a close relationship with the books. It stands to reason The Cornerstone would pick up on that.'

Merelie.

It was a very pretty name, Max decided. 'That's her name, is it?'

'Yes it is, but that's not important right now.'

It was the most important thing in the world as far as Max was concerned.

'Sit down and let's see if it works for you,' Imelda demanded, impatient to see if he had any more luck.

Max sat on a comfy brown sofa and Imelda thrust The Cornerstone at him.

'Now, hang on a minute!' he objected, holding his hands up to ward the book off. 'The last time I touched that thing I went blind, deaf and was half suffocated.'

'The *aaaahhh*-ing?'

'That's the one.'

'Yes. I said it had a personality. I didn't say it was a subtle one. When it wants attention it can make a right racket.'

'That was *attention seeking?*'

'Of a sort, yes. It wanted you to find it... and it usually gets its way.'

Max gave The Cornerstone a long look. 'Got a personality, you say?'

'Indeed,' Imelda replied, still holding it out.

Feeling a little silly, Max leaned forward and addressed the book directly. 'Now listen here, you. This Merelie's in trouble and I want to help her. From what the librarian is saying, it sounds like you want me to help her too.' Max gave the book the pointy finger treatment. 'Having said all that, let's skip the theatrics, eh? No choral singing, no suffocating, no weird glowing and definitely no blinding white light... it gave me a headache. Got it?'

The Cornerstone showed no sign that it understood - let alone agreed - but Max hoped his admonishment had done the trick.

'Be careful,' Imelda warned. 'And don't do anything stupid over there. Just find out what's going on and come straight back, understood?'

Max nodded, opened the book, took a very deep breath and started to read.

- 4 -

'Be careful,' Imelda warned. 'And don't do anything stupid over there. Just find out what's going on and come straight back, understood?'

Max nodded, opened the book, took a very deep breath and started to read.

The process was easier this time. The Cornerstone had apparently listened, because there was no choir and no exploding universe. While there was still some silver light, it was far less blinding and the trip didn't include another visit with the evil purple space monsters.

As the book did its thing, Max hoped he wouldn't arrive in the enormous, mist-wreathed library with its unseen terrors. His hopes were answered as the light faded and he could see again.

It was a square, stone courtyard, surrounded on all sides by corridors visible through tall, narrow windows. There was an archway in each wall allowing access to these corridors, which went who knows where.

The place had a medieval vibe to it, but didn't look rustic or run-down. In fact, it seemed well-kept and quite tidy. Warm sunlight filtered in through a wide skylight above. Max could see deep blue sky and a single white cloud scudding happily along in the gentle breeze.

He stood on a neat square patch of grass, split down the middle by a shallow canal of running water. The water came from a plain stone fountain at one end of the courtyard and flowed into a drain at the other.

Picturesque was the best way to describe the place... with a little quaint thrown in for good measure.

The patch of grass Max stood on was bordered by smooth, grey flagstones and he stepped over onto one, stamping his foot down.

Seems real enough.

This was certainly a better place to materialise than the gloomy library. The chances of a hideous tentacle monster smashing through the skylight and sucking his eyeballs out were quite remote, he felt.

'You're back!' a voice said from behind him.

Max spun around. Standing in the nearest archway was Merelie.

This was the first opportunity Max had to get a good look at the girl and he was struck by how beautiful she was. Her deep blue eyes were exquisite and her hair was a glorious honey-blonde.

She was quite breath-taking, all things considered.

Merelie was dressed in simple black trousers and a pale green shirt. The cut of the fabric was a little odd, but despite being from another dimension, the girl wouldn't have looked out of place walking through John Lewis on a busy Saturday afternoon.

Ordinary looking clothes or not, she was quite stunning, leaving Max at a loss for words.

'Um... er... '

Merelie walked over.

'Did Borne hurt you?' she asked with concern. 'He can be a bit heavy handed sometimes... but it was an emergency.'

Max supposed that Borne was this Arma thing Imelda Warrington had mentioned.

'Er... no, I'm ok thanks. Just gave me a bump on the head.'

'Thank goodness!' Her smile was like the sun coming up. 'I thought I'd make sure The Cornerstone was somewhere more pleasant for you to arrive this time around.'

What Merelie did next was very nice, but at the same time *deeply* traumatic. She leaned forward and gave him a gentle kiss on the cheek.

This turned Max redder than an angry beetroot.

'Thank you for reading my message and coming here,' she said.

'S'not a problem, really... wasn't doing much else,' he replied, now completely unable to make eye contact.

'What's your name?'

'Max... M'name's Max.' he said, looking at his feet.

'Max. That's a nice name.'

'Thanks,' he said, looking at the wall.

'Mine is Merelie.'

'I know. The librarian woman told me,' he said, looking at the other wall.

'Did she?' Merelie's expression darkened.

'Yeah. She told me a lot, actually.'

Max failed to see Merelie's reaction as he was looking at his feet again. 'Well, I'm not sure how she could,' she replied, 'stuck over there... not knowing what's been going on.'

There were a few awkward moments as he tried to get over his embarrassment and she seethed privately over Imelda's interference.

'Er... where am I, exactly?' he asked, breaking the silence.

The sun came up again. 'Sorry, Max. This must be all very confusing for you.'

'You've got that right,' he replied, looking into her eyes for the first time.

She took his hand in hers, causing embarrassment levels to peak. 'Come on, we'll go somewhere a bit more private to talk. A Chapter Guard could walk by any time and explaining you away would be a real problem.'

'Ok.'

Max had no idea what a Chapter Guard was, but had heard so many strange things over the past couple of days he'd given up on asking and had just elected to go with the flow.

Merelie led him through the archway and along one of the corridors.

'What is this place, Merelie?' It felt nice to use her name.

'This is the Chapter House... our Chapter House I mean... my family's.'

There was a note of pride in her voice that suggested being in a family with a Chapter House was a very good thing indeed; like having a swimming pool or a pony.

She led him down several more corridors. All of them were lit from above with the same type of skylight as the courtyard, and there were large windows spaced regularly along their length. Soft, glowing blue orbs sat on metal sconces attached to the walls, augmenting the natural light provided by the skylights. Many rooms and other courtyards led away, giving Max the impression he was in a very large building.

As Merelie guided him along, he looked out of the windows and was offered a snapshot of the surrounding environment. They were in what appeared to be the tallest structure of an elegant city. Most of the buildings looked built of stone, but there were a few metal and glass constructions dotted about.

Neat parkland areas were spread throughout the section of the city he could see and the streets were lined with healthy, stout trees. Long, sleek airships floated above the buildings, most of them coloured a deep, rich green. Some were moored at the top of the highest buildings.

Max could see people teeming in the streets below, going about their business on this sunny day. While there was nothing he could recognise as a car, there were vehicles down there, trundling along the wide, paved avenues on tracks - like the trams he'd seen on a trip to Blackpool a few years ago.

Between the buildings he could see green rolling hills behind the city, which gave way to the sea a couple of miles beyond.

The whole place looked sickeningly clean and tidy.

Max got the distinct impression that the city was new and hadn't had time to get grimy and stained yet due to centuries of accommodating messy human beings. He would've liked to study his surroundings a bit more, but Merelie was in a rush, so there wasn't much time for sight-seeing.

They went through a set of heavy green marble doors and entered a large hall, which had a grand looking wooden staircase at one end and several comfy looking chairs and tables dotted about for anyone who fancied a sit down.

On the walls were several large paintings, depicting strong and handsome looking people, staring off into the middle distance. They were dressed in a variety of styles, continuing the elegant, simple look of Merelie's clothing.

Some paintings looked quite new - especially the one of a tall, thin bald man with piercing blue eyes. Others looked older, with a distinct patina of age.

The one constant in all the portraits was that every person had their left hand resting on a leather bound book sat on a tall plinth beside them. It looked a little like The Cornerstone, but much larger and more ornate.

'You lot really like books, don't you?' Max said, as Merelie hurried him across the hall.

She glanced up to the paintings. 'It's more than just liking books, Max. Our world wouldn't exist without them. I'll explain more, but I don't want us to be caught here... come on.'

She pulled him up the flight of polished wooden stairs and underneath a large, lavish tapestry that depicted the world, hanging right above the landing where the staircase split to the left and right. Merelie yanked him left and headed along a gallery running above the hall.

They stopped at a pale green set of double doors and Merelie pushed one open, leading Max into what looked like her private rooms.

The chamber was large and circular, with two other rooms accessible from a couple of doorways. The plain interior design of the Chapter House continued here, though there were more flourishes of colour and personality, with several hangings and pictures adorning the walls. Tall bookcases were set against the wall at regular intervals, stretching all the way to the ceiling. They were crammed with books of all different sizes.

I'm in a pretty girl's bedroom... and all it took was travelling to another world.

Merelie closed the door and breathed a sigh of relief. 'Thank the Writer for that. Nobody saw us. We're lucky my parents are at negotiations with the other Chapter Houses in the Great Hall, otherwise there'd be far more people about.'

'Are your parents important then?'

'My father is Chapter Lord here. He rules this land.'

'Of course he does,' Max sighed. That was it then, he had no chance with her. She was even more out of his league than he thought. 'Why aren't you there with them?'

Merelie laughed bitterly. 'I'm not exactly my father's favourite person at the moment. My presence wouldn't go down well. I have opinions that aren't shared by others.'

Max remembered what Imelda had said. 'You sent that note because you think something bad is going to happen here... that *they're* coming? Something awful?'

'That's right.'

'Nobody believes you?'

'No, they don't.' Merelie said, slamming a bolt at the top of the door into place. She moved away and sat at a long low table in the centre of the room, which was covered with paper, pencils and books.

Max joined her and put The Cornerstone down between them.

This seemed like a good time to kick start the conversation he was desperate to have.

'What's going on, Merelie? Why did you ask for my help?'

'It wasn't really you I was asking for help from, Max. It was anyone suitable I could find from your world.'

That was a bit disappointing. 'Oh, ok.'

'Don't worry! I'm very glad somebody like you came. You look clever and brave, and that's what we need right now. I guess I got lucky. And anyway, The Cornerstone seems to like you.'

'Like me? It nearly killed me!'

'Well there you go then. If it hadn't liked you, it would have killed you.'

'Great. That's very comforting to know. Why did you send that note in the first place?' Max asked. 'And how the hell did you get it into Farefield library?

'Is that what it's called? The library you came from?'

'Yep.'

Merelie's eyes went misty. 'Is it beautiful? Your library? I bet it is.'

Max pictured Farefield library in his head: The woeful window displays. The lack of decent books. The grey concrete walls. 'I wouldn't quite say beautiful, no.'

'Anywhere there are books is beautiful, Max... because they are.'

'You obviously haven't read anything by Clive Bonnet,' Max muttered under his breath.

'What?'

'Doesn't matter. How did you get the message through?'

'You just have to know how to craft the words, that's all, and know how to access the doorway.' She said this like it made any sense whatsoever.

'That doesn't make any sense whatsoever.'

Merelie looked at him with disbelief. 'I know your world doesn't work like ours, but I had no idea it was this bad.'

He gave her a blank look.

She sighed and continued. 'Words have weight, Max. They have power. All written words capture the thoughts and dreams of the people who write them. When enough of them are collected in a book, their weight grows.'

Merelie paused, giving Max time to digest this.

'The more you have in one place,' she explained, 'the heavier they get. The *stronger* they get. Understand?'

Max nodded. He didn't want her to think he was an idiot.

'Books gain energy from one another, the same way we gain energy from each other, like this.' She took his hand in hers. It felt a little cold. 'If I keep my hand in yours for long enough, it'll get warm like yours, yes?

'Um... yeah.'

'Words work the same way.'

'That's silly. You're talking like they're living things.'

'They are! If you understand them, anyway.'

Merelie picked up a piece of paper from the table and gave it to Max. 'Hold this up for me, and keep it flat.'

He did so, wondering where this was going.

'When you get enough books in one place - thousands and thousands, I mean - they can get so heavy that with a little help they can... well, rip through space itself.' She prodded the paper with one finger, tearing a hole in it. 'Those rips always go somewhere else. Once you know that, it's just a question of finding out where. One rip leads to your world and I sent the note through it.'

'So you knew it would end up in Clive Bonnet's book?' This was a weird choice to Max. He thought she would have picked something more appropriate. Alice in Wonderland, perhaps.

'I've never heard of that book. I couldn't be that accurate. The whole thing was random... a bit hit and miss. I just knew the note would end up in the same library The Cornerstone was in.'

'But it might never have got read,' Max pointed out. 'It could have been a waste of time. It could have taken ages for anyone to see it, if nothing else.'

'True, but I had no choice. Contact with your world is so restricted. I had to hope The Cornerstone would help me. It helped me write the note, after all.'

'What do you mean?'

'Flick to the back page,' Merelie said, a guilty look on her face.

Max saw why as he opened The Cornerstone and saw that the last page had been ripped out. A ragged sliver of paper was still visible, poking out from the binding.

'Defacing a Cornerstone like that is a horrible thing to do,' Merelie said, 'but I had no choice... and it let me do it. I knew someone would find the note sooner or later, and here you are!'

'Yeah, here I am,' Max said with uncertainty.

Something else occurred to him. 'We've got The Cornerstone here, right?' he said, giving it a poke.

'Don't poke it, Max.'

'Sorry. If it's here, how can it also be back in the library in Farefield?'

'It's the same book, Max. Two ends of the pathway between worlds.'

'It's the same book, but there's two of it.'

'Exactly!' Merelie beamed, thinking Max understood.

He didn't, of course.

'Forget it!' he said, before Merelie could launch into another explanation. 'I'll just pretend I understand and we'll call it quits for now.'

'If you say so.'

'How did you know the other book - that's actually also this book, but isn't – was in Farefield?'

'I've always known The Cornerstone was there, along with someone from my world.'

'You mean Imelda the librarian?'

'Yes. She protects the book and uses it to communicate.'

'...through the doorway it creates.'

'That's right! No-one can open it by themselves. You need The Cornerstone to do it. That's why it was created - as a means for people to travel between worlds.'

'Which brings us back to my main point,' Max remembered. 'Why did you bring me here? Why do you think I can help you?

'Because only someone from your world can stop them Max, that's why.' Merelie looked frightened for the first time.

'Stop *who*?'

'MERELIE!'

Max jumped two feet in the air and Merelie let out a yelp of surprise as the marble doors slammed open and a wall with arms ran in.

Actually, it wasn't a wall with arms - but a tall, broad shouldered man, of a size that'd make Arnold Schwarzenegger think twice about starting something.

'Borne!' Merelie exclaimed.

Borne was the kind of square-jawed, muscle-bound idiot Max could really learn to despise.

He had short cropped brown hair, arms like a sack of walnuts and a definite military air about him. He wore a dark green leather tunic, black combat trousers and polished black boots.

'Merelie! Your father is on his way up!' Borne thundered. He stabbed a finger at Max. 'He should not be here, girl!'

'We need him!'

'Your father doesn't agree.'

'My father has his head in the sand, Borne. You know that!'

'I'm your Arma Merelie, not one of your little friends. I keep my opinions to myself.'

Max guessed an Arma was a bodyguard of some kind. This Borne looked liked he could guard several bodies at once.

Merelie looked at Max in panic. 'He mustn't find you here! I used The Cornerstone without authorisation,' she said, sounding almost hysterical.

'We'd better leave then, yeah?' Max said.

Borne gave him a look that made his eyes water.

'Come on Merelie,' the big man said. 'We'll head out of the Chapter House and into the city. We can say you were in the commerce square again. Once we're out, we can send this one back to where he comes from.'

'But I haven't told him everything yet! He needs to understand if he's going to help!' Merelie's voice had risen to an octave range that was bordering on painful. Max had heard the same tone from both his mother and sister at one time or another – usually when they thought he'd done something wrong.

'We don't have time to discuss this!' the Arma roared and took Merelie's arm, pulling her to her feet. 'Come on both of you!'

Borne marched Merelie away and Max - still frustrated that he understood so little - gathered up The Cornerstone and followed them out of the chamber.

All three walked at a brisk pace towards the stairs leading to the large hall below. The Arma looked in every direction as he went, as if on the look-out for an ambush.

Max was feeling decidedly put out at this juncture.

Considering he hadn't asked to get caught up in this mess, he'd been led around by the nose and kept in the dark about proceedings for far too long now. It was really starting to grate. About the only thing Max was sure about was that he was so far out of his depth he was bumping into giant squid and angler fish.

Thinking things through caused his pace to slow. Borne noticed the drop in speed and glared at him.

'Keep up boy!' he ordered, between clenched teeth.

Right, that's bloody it!

The Arma continued up the corridor a few steps dragging Merelie along, before he realised Max had stopped.

'What are you doing, boy?!' he hissed.

'Max?' Merelie said, in a small voice.

'You know what?' Max said in a matter-of-fact tone. 'I don't like being confused... and I really don't like being scared. Especially when I've got no idea what I'm supposed to be scared *of.*' He warmed up the pointy finger. 'I'm also not keen on running around like a headless chicken in a place I've never been before, having no idea where I'm going!' The finger not only pointed now, it waggled a bit too. 'But most of all, I really, really don't like being ordered around by people *I've only just met!*'

Borne looked surprised, like he'd just been attacked by a wet flannel. Merelie looked half way between shocked and amused.

'I can see why The Cornerstone likes him,' Borne said. 'They've got the same temperament.'

'They have, haven't they?' Merelie agreed, smiling despite herself.

'Oh, I'm glad you're both finding this funny,' Max said, his temper now at boiling point. 'Let's laugh at the idiot from another dimension shall we?'

'I'm sorry, Max' Merelie apologised.

'Are you really? Well then Merelie, if Captain Steroid Abuse will let you, could you please tell me why the hell you brought me here?'

'Because my daughter thinks she knows better than her elders, boy,' said a calm, clear voice from behind him.

- 5 -

Ten minutes later, Max found himself in a large, book-lined study. The room was dominated by a large, highly polished marble desk in a deep sea green colour, with a high backed chair in the same shade behind it.

Embossed on the front of the desk and back of the chair was a large circular symbol. To Max it looked like a pair of antlers crossed with one of those tribal tattoos people have. He supposed it must be a coat of arms for Merelie's family. All four walls of the room were covered in book cases, carrying on the love affair these people had with the written word. It reminded Max of his grandfather Charlie's front room.

It was just as well the study was large, as it had to contain a lot of people this morning. Max and Merelie sat in front of the massive desk, like school children called to the headmaster's office for letting off stink bombs. Borne stood between them - arms crossed and looking slightly ashamed of himself.

The Cornerstone sat on the desk, having been taken away from Max the second they'd been captured.

Lined up along the back wall were several enormous men in armour - the Chapter Guards Merelie had been afraid of running into. They'd marched Max up to this room against his loud protests.

He could attest to both the strength of their grip and the hardness of their armour - nursing a painful bruise on his left elbow due to the latter. It was like the Kevlar bullet proof vests he'd seen American soldiers wearing, but coloured the same green as the desk. They wore helmets as well, adorned with the odd looking coat of arms.

Sat behind the desk was a man looking at Max and Merelie over steepled fingers. He was tall, thin - just this side of gaunt, in fact - and bald, with a wreath of short grey hair at the sides. He had the same piercing blue eyes as Merelie.

He wore a long cream coat, buttoned to the neck and dropping almost to the floor. The coat of arms was embroidered in green on the left breast.

This dude looks like he should be standing on the bridge of the Enterprise, telling that one with the pastie on his head to 'make it so'.

The man noticed Max's attention and focused his gaze. 'Has my daughter even bothered to tell you whose house you've trespassed in, boy?' he said, cutting through any pleasantries.

'No she hasn't,' Max replied, adding a hasty 'sir,' at the end, because good manners couldn't hurt in a situation like this.

Merelie's father favoured her with a stern look. 'I'm not surprised at all,'

Merelie said nothing.

'My name is Jacob Carvallen, Chapter Lord of this House,' he announced.

Max felt something was required of him at this point. 'Erm. Ok. Good name... sounds impressive.'

'And you are?'

'I'm Max Bloom. I come from Farefield. In England. Er... on Earth.' There wasn't much more he could add.

'I know where you're from, boy. It was our House that discovered the pathway to your world.'

'Right... gotcha. Good for you.' This wasn't going well at all.

'How is it we have not heard from the Wordsmith appointed to watch the doorway?' asked Jacob Carvallen. 'Why did I have no warning of your unauthorised use of The Cornerstone?'

'Imelda, you mean?' Max looked at Merelie, who nodded. 'Well... the book wouldn't let her contact you.'

'What do you mean by that?' Jacob asked, looking down at The Cornerstone.

'It wouldn't let her use it. She said it was being stubborn.'

'It knows father, The Cornerstone knows!' Merelie blurted out. 'It knows something's coming... that's why it wouldn't let your spy talk. That's why it brought Max here!'

'Be quiet Merelie!' Jacob snapped and looked at Borne. 'Arma, how could you allow this? She should have been under your supervision at all times.'

'Your daughter is more than smart enough to elude me when she wishes to, sir.' Borne replied. 'She's committed to her cause and believes everything she says. Perhaps you should listen before dismissing her fears completely.'

'I *have* been listening for a long time Borne and there is no evidence that this great evil of which she speaks exists!'

Max lent forward in his chair. Merelie's angry father looked like he was about to spill the beans.

'I have had the custodians searching the void,' the Chapter Lord continued, 'Wordcrafting for days at a time, and they have found nothing!'

Merelie jumped out of her seat. 'Father, you never told me that!'

'I'm not a stupid man, Merelie. If someone I trust warns me of impending doom, I look into it.' Jacob gave Borne a meaningful look. 'I listened and did what I thought was appropriate.' He turned his attention back to Merelie. 'But there's been nothing. No sign that the void between worlds is about to spill out a monstrous evil that will lay waste to us all.'

Merelie sat back in her chair, deflated. 'But the dreams, father. The way the words have come to me... it must be true.'

'I don't know what to tell you, Merelie. I really don't,' Jacob replied, a little compassion slipping into his voice for the first time.

He got up, walked around the desk and took his daughter's hands. 'This has to stop now. You have to send this boy back and forget these nightmares. Nothing is coming to kill us. We're safe.'

Merelie's eyes filled with doubt. 'It's been so clear father, for so long. I see them breaking into our world. Invading our minds and twisting us until - ' The fear etched across her face was horrible. 'You asked me why I brought you here, Max. Why I needed somebody from your world?'

Here we go!

'It's because only someone like you can stop it. When the darkness spreads, only a powerful Wordsmith from your world can save us.'

Max looked blanker than a gambler's cheque.

'Right,' he said, digesting this. 'Just one question?'

'Yes?'

'What's a Wordsmith?'

Jacob Carvallen tutted and looked at Merelie. 'You didn't tell him much, did you?'

'She's tried,' Max said in a strained voice, resisting his natural urge to start chucking insults about. 'We keep getting *interrupted.*'

'A Wordsmith is one blessed with the natural talent to shape words and grasp the power they hold... and the training to do it properly,' Jacob told him.

'A wizard, then?' Max felt on slightly firmer ground here.

'That's a word from your world, boy. Not ours.'

Stop calling me boy.

'Whatever! Wizard or Wordsmith. I'm not one, I know that much.'

'But you will be!' Merelie exclaimed. 'You *have* to be. Your world has so many books... so many words, so much potential power. You should *all* be capable of word shaping. That's why I brought you here. You can save us, Max. You alone can stand against the darkness I've seen coming!' Her eyes gleamed with hope.

'Right... so what happens to me if I'm not an ultra super powerful Wordsmith when this darkness turns up?' Max asked, dreading the answer.

Merelie looked non-plussed. 'Why, you'd… you'd die. We all would.'

I should have stayed in bed this morning.

Jacob gave him a sympathetic look. 'I'm sorry boy. I've known my daughter's intentions for a long time. She believes that you - as a citizen of your world - are the saviour of my people. With The Cornerstone colluding with her, your presence here was guaranteed.'

Max Bloom drew himself up to his full five foot eight inches, took a deep breath and aimed the pointy finger of doom at Merelie. 'You're telling me you dragged me into this stupid dimension to stop some indescribable creatures from sucking your brains out 'coz you think I can be some kind of magical wizard, shooting lightning bolts out of my arse? And you reckon I can *single-handedly* save your entire race. Have I got that about right?'

'Yes, Max. That's right,' Merelie said with a smile, happy he understood his part in the grand scheme of things.

Max's face had gone an alarming shade of red.

'Did it not occur to you,' he continued. 'That I – and every other berk from my world – might not have any super-duper magical powers, and that if I go up against your evil monstrosities, I'll get skinned alive in thirty seconds flat?'

Merelie looked confused. 'No, Max. That's not how it's supposed to happen.'

'*Supposed* to happen?? You… you… ' He was so angry the power of speech was starting to desert him. 'You're bloody nuts!'

Jacob and Merelie were both taken aback.

'There's no need to talk to my daughter that way,' Jacob warned.

When Max gets a temper going, his instincts for self-preservation get sidelined. 'Oh shut up, baldy! If you could control your bloody kids I wouldn't be in this mess!'

'Don't speak to me in that tone, boy!'

'Stop calling me boy! I'm not your bloody servant!' Max grabbed The Cornerstone and shook it at Merelie. 'Send me home. Send me home now!'

Merelie actually had the decency to look a bit scared. 'Ok, Max. I will… but without you, we're all dead!'

'Well without you, I'm not! I should - '

We don't get to hear what Max should or shouldn't do, as Borne - who'd had quite enough of his mistress being insulted - gave Max a smart whack across the back of the head. Nothing too damaging, you understand. He isn't a barbarian. However, the blow was more than hard enough to send Max from standing indignantly in a rage, to laid out on the floor unconscious.

Borne had actually done Max something of a favour, as several Chapter Guards had started drawing unpleasant looking crossbow guns from their holsters.

One lunge from Max at either of the Carvallen family members and he'd have been turned into a pin-cushion with frightening speed and accuracy.

Jacob Carvallen was not the sort of man who got shouted at a lot and nobody had ever called him baldy before. It was an experience he was still trying to process as he looked down at the incumbent form of Max Bloom. 'He certainly is a strong-willed one. I can see why The Cornerstone likes him.'

'That's what I said, sir,' Borne pointed out.

'He could still help us,' said Merelie.

'I rather think not,' her father said. 'There's no need for this boy to go into battle and sacrifice himself. No darkness is set to engulf us - the custodians have proved it.' Jacob knelt and checked Max's pulse. 'I think you'd have a very hard time convincing him to help us now anyway,' he added, satisfied the boy's heartbeat was strong and regular.

Everyone's heartbeat shot up as the large study doors flew open and a grossly overweight man in a billowing blue suit waddled in, flanked by several guardsmen, also clad in blue.

'Carvallen! What the hell's going on?' the fat man roared. 'You've been away from the table for too long! Falion is spouting her drivel about equality for the masses again and Lord Morodai objects. We need you to mediate!' He caught sight of Max lying on the ground. 'Who in the Writer's name is that?'

'Apologies Osgood,' Jacob said, 'I shouldn't have absented myself for so long. You needn't worry about this boy. He's a problem of my daughter's making, but I think we've managed to clear it up... haven't we Merelie?'

Merelie said nothing. She was concentrating too much on glowering at the fat newcomer.

'Hello Merelie,' he said, seeing her for the first time.

'Good morning Chapter Lord Draveli,' Merelie responded, with enough ice in her voice to go well with a shot of whisky.

Osgood Draveli looked at Max and back at the two Carvallens standing over him. 'Let me guess Merelie,' he sighed, 'this has something to do with your insistence we're all doomed, hasn't it?' He snorted like a pig. 'You finally did it, didn't you? Dragged some poor fool from that charmless little existence over here to be part of your delusion.'

'That will do Osgood,' Jacob said. 'My daughter has had the facts laid out to her and I'm confident this is the last we'll hear of this.' He looked at Borne. 'Arma, take my daughter to her rooms. I will oversee this boy's passage back through The Cornerstone. I want his return properly supervised by the custodians. Until then, I'll have him held in the cells.'

'Father! He isn't a prisoner!'

'What do you suggest, then? This is a problem of your devising.'

Merelie thought for a second. 'Let me take him down to the Library. The Cornerstone will need replenishing anyway, so I might as well.'

Carvallen looked at his daughter with suspicion.

'Trust me father,' Merelie said, 'I know I've gone too far. I'll send him home as quickly as possible.'

'Time is of the essence, Jacob,' Osgood piped up again. 'The talks are at a very critical stage and you left at a most inopportune moment. If this doesn't work out, it could mean war between the Chapters!'

'It won't come to that, Osgood,' Jacob said. 'Merelie, I'll trust you to get rid of this boy. Don't disappoint me please... Borne, make sure she keeps her word.'

Without waiting for a response, Jacob strode out of the study with the corpulent Osgood Draveli in his wake.

'Blrhrmfrhm,' Max said as he came to while slung over Borne's sweaty back.

He felt lifted, then dumped unceremoniously into a large chair, which at least had the good grace to be soft.

'Go easy with him Borne,' Merelie told her Arma.

'He insulted you, Merelie. I don't like that.'

'He was angry.'

'Manners are manners.'

'Where the hell am I?' Max said.

'We're in the entrance lobby to the Library,' Merelie said, walking over to a large door at the back of the room.

'Library?'

'Yes, the one you were in the last time you came here.' She knocked on the door gently.

Despite the smack on the head and subsequent grogginess, Max was up like a shot, looking for invisible library monsters.

'Relax boy,' said Borne. 'The guardian is nowhere near us. It patrols the sections of the library where the mystical books are. We're quite safe here.'

Max looked at him with deep suspicion, but relaxed his guard. He had to admit the room they were in didn't look the type favoured by your average invisible creature from Hell.

It was spacious and well appointed, laid with luxurious green carpeting with the Carvallen coat of arms stitched into it, and containing several plush cream coloured couches and chairs.

It was a bit like the waiting room of a particularly upmarket plastic surgeon's office. The kind celebrities go to when they want to shave off a few years.

Merelie walked back, her shoes making no noise on the thick carpet. 'It shouldn't take too long,' she said. 'The head custodian will know we're here and will be up shortly.'

'Whoopee crap,' replied Max, sitting back on the couch in a huff.

Merelie sat and looked at him with her big, blue eyes firmly set on stun mode. 'I know you don't believe me Max. You don't think you have this power in you, but I know I'm right. When the evil from my dreams is unleashed, it's you who will save us.'

'But your old man says there's nothing to worry about!' Max argued.

'I still think he's wrong,' she replied, but there was doubt in her eyes.

'He's a powerful bloke, though,' he pointed out, 'being in charge of this place and everything. Maybe he knows better than you?'

'He hasn't had the dreams… and neither have you.'

'Oh, here we go with the dreams again.' He shook his head. 'Dreams are stupid, Merelie. My mate Figgy says they're just your brain taking a dump.'

She didn't quite know how to respond to that.

Max, knowing how idiotic that had sounded, tried to regain some momentum. 'What I'm saying is… dreams don't mean anything. It's just your mind processing the rubbish floating round. Figgy says you'd go mental if you didn't dream. There's nothing more to it than that.'

'Not my dreams, Max.'

'Really?' he said, folding his arms and sitting back.

Merelie's eyes narrowed. 'Borne? Give me The Cornerstone!'

'Merelie, that's not wise,' the Arma replied. 'We should wait for the custodian.'

'Give it to me Borne… now!'

Borne heaved a sigh, fished the book out from one of his large trouser pockets and handed it over. 'I don't know what you expect it to do, Merelie. It probably needs charging.'

'Not for what I'm going to do. The door I'll be opening isn't to another world,' she said, flipping The Cornerstone open.

Despite himself, Max leaned over to see what was going on.

Merelie stared at the blank pages of the book, whispering under her breath.

Words began to appear on the paper at great speed, the page flipping over once it was full. Max couldn't make out what was being written, but whatever it was, it filled the whole Cornerstone from cover to cover.

The book was glowing in Merelie's hands as she continued to speak under her breath, eyes closed in concentration.

When the last page was reached, she gasped and slammed the book shut.

'Merelie! What have you done?' Borne demanded, trying to take The Cornerstone back.

'No! He needs to see!' she cried, opening the book again and thrusting it at Max. 'Read!' she commanded.

Max made a face, but then looked down, doing as he was told:

The first time I had the dream I was six and could barely understand what I'd seen.

This was different. It wasn't describing what had just happened.

In the years that have passed however, I've become more and more aware I was seeing the end of everything, and I knew I had to do something to stop it.

This was Merelie speaking.
Good grief, am I about to see her dreams?
Sure enough, silver light enveloped Max and he entered Merelie's subconscious.

- 7 -

Max materialised out of the light into the girl's chambers, which now looked quite different from the rooms he'd visited earlier.

Stuffed animals gave him glassy looks from every available flat surface and a huge doll's house sat in the centre of the room. It was actually more of a tower, reaching a good six feet from the bedroom floor. Max wondered if this was a representation of the Carvallen Chapter House. If it was, the real building must dominate the skyline. It looked imposing, even in miniature form.

The rest of the floor was covered in brightly coloured cushions and a variety of dolls, discarded as their owner got bored with them.

This was the domain of a child, and Max wasn't surprised to find that when he tip-toed over to the bed, he could see a little blonde girl of about six sleeping peacefully, her arms wrapped around a stuffed horse.

The mini version of Merelie started to twitch, entering what appeared to be a vivid dream. It evidently wasn't a good one.

She started to whimper, her eyes trembling back and forth beneath the lids. Max lent forward and shook her shoulder, trying to bring her out of the nightmare. Her eyes snapped open and she screamed at the top of her lungs.

The bedroom dissolved, like smoke blown away in a gust of strong wind, leaving only Max, Merelie and the large bed she lay in.

What replaced the room was very strange indeed.

Max stood on a soft white surface of woven material. It looked like wood, but felt quite springy underfoot.

The sky above was the same writhing purple mass as the void The Cornerstone had sent him through the first time he'd used it. Flecks of bright silver rolled and spun in the dark mass, creating a night sky alive with light, under which rested this odd, silent landscape.

It was all very eerie.

'Hello Max,' said a tiny, piping voice from behind him.

He looked at the bed where the mini version of Merelie was now awake.

'Merelie?' he asked.

'Yes, it's me. This is how I looked when the nightmares first started.'

'But... you're talking to me as you are now and not as you were then, even though you look like you did then and not like you do now?' Max was quite pleased with the way he'd negotiated his way through that sentence.

'Yes, that's right... I think.'

'Where are we exactly?' he asked, trying to get back on firmer conversational ground.

'This is how the nightmare always starts.' She looked up at the moving night sky. 'Seems quite peaceful doesn't it? It doesn't stay this way, though.'

'Brilliant. My nightmares usually start with me butt naked in front of my old geography class. If I'm really unlucky there's a giant pair of scissors outside waiting to attack me.'

Merelie gave him a perplexed look.

'Er... so why does your nightmare start like this?' he said, changing the subject.

'Books mean so much to my people Max. They shape the way we look at the universe. There's nothing more sacred to us than the blank pages of a new book, waiting to be filled with the words from someone's heart.'

It clicked in Max's head what the odd, weaved, white surface was.

I'm standing on a gigantic book, floating in space. I will never need to take drugs in my entire life.

'Is this The Cornerstone?' he said, prodding the vast white sheet of paper with a tentative foot.

'I don't think so. It doesn't feel like The Cornerstone. That's created to open doorways to other worlds... or in this case to my dreams. This book was created in my mind. It's a book of prophecy. You'll see what I mean. '

'It's all about the books, eh?'

'They're my world.' she said. 'From an early age, I was taught to respect and learn from the words written by those who came before me. I was told to read as much as I could - and to always keep an open mind. My people form our beliefs and morality that way. Everyone comes to their own conclusions, based upon what they've read.'

'That makes sense, I suppose,' Max said, gazing up into the sky. 'Let people make up their own minds.' It certainly sounded better than the way they did things back home, he had to admit.

Feeling a sudden attack of agoraphobia, he sat on the bed and focused his attention on the little girl.

'Most people are only affected by the power of words inside,' Merelie continued, putting her hand to her heart. 'Like when they read a sad story and cry... or read something stupid that makes them angry.'

'Yep... with you so far,' and he really was - thoughts of Buck the sled dog ran through his mind.

'But some can use this power to affect the outside world… use it to do amazing things.' Merelie's face lit up as she spoke.

'Like punch holes in space, right?' Max said.

'Yes, just like that!'

'You're one of these special people, I suppose?'

'I am. They saw I had the talent when I was about the age I look to you now. I'm a Carvallen, so it's not that surprising. I've been in training since then.' A note of pride entered her voice. 'I'm pretty much the youngest Wordsmith in history.'

Wordsmith.

There was that word again.

Like a blacksmith… only with words on a page, rather than metal in a fire.

It had a ring to it.

'So you think I'm like you then? You think I can be a Wordsmith?'

'Yes, I do.'

'More powerful than you? Just because I come from a place where there are loads of books?' This was the part Max couldn't get his head around.

Little Merelie's eyes lit up.

'Oh yes. There are millions where you come from. It's incredible!'

'Well, I still think you're a bit mental,' he said, automatically feeling bad about having a go at what was ostensibly a six year old girl.

Merelie looked hurt and they both lapsed into a brief silence.

'When's this dream start then?' Max asked.

At a speed so horrific it could turn milk sour, the book below the bed fell away, leaving it floating in space. Max clung to the duvet, making a strangled noise at the back of his throat.

The giant book ceased its rapid descent, spun itself upwards through forty five degrees and shot forward until it filled their field of vision.

'Why the hell did that happen?!' Max screamed, trying not to look down into the enormous purple gulf below.

'I have no idea, Max… nightmare, remember?' said Merelie, looking at the book, her voice trembling with dread. 'It's starting.'

There was nothing more Max Bloom would like to do right now than to climb under the duvet, fall asleep and wake from this nightmare in his own bed - in his own house, in his own reality.

He followed Merelie's gaze up to the huge floating book.

Something began to write on it.

- 8 -

Across the sixty foot high page, thick black writing started to appear.

Max held his breath as a message scratched itself across the page, scrawled in ugly, ragged letters by a great unseen hand:

We see you...
We hear you...
We watch as you cross the spaces between.
We dwell in the dark - and we are **hungry.**
We will eat the words from your mind and walk in your skins.
We will walk through all worlds - and we will feed...

Max heard crying beside him.

'Merelie?' he said, but the little girl didn't reply.

'Merelie?' he repeated, still with no response. She was transfixed.

One more sentence etched its way across the bottom of the gigantic page:

This is how your story will end...

With a gut-wrenching roar, a huge slash ripped across the page, quickly followed by another and another, as if huge, invisible claws were attacking the book. It was shredded in front of their eyes in an assault fuelled by some apocalyptic rage they had no way of stopping, or surviving if it turned on them.

Merelie screamed as the massive book hanging in front of them was eviscerated – huge, ragged pieces of paper beginning to rain down around them.

———

73

Then the bed dropped like a stone.

As they plummeted, Max glanced over the edge in terror to see the ground flying up to meet them at an impossible speed.

There was a huge lurch and a nauseating sensation in the pit of his stomach as the bed came to a juddering halt. It clattered down onto flagstones in a vast courtyard lying in front of a gigantic stone tower. Max relaxed the death grip he had on the duvet and tried to sit up straight for a better look. All this whooshing about at stupid speeds had done nothing for his inner ear balance though, so he promptly fell off the bed.

Letting out a cry as his backside made contact with the flagstones, Max made a grab for the duvet. Muttering in discomfort, he pulled himself back up and had another go at looking around.

On the wall in front of him was a massive plaque bearing the Carvallen coat of arms, underneath which was written 'Main Courtyard'. Below this was an enormous set of doors that looked strong enough to stop a nuclear bomb.

Mini-Merelie climbed off the bed, walked over and pushed one open with no effort. As it swung open in silence, Max could see what lay beyond.

He'd seen quite a few horror movies in his life, ranging from gross-out numbers like Day of the Dead and Saw, to the seemingly endless sequels to Friday the 13th and Halloween. None of these movies had bothered him a bit.

You'd have thought all that would prepare him for the sight that met his eyes just beyond the open doorway.

It didn't.

Not by a long shot.

There were monsters in that room. Monsters with human faces.

Several hundred were packed into the cavernous hall, silent except for the rustling of clothes as they swayed and rubbed against one another like grass in a soft breeze. None had blood running down their faces, limbs missing or chunks of flesh torn out, but they still looked more terrifying than anything lurking in the horror section at Amazon. Their eyes sockets boiled with a hideous purple and black smoke, their collective gaze locked on little Merelie. Each of them was holding a book, and one by one they started to tear the pages out, stuffing the paper into their mouths with ravenous pleasure.

Max recognised one pallid grey face in the crowd. Borne was eating slowly and leering at the girl.

A woman - who looked so much like Merelie it could only be her mother - stood in the centre of the silent horde, methodically chewing paper ripped from the mangled Cornerstone, which she held shut in one grey, withered hand.

She moved to one side and the crowd parted.

A younger version of Jacob Carvallen was thrown forward out of the throng to fall at his wife's feet.

'Daddy!' little Merelie cried.

'Merelie?' he said, eyes widening as he realised how close his daughter was to danger. 'Run Merelie! Run before they get into your head!'

With a hiss, Merelie's possessed mother opened The Cornerstone. Thick, black and purple ribbons of smoke streamed from it, directly into Jacob's eyes. His body jerked and twitched for a few moments and he screamed in agony, before becoming silent and still.

Then, as if a lightning bolt had passed through him, Jacob jumped to his feet and stared at his stricken daughter. 'Come here, child.' His voice was guttural and rasping. 'Let me feed on your thoughts… on your dreams.'

The Jacob-thing walked forward, grabbing at Merelie with clawed hands.

Max moved quickly to stand between Merelie and her possessed father. 'Not so fast, you demonic git!' he shouted and kicked Jacob so hard between the legs, the man's feet left the floor. The Jacob-thing looked about as surprised as a purple-and-black-smoke-eyed-demon-from-beyond-space can when it gets kicked in the cobblers.

Max stood triumphantly over his vanquished enemy for a moment, before realising that the rest of the evil hoard were starting to creep towards him, snarling like dogs.

He looked down at Mini-Merelie, who was now clinging to his leg. 'Um… if you've got any ideas how to get us out of this, now's the time,' he said.

Mini-Merelie looked at the ravening hoard and let out another high, piercing scream.

The universe took this as a cue to explode again. It'd happened so many times by now, Max was starting to find it a tad boring.

- 9 -

Max awoke back in the plush entrance hall to the Library, sat next to Merelie. He gave his rear end a rub, which felt like it had recently made contact with something hard and flagstone shaped. Merelie was staring at him.

'What's the matter?' he asked.

'You kicked my father between the legs,' she said in disbelief.

'Technically, I kicked a purple-and-black-smoke-eyed-demon-from-beyond-space in the shape of your father between the legs, I think you'll find.'

Merelie looked down at The Cornerstone. 'The dream's never finished like that before. I usually just scream and wake up as my father's hands close round my throat.'

'Glad to provide a bit of variety then.'

Borne came over and put an arm around his mistress. 'Are you alright, girl? I told you that wasn't a good idea.'

'I'm fine Borne. I've been through that so many times now I'm more than used to it.'

'You've had the dream a lot then?' Max said.

'At least once a week for ten years. Others like it, too. They always run along the same lines, though. You were in the version I tend to have the most.'

'Nasty.'

'Do you understand now?'

'Yeah, I get what you're on about. There are things out there in this place between worlds that have noticed you lot monkeying about creating doorways and they want to suck your brains out through your eyeballs. That about cover it?'

'It's one way of putting it,' said Merelie, frowning.

76

'Fair enough. I can understand why you'd want help with that and I guess a mega powerful Wordsmith from another dimension would fit the bill.' Max gave her an incredulous look. 'Why the hell you'd think it would be me is bonkers, though. There's no magic in my world – from books or anywhere else.'

'But there is my boy,' a cracked and aged voice said from over by the door, 'you just have to know where to look for it.'

Max looked round.

If it were possible to splice a human with a frog and a prune, this person would be the result. Tiny and wrinkled, it looked like he'd been left on a hot wash for half an hour too long.

The little man wore a serviceable plain robe in the dark green that denoted membership of the House of Carvallen. He also wore round-rimmed spectacles and had hair as white as snow, cropped close to his head. His face looked a bit like a new born baby's.

'You're not a fan of dramatic timing then, Mr Bloom?' said the frog prune as he floated over.

'You what? How do you know my name?'

'Timing is the essence of a good story... fictional or otherwise, Max,' he explained. 'I've read more than enough to know that. As to your second question, let's just say I'm in the position to know most of what goes on in and around the Chapter House... and who's involved,' he said and offered Max a wise smile.

Good grief, this one's going to be annoying.

Merelie moved closer to the walking wrinkle and took his frail looking hands in hers.

'Garrowain, it's so good to see you again.'

'And you too, child.' He looked over at Max. 'You've been busy I see.'

'Yes, but I'm not sure it served much of a purpose.'

'Purpose only chooses to reveal itself at the right time, child,' the old man said, so wisely it was nauseating.

'This is Garrowain, Max,' Merelie told him. 'He's the head custodian of the Carvallen Library. He oversees all those who look after the books in our Chapter House. He's a dear friend and has helped me interpret my dreams. Without him, I'd know nothing of your world and you'd never have seen my message.'

Max rolled his eyes. He wasn't much of a book reader, but he'd seen enough movies to know this old codger was revered by everyone and could probably provide a sage and apt quotation for any situation.

'So let me get this straight, it's your fault Merelie thinks I'm Captain Magic – and the reason I'm going to get skinned alive by purple monsters?'

'As I'm sure you're aware by now, it isn't about you specifically Mr Bloom,' Garrowain said, in a level tone. 'We believe the potential to be a great Wordsmith may exist in many of your race. You were just the one lucky enough to find Merelie's plea for help.'

'Lucky?'

'Indeed! To learn Wordcraft is a great honour. You will be the first from your world to do so and will tap a source of power as yet untouched by your people.'

'Will I?'

'Indeed. We will open both your eyes and your mind to the power we believe is within you. You will be able to face any horrors the void can muster.'

'And what if I can't? What if I'm about as magical as a drunk squirrel in leg warmers?'

Garrowain's train of thought was somewhat derailed by this. Merelie – who was getting used to Max's turn of phrase – answered for him.

'We don't believe that's possible. It simply can't be. All those books, all that potential power…'

'See, this is the bit I still don't get.' Max said, throwing his hands up in frustration.

'You're still confused about how we regard your world, Mr Bloom?' the custodian said, having finally pushed the vision of an inebriated tree-dwelling mammal out of his head.

'That's a wild understatement.'

Garrowain narrowed his eyes, assessing the irate teenager. 'Come with me,' he ordered and turned on his heels, floating back in the direction of the doorway.

This is the last time I'm blindly following somebody into a strange place.

Max made his way over to the door, into the library proper and whatever awaited him on the other side.

The dreadful mist was back.

It hung high in the large circular room they all now stood in, blanketing the ceiling and defying all laws of precipitation.

The room itself looked much more old fashioned and gothic than the rest of the Chapter House. It was all sweeping buttresses and knobbly stonework. Several arched doorways were sat at regular intervals in the smooth, grey stone wall and tall metal sconces were placed between them. They were the same as those on the upper floors, containing orbs of light which gave off a pleasant blue glow, illuminating the large chamber and the underside of the disconcerting mist.

The temperature had dropped several degrees and Max was glad he'd elected to wear his hoodie today.

'It's so good to be here again,' said Merelie.

'You absent yourself for too long these days, my girl,' Garrowain agreed.

'Circumstances have been against her, custodian,' Borne said, defending his mistress.

All three of them were acting like devout parishioners in a church; speaking in hushed tones and moving around in a careful, quiet manner. This was obviously a sacred place to the people of the Carvallen Chapter House.

Max was having none of it.

'What's this gaff, then?' he said in a loud voice.

'This is the Main Hub of the Carvallen Library, Mr Bloom,' the custodian replied. 'From here we can visit any section we desire.'

'Ah, right. Does that include the one with the invisible book chucking lunatic?'

'You refer to the Guardian of the Stacks, I assume? That entity only roams the corridors of the Library devoted to supernatural texts. It is the physical embodiment of dark writings, produced by many disturbed individuals.'

'Ah... nut jobs.' Max flashed the old man a quick grin.

Garrowain chose to ignore this and walked over to a pedestal in the centre of the room on which – naturally - sat a book. This one looked properly magical in Max's opinion. Not boring and ordinary like The Cornerstone.

It was huge, with an ornate silver and green cover, replete with embossed writing, curly filigree and other somewhat unnecessary artistic flourishes. The pages inside looked like they'd been dunked in tea for a fortnight. It even had an ostentatious padlock, keeping the book's secrets from all but those with the appropriate levels of wisdom and glaring self-righteousness.

Garrowain fished out an elaborate silver key from his robe, twiddled it in the lock and opened the great tome.

'This another magic book then, Gandalf? What are you gonna do with it, turn me into a banana?' Max asked.

Garrowain picked up a long quill from the pedestal and paused to look at him. 'Mr Bloom, I can assure you the rise you are attempting to get out of me with your rather coarse behaviour will not manifest. I take no pleasure in the situation we find ourselves in, nor in what must be done to resolve it. Therefore, directing your anger at me is pointless. You should learn a little trust.'

'If you say so, Yoda. But if you don't mind, when it comes to trusting what people say around here, I'll keep my options open, alright?'

Merelie touched him on the arm. 'He's telling the truth, Max. Garrowain wouldn't lie.'

'Your caution does you credit, young man,' the old man said and turned back to the great book on the pedestal.

He opened it to a page about halfway through. Max peeked over his shoulder.

Several entries had been made in a variety of hands:

Information on the fermentation of alcohol from summer fruits.
The story by Mecledies about the formation of House Wellhome.
The Siren and the Sailor by Halbroke.
The nomad settlements and geography of the Northern Carvallen plains, circa Year of Writing 1,958.

Below the last entry, Garrowain wrote:

Earth: its discovery, people, and relationship with our own world.

As the custodian completed the 'd' of world, the letters flashed in the same silver light that came from The Cornerstone. Then there was a loud grinding noise coming from somewhere beyond the stone walls.

Merelie, Borne and Garrowain seemed to take this in their stride, so Max guessed it was meant to happen and that the ceiling wasn't about to fall on his head.

'What's going on now?' he asked Merelie.

'The Library is finding the right section,' she shouted over the din. 'Garrowain wrote what he wishes to view in the Codex and the Library will bring it to us.'

'The library takes *you* to the book you want?'

'Yes, of course! That's how libraries work.'

Max started to ask another question, but stopped himself. 'This is more weird magical stuff I'm never going to understand, isn't it?'

Merelie smiled.

The grinding subsided. The door directly opposite the pedestal flashed silver along its edges.

'The centre door today, it seems,' Garrowain said and walked over to it.

Merelie and Borne followed with Max in tow, a look of deep distrust on his face. The old man pressed a hand to the door, muttered softly under his breath and it swung open.

It led onto a long corridor of bookshelves, much like the one Max had materialised in yesterday. The only difference he could spot was that here the books looked more colourful and a tad friendlier.

'Follow me,' said Garrowain, 'it won't be far along.'

The little man strode away with the assurance of someone who had done so a thousand times before. Merelie and Borne followed with similar confidence.

Max *crept* across the threshold, eyeing the doorway and poised to run like a scalded cat the second he spotted tentacles. As he forced himself to speed up to catch the others, he was surprised to see books he could actually read. Not only could he read them, he'd seen a lot of them before.

'Er… where did these come from?' he said to Garrowain, as they walked past the entire Wilt saga by Tom Sharpe. 'These books are from my world.' He glanced over at the complete works of Barbara Cartland. 'Why are they in your library?'

Garrowain stopped just opposite Men Are From Mars and Women Are From Venus. 'We can't understand a society without reading its words.'

'It's a weird selection,' Max critiqued, wondering if the Haynes Manual for the Austin Montego was in here anywhere.

'Your world is a new find and we are a relatively young House, Mr Bloom. We are still learning and discovering which texts to embrace. There's been so much written by your people over the centuries.'

'You're not going to learn much from that one, chief,' Max said, pointing at a copy of Paris Hilton's biography.

Garrowain gave him another one of those insufferable smiles and continued his way along the corridor.

There were many books here, in many languages. Max supposed there was probably a sample from every country on Earth. As they progressed, he noticed the books becoming incomprehensible again. They were evidently leaving the part of the library where books from Earth were stored and moving into a section Max guessed was full of books *about* Earth, written by the people of this world.

There were a lot of them. Earth looked to be quite a popular place.

He mentioned this to Merelie.

'It is,' she said. 'It's a recent discovery, fascinating to read and write about.'

'Recent discovery? Like when?'

'Two hundred years, more or less.'

'That's *recent* is it?'

'Oh, yes. Very recent compared to the others.'

'Others?'

Merelie was about to respond when Garrowain stopped next to a bookshelf with some particularly thick volumes stuffed into it.

'Ah, here we are.'

He pointed a finger at by far and away the largest book Max had seen on this fun little excursion.

It was a good foot thick and four feet high. There was no writing on the spine, just an embossed image of Earth, detailed enough to have individual continents picked out in the stitching.

Looks like we found the Rough Guide to Earth, then. How's the little bugger going to lift it?

He expected Borne to step forward and heave the book down for Garrowain. The Arma had been silent during the whole trip and hadn't served much of a purpose. Heavy lifting looked to be the best use of those ridiculously muscular arms, so Max supposed the giant was about to do his thing. He was therefore surprised when the big man didn't budge and Garrowain stepped forward, holding his hands out.

'You'll give yourself a hernia trying to lift that,' Max warned.

'That is not how we read books of this type, Mr Bloom.'

'Then how - ' Max stopped, his head snapping around. 'Is the universe about to explode?' he asked, squinting in preparation.

'I rather think not,' Garrowain said. He placed his hands on the book, muttered briefly under his breath and stepped back as the familiar silver light played along its spine.

The great tome slid out of the shelf and hung in the air, bobbing up and down. The cover opened with a slight creak as Garrowain moved closer.

'Blimey,' Max said, more than a little awestruck.

Merelie smiled. 'This is the power I was on about, Max. You take the weight of the words and build a foundation with them. Anything is possible if you shape them well enough.'

'And Marrowbone here is good at it, I take it?'

'It's Garrowain… and yes, he's very good.'

Max's dad had recently been promoted, for being good at whatever it was he did for a living. To celebrate this, Peter Bloom had bought a lovely new fifty inch widescreen LCD telly with full HD.

He'd shown off the high definition glory with a wildlife documentary. It was so bright and crystal clear on the massive screen that after ten minutes Max's eyeballs had begun to ache and he'd had to go for a lie down.

The effect produced between the covers of this floating book was similar.

—

A glistening star field appeared on the double page spread. Comets streaked across the page and Max couldn't help but hear Captain Kirk's famous monologue in his head.

A slowly revolving planet Earth zoomed into view.

Golden writing appeared above it, floating just off the page:

'The planet Earth exists in the most recent dimension discovered by the shaping of words.

'Symon Carvallen created the gateway to this reality from the Chapter Lands in 1823 Y.W and commissioned a new Cornerstone book to facilitate a permanent and stable link.

'Each Chapter House retains its own Cornerstone, linked to their respective dimensions. As our knowledge has increased, so has the complexity of each Cornerstone book that has been created. The Carvallen is the fifth and most advanced.

'Symon Carvallen founded the fifth Chapter House - as was his right upon the creation of a new gateway - and the House of Carvallen has henceforth flourished under the guidance of - '

Garrowain gestured and the pages started to flick over. 'Apologies, the introduction takes quite a while. I'll forward to the passages we require.'

The pages stopped turning about midway and the interior of a large building swam into view.

The place was cavernous. Obviously a library, it had massive bookcases along the walls and the architecture was clean, white and thoroughly modern.

'In their research of this world, the Chapter House of Carvallen discovered a wealth of knowledge in written form, unheard of in The Chapter Lands, or in the other four existences overseen by the older Chapter Houses.

'This image shows The British Library, situated in the capital city of the nation known as Great Britain, where the gateway from our world leads.

'It is a repository of knowledge so huge it contains millions of texts, both factual and fictional, all written solely on Earth.

'Unlike our world, where only five libraries exist, Earth has **thousands**, *full to the rafters with books.*

*'This indicates that millions – if not **billions** – of their people are able to both read and write! The possibilities for word shaping from this are staggering!'*

The picture changed from the British Library to the Google Internet homepage. As the writing continued to spiel out, images flicked through thousands of internet sites at high speed.

'Not only do they have more books than the other worlds, they have a vast web of knowledge they call the internet, which is theoretically accessible to everyone. However, at this stage, the validity of the information included on this is in doubt. Any attempt at word shaping from such a dubious source could result in injuries... both mental and physical.'

Max chuckled as he pictured somebody trying to punch holes in reality using the words they found on the average sci-fi blog or gentleman's entertainment page. Mental and physical injury sounded like a tragic understatement.

'It should be noted that at this stage in the Carvallen research – some two hundred years of undertaking – not one individual from this world has displayed any evidence of talent for the use of Wordcraft.
*'This is **unprecedented**.'*

The last three words hung in the air, glowing in an almost accusing fashion. Max stared at them, trying to marshal his thoughts. This was quite an effort, as his thoughts didn't want to be marshalled in the slightest and were in danger of going AWOL any second.

He'd never thought much about the importance of books. To him they were just... there. It never occurred they might be special in any way.

And yet here he was: in a world where books were virtually worshipped - not least because they could somehow be used to perform magical and incredible feats.

He looked at the frail custodian. 'So my world's amazing because it has all those books?'

'That's right.'

'But this library's enormous!'

'Indeed it is, but it is only one of five in the whole of the Chapter Lands. Every book ever written in this world is contained within them - as well as those culled from the dimensions joined to each Chapter House. Very few books have more than one copy. Compared to Earth, the amount of books we have is tiny.'

'Books are rarer here?' Max said, starting to get the point.

'They are. Considerably so.'

'The guide sounded surprised that so many people on Earth can read and write,' Max pointed out, 'it's not the same here, then? Even though you hold books in such high regard?'

Garrowain nodded. 'Quite right. Because words have so much power and can be used to do great or terrible things, the amount of people who can read and write is controlled.'

'Controlled?' Max didn't like the sound of that.

'Yes. Otherwise there would be anarchy.'

'How many of your people can read and write?'

Garrowain thought about this for a moment. 'A few hundred thousand, I'd say.'

'That's all? How many people live on this planet?' Max asked, knowing he wasn't going to like the answer.

'Oh, about half a billion.'

Nope, he didn't like it one bit.

- 11 -

Several floors up in the cavernous Great Hall of Chapter House Carvallen, there is an important meeting going on.

At the summit, representatives of all five Chapter Houses sit around a large table in the centre of the hall. The table is that same deep shade of Carvallen green, and a few hundred tins of Pledge must have been used to make it so shiny. You could eat your dinner off it.

The room itself is an amphitheatre - the massive table ringed by rows of stone seats, beneath a high-domed glass ceiling that bathes the hall in warm sunlight.

The five people sat at the table are the Chapter Lords; the four men and one woman who run this entire civilisation, collectively known as The Chapter Lands.

Each is dressed in the colour of his or her House. We know the deep green of Carvallen and the blue of House Draveli - but alongside these are the red of House Wellhome, the purple of House Falion and the gold of House Morodai.

Behind each Lord there are five Chapter Guards, standing with varying levels of discipline, depending on which house they represent. Morodai's are the stiffest and Draveli's are all slouching.

It's rare for the Houses to meet in this fashion and even rarer for the youngest of the five to host such a meeting.

These are fraught times and Jacob Carvallen is seen as a moderate man and a cunning negotiator, so custom has been suspended for the sake of accomplishing a lasting peace.

The five Houses have always had a fractious relationship, but current levels of animosity are unheard of. Falion and Morodai are at the centre of the conflict as usual. Wellhome backs their cousins in purple and Draveli acts as side-kick to their Morodai masters.

This latest battle - one of words and not arms, so far - concerns House Falion's desire to teach more of its people the skills of reading and writing. Morodai stands opposed to this, surprising no-one. If Falion's people learn to read and write, Morodai's will no doubt want the same privilege.

This is a potential state of affairs that Chapter Lord Lucas Morodai is less than happy to entertain. An illiterate work force is a controllable work force – and one unable to word shape. He'll never agree to educate his people, and has just announced this to the hall, in tones that brook no argument.

'But the benefits of allowing my people these rights are clear!' said Bethan Falion, head of her House and most forward thinking of all five Chapter Lords. 'They will be educated and better able to serve us. The same holds true for your citizens, Lucas!'

Morodai sneered. 'More able to cause destruction and panic, you mean. Give them this power and the Houses will be reduced to rubble!' He addressed the whole table, running thin fingers over his close cropped black beard. 'Maybe Falion and her family - with its rampant liberalism - would embrace this, but I certainly do not! This is just the latest example of idiocy from their House.'

'How dare you!' Falion jumped to her feet.

Jacob Carvallen held his arms out in a calming gesture. 'Now let's try to be civil about this. Nothing will be resolved with insults and shouting,' he said, trying not to stare directly at Morodai.

Morodai gave him a look that clearly stated he couldn't care less what Jacob Carvallen thought and gave Osgood Draveli a sharp nod.

Draveli got the hint.

'I agree with Chapter Lord Morodai,' he piped up. 'House Draveli does not wish to risk teaching its chattels the use of words either. The potential dangers outweigh the perceived benefits.'

Aaron Wellhome snorted into his wine glass. 'There's a surprise,' he said in a voice that rumbled like thunder. 'Draveli sides with his master again.'

'And you automatically agree with the Falion woman, Aaron. That too is *quite* the surprise,' said Morodai, causing more uproar from the table.

Once again it fell to Jacob Carvallen to cool his fellow Chapter Lords before the whole thing got out of control. The Chapter Guards were starting to look decidedly twitchy and this whole thing could degenerate into an ugly punch-up if he wasn't careful.

As he calmed his colleagues, his lovely wife Halia - sat in one of the packed galleries behind the conference table - leaned over to her Arma Elijah, a deep frown on her face.

'This is going nowhere,' she said. 'They squabble like children, with Jacob acting as parent.'

'Indeed,' said Elijah, a grizzled veteran of many conflicts. An ugly, jagged scar ran down the left side of his face, a souvenir of the last argument between Chapters that had come to blows. 'They snivel and moan, waiting for the other side to back down... but they never will. This meeting is pointless.'

'At least Bethan's wish to teach her people is valid. It's about time this discussion was aired among us again.'

Elijah snorted. 'You think so? Morodai will never budge. He treats his citizens like sheep... to be herded and kept in filth. Without his approval, Falion's plan will never come to fruition, whether it's wise or not.'

'You don't believe the people have a right to the words, Elijah?' Halia said with some surprise. Her Arma always seemed so level-headed and sensible. Surely he thought this move towards an educated populace was a good thing?

'I believe knowledge can be a dangerous thing if not controlled. While teaching the masses sounds a good idea, I wonder what'd happen if enough of them had the talent to word shape.'

'I'm not suggesting we give them free reign, Elijah.'

'No? Then how will you control what they learn?' He clenched a fist. 'Will you punish them if they learn something you don't want them to? Kill them if they start using Wordcraft and become too powerful to control?'

'I would never kill my own citizens, Elijah!' Halia sounded horrified by the suggestion.

'Truly, ma'am? Even if they threatened the very existence of Carvallen?'

'It would never come to that.'

'No? You're sure? You had better be before you give them the power to use words. You'd be putting them on a level playing field, and that could come back to bite you.'

'You're a cold man, Elijah.'

The warrior shrugged his shoulders. 'You don't employ me for my cuddly personality, Halia.'

She laughed despite herself and returned her attention to the floor, where Jacob had managed to restore a moderate level of calm to proceedings.

'This is a subject that raises many concerns,' he said.

'Of that there is no doubt,' Lucas Morodai agreed.

'We have vastly opposing views on whether our people should be allowed the chance to share in the gifts of reading and writing, enjoyed by the Houses for so long.'

'We, Jacob?' said Bethan Falion. 'Your house sits on the fence, I think.'

'Carvallen has always tried to keep an objective view, Bethan. We are a careful and patient people.'

'You'd have to be with that backward reality of yours, Jacob,' said Osgood Draveli, never one to pass up an opportunity to snipe.

Morodai chuckled and even the mouths of Bethan Falion and Aaron Wellhome went up at the edges in disguised smiles.

It was well known that Earth had no-one with the ability to word shape, despite its incredible population size and wealth of knowledge. This served as constant amusement to the other Houses, who thought of the people of Earth as dim-witted monkeys - with Carvallen acting as the zookeeper.

The other Chapter Houses had no such problems with the dimensions they'd broken through to centuries earlier. Those with the talent to read words and craft magic existed in every one - and were plucked from their lives to be trained as Wordsmiths in the service of the House.

Morodai's world had been a stone-age civilisation, as had Wellhome's. Both Houses now ran their respective worlds entirely - having infiltrated every level of society thousands of years ago. Morodai regarded their planet as a resource to be used as they saw fit, ruling it with a rod of iron. Wellhome were kinder leaders, but their authority was just as absolute.

The dimension discovered by Chapter House Falion seven centuries ago had been more advanced, so the relationship they shared was more one of mutual respect and equality. A partnership, rather than a dictatorship.

Draveli's was a dirty, dark industrial nightmare of a place, where they'd still not openly revealed their existence to the planet's general population. They had managed to weasel their way into the planet's governments over the past five hundred years however - stealing or bargaining for whatever took their fancy. Even Draveli felt comfortable looking down on the plight of Jacob's House.

Carvallen suffered with an entire planet of people too stupid to grasp the skill of word shaping - but far too advanced and well developed in other ways to conquer. It was a lose-lose situation, any way you looked at it.

Jacob was well used to these jibes, so made no attempt to respond to Osgood's insult. Instead, he addressed Falion.

'If your idea is to allow your citizens the skills of basic reading and writing, that is one thing Bethan, but surely allowing them to word shape is going too far?'

'Nonsense! They have as much right to the power as we do!'

This was met with a chorus of disapproval.

Bethan raised her voice to be heard. 'They are the same as us and deserve the same rights we have! Word shaping is a gift from the Writer and should be freely available to all!'

Lucas Morodai leapt to his feet, closely followed by Osgood Draveli.

'You're delusional, woman!' Morodai said.

'Yes! Delusional!' Draveli parroted.

Falion banged her fist on the table. 'How dare you speak to me like that!'

'I'll speak to you however I please, if you continue to talk such rubbish. This kind of woolly-minded, liberal thinking is dangerous and should be silenced!'

'Is that a threat, Chapter Lord?' Bethan said, her eyes narrowing.

Morodai smiled with absolutely no humour. 'Only if you want it to be, woman.'

'Call me *woman* again, Morodai and you'll be singing like one in a heartbeat.'

The Chapter Guards from both houses put hands to sword scabbards and bow gun holsters, knowing where this was going.

'Enough!' Jacob ordered. The Chapter Guards of Carvallen, who outnumbered their counterparts twenty to one in the hall and had been placed in strategic positions by their master, now stepped forward and drew their weapons simultaneously. Jacob had evidently prepared for this kind of confrontation.

Aaron Wellhome looked furious. 'You go too far, Jacob!' he rumbled.

'No, Aaron. I don't. I will not have Chapter Lords threaten each other like children under my roof. No guards other than mine will come to arms in this hall!' he warned, glaring at Falion and Morodai.

Morodai smiled in conciliatory fashion and sat back down. 'Fair point, Carvallen. This is your house after all,' he said, smoothing the front of his long coat.

'Thank you, Lucas,' Jacob said and turned to Falion, who still stood. 'Bethan?'

The Falion Chapter Lord bowed her head. 'I can see that attending this farce was as big a waste of time as I thought it would be. It's evident no progress can ever be made if a consensus must be reached between all five of us. Therefore, I will make my own decisions and take action independently.'

Jacob walked around the table and stood next to her. 'What are you saying, Bethan? You'll break hundreds of years of custom and law?'

'If I must. This system is antiquated and can never function properly while these attitudes prevail.'

Falion lifted her head and looked around the table, challenging anyone to speak against her.

Lucas Morodai was more than happy to accept. 'What you are saying Chapter Lord, is that you intend to teach your subjects the use of words, despite the strongest objections of this council?'

'The only objections I hear are from you and your lap dog, Morodai.'

Osgood tried to argue with this, but Morodai spoke over him. 'Regardless of who wishes to veto the notion Falion, our rules dictate that all of us must reach consensus and that no action can be taken without it. If any one of us breaks this rule, it is grossly offensive... and in the worst case can be provocation for armed conflict.'

Bethan Falion leaned forward. 'Are you threatening war on me if I choose to treat my people better than dogs, Lucas?'

Morodai's smile was vicious. 'If I must, Falion.'

The other three Chapter Lords had watched this exchange with fascinated horror. It was no secret these two houses benefited from the largest armies and most Wordsmiths, so any conflict could be catastrophic.

Morodai's cruel reign had bred strong, brutal soldiers and devious Wordsmiths. Falion's were considered the most talented in Wordcraft and she too had a well trained standing army. Such well matched opponents would start a protracted war that could engulf the whole of The Chapter Lands.

Jacob Carvallen tried one last time to cool things down. 'Bethan, Lucas, please! We must work this out as civilised people. War is no answer.'

'Oh, be silent, Carvallen,' Falion said. 'I'm sick of your fence sitting and so is everyone else. This meeting was – as ever – a waste of time. Actions speak louder than words. I will return home and begin the process of educating my people.' She gave Morodai a look that could cut glass. 'And if anyone wishes to object to that, I invite them to mount as vigorous a protest as they can muster. I can assure them the response they receive will be *equally* vigorous.'

Morodai chose to remain silent, but flashed a dead eyed smile at her.

Falion stormed off in the direction of the main doors, her Chapter Guards trailing in her wake. Her whole entourage left the hall in quick succession, leaving the remaining Chapter Lords in stunned silence.

Three of them anyway. Morodai was sat back with a sly grin on his face.

Aaron Wellhome stood and spoke. It sounded like someone gargling with gravel. 'I think this also concludes my contribution to the meeting. I'm not sure whether Bethan's going too far, but I know I'd rather not spend another moment in the company of men like you.' He stabbed a meaty hand at Morodai and Draveli, before looking back at Carvallen. 'I bid you good day, Jacob.'

He walked away from the table and exited the hall with his people.

'Well,' Lucas Morodai said with veiled glee as he rose from his seat, 'it looks like our little get together is over.'

'Yes, indeed,' Draveli agreed.

'You must curb these instincts for war, Lucas,' Jacob told him. 'Bethan can be calmed down... reasoned with. But if you challenge her, she will dig her heels in and conflict will be inevitable.'

'So be it!' Morodai hissed. 'Her ideas are ridiculous and dangerous. If Falion steps back from her madness, no arms will be brought to bear. If she doesn't, I will do everything in my power to stop her.' He regained his composure somewhat. 'Goodbye Jacob, I trust we'll be in contact again soon.'

Without waiting for a reply, Morodai was gone with Draveli behind him, following like a faithful hound.

Jacob Carvallen took a deep breath and looked over to where his wife and her Arma sat, his face etched with disappointment. He'd wanted to achieve so much from this meeting, but Bethan's insistence on bringing up such a controversial subject had derailed any chance of progress on other matters. Instead of brokering new trade accords, the meeting had instead set the scene for war between the Houses.

Halia gave her husband a sympathetic look, rose from her seat and came down. He met her beside the conference table, taking her hands in his.

'I'm sorry, Jacob,' she said. 'That shouldn't have descended into such farce. They're as stubborn and as foolish as one another.'

'Maybe,' he agreed, 'yet I can't help thinking this was always likely to happen. Such massive differences of opinion may never be overcome. History shows us that.'

'But this is the modern world. If we can't find a happy middle ground in this, then we're no better than our predecessors.'

'I know Halia, but I don't know what to do. We're a young house and haven't the power to keep the others in line.'

Jacob was acutely aware that his forces weren't strong. The House of Carvallen had the fewest Wordsmiths, and Earth offered them no conduit to find more. It was at times like this he wished his daughter's delusions were true; that the Earth really was capable of birthing a Wordsmith with the power to eclipse all others. Delusions they were however, and Carvallen could do nothing to stop the war that now threatened like a storm on the horizon.

Outside, Lucas Morodai swept down the corridor towards the airship port where his luxurious transport lay in wait to take him and his staff home. He could see the party of that fool Wellhome as it disappeared round a corner and was glad he wouldn't have to look the big, hairy idiot in the face again today.

Osgood Draveli bobbed along in Morodai's wake, wondering whether he should open his mouth.

They reached the long gold and blue airships – Morodai's at the front, naturally - and while the Chapter Guards made them ready, Draveli finally worked up the courage to speak.

'Do you think Falion will take the bait, Lucas?'

'Of course she will, you fool,' Morodai spat. 'That woman can't wait to go to war over her principles and will commit to any battle we care to conjure up.'

'And that's when we allow our new allies out of the bag,' Draveli said, in such an overtly conspiring manner, it made Morodai roll his eyes in disgust.

'Would you like to say that any louder, Osgood? I don't think everyone else in this dirty little Chapter House heard you,' he said venomously.

Osgood cowered like a whipped dog.

'While we're on the subject,' Morodai continued in a low voice, 'what did you discover when you went to Carvallen's rooms? Why was he called away? Was it that annoying daughter of his?'

'Yes, Lucas. It appears she managed to draw someone over from the Carvallen world, as we suspected she might.'

'She still believes that dim little place can muster up a Wordsmith strong enough to stop our new allies?'

'Oh my, yes. She's insane.'

'True, but her insanity may cause problems. It might be time to start thinking about her removal. Does she suspect anything of our involvement? Does her father believe anything she says?'

'Not at all. She still spouts her ridiculous notions that we're all doomed if the Dwellers are allowed in to this world. She has no idea they'll do the both of us no harm,' Draveli said, with mischievous glee in his eyes. 'Her father thinks she's mad.'

'Our Wordsmiths continue to hide the Dwellers successfully, then?'

'Indeed, no one will be any the wiser until they are unleashed.'

Lucas Morodai looked across the Carvallen city, the gentle breeze ruffling his black hair. 'Good,' he said, feeling genuinely content for the first time since Falion had opened her fat mouth. 'Then the other Chapter Houses will fall and I will take up my... sorry, *we* will take up our rightful places as rulers of all five Chapter Lands.'

Back in the Library, Max Bloom has had an education in the Chapter Lands, with Garrowain spending the last few minutes explaining how the Houses function and why most of the populace don't read or write. Max has listened very carefully, and chooses to sum it all up with the following witty epithet:

'What a load of pony's knackers.'

Merelie gasped. 'Max, that's our society you're talking about. It's functioned well for thousands of years.'

'It's still stupid. I agree with that woman. Fa… Fal?'

'Falion. Bethan Falion,' Garrowain supplied.

'Yeah, her. I reckon she's right. You can't stop people reading. Everyone's got a right to stuff like that,' Max said with conviction, choosing to leave out the fact he'd only ever read three books.

'But the dangers of everyone having such knowledge are too great,' Garrowain replied. 'If everyone can read and write, more will develop the ability to Wordcraft. Not everyone can handle it and not everyone would use it constructively.'

'Who decides who gets to learn it, then? *You*, I suppose?' Max said, shooting an accusing look at all of them.

'The Chapter Houses,' Merelie said. 'They control who reads and writes for the good of everyone.'

'The people must be controlled,' Garrowain said again, starting to sound brainwashed.

Max gave all three of them a long hard look up and down.

'What are you doing?' said Merelie.

'Checking for swastikas.' He threw his hands up. 'Look, I'm done. I've listened to everything you've said. I've tried to pay attention and I get it. But when you get right down to it, this isn't my world and it isn't my problem.' He folded his arms and rocked on his heels. 'I reckon from the sound of it, you lot deserve a kick up the arse by monsters from the twilight zone… treating your people like idiots and mucking about with the space-time continuum.'

'Max, that's a horrible thing to say!' Merelie cried.

'Sorry, but that's the way I see it.' He scratched his chin. 'Look, we never asked you to punch a hole into our reality and spy on us. Maybe if you'd come clean in the first place and said hello, then things might be different. As it is, we're nothing more to you than a bunch of apes who can't do your silly magic tricks.'

Max knew damn well he was offending them, but once you've started on a rant, it's vitally important to see it through to the end.

'The same goes for all your other Houses and their little playgrounds off in other dimensions. I'm not a Wordsmith and don't want to be. I just want to go home and forget all this weird stuff ever happened,' he finished in a low, tired voice and looked at the big floating book.

The words 'This is unprecedented' still hovered in mid-air.

You got that right.

Merelie stepped forward. 'But Max...'

Garrowain cut across her. 'Mr Bloom has said his piece, Merelie. He does not believe he can help us and by the sounds of things, would be highly uninterested in doing so even if he could. Correct?'

'Yep.'

'Therefore, we send him back to his world so he can 'forget about the whole thing' as he says. Maybe there will be somebody else more willing to assist.'

'Don't bet on it,' Max said, knowing his species well.

'We shall see.' The custodian turned to Borne. 'Put The Cornerstone on the shelf Arma. Let's get Mr Bloom home as quickly as possible.'

Borne did as he was told, wisely remaining silent.

Max groaned inwardly as he saw the look of hurt on Merelie's face. 'Look I'm sorry,' he said to her, 'but I can't help the way I feel.'

'Please don't do this Max. I thought you understood?' she pleaded.

'I do understand... sort of.' He gave her a half-hearted smile. 'There's nothing wrong anyway! You've just had some bad dreams. You don't need a powerful Wordsmith from Earth, just a good night's rest and a nice holiday somewhere.'

Her face hardened. 'You're just like the rest of them! Go on... go away! I don't care anymore!'

'Well... well... neither do I!' he shouted back, reaching out and grabbing the recharged Cornerstone.

'Thanks for nothing the lot of you! You're all bloody bonkers and I'm off!'

Max opened the book and read:

Her face hardened. 'You're just like the rest of them! Go on... go away! I don't care anymore!'

'Well... well... neither do I!' he shouted back, reaching out and grabbing the recharged Cornerstone.

'Thanks for nothing the lot of you! You're all bloody bonkers and I'm off!'

Max opened the book and read:

Boom! went the universe.

Part Three

From the stressful, misty corridors of the Carvallen Library to the peaceful environs of the brown Farefield library staff room, Max Bloom plopped into existence, making Imelda Warrington spill her tea.

'Good grief!' she yelled as he chucked The Cornerstone onto the coffee table, vowing to never pick it up again.

'Wotcha... *Wordsmith*,' he said, putting a heavy accent on the second word.

Imelda got the hint. 'So, you've found out lots of interesting things over there, have you?'

'You could say that,' he replied, looking up at the clock. 'I was only gone for five hours? It felt like a bloody century.'

'Time can be funny when you're inside The Cornerstone,' Imelda said.

'Oh no, don't you start! I've had enough 'wisdom of the ancients' rubbish from that Garrowain bloke without you joining in.'

'Garrowain? You met the head custodian?'

'Met him... listened to him... mortally insulted him. Not necessarily in that order.'

'So you know about Merelie's nightmares? The prophecy she's been trying to sell all these years?'

'I take it you don't believe her either, then?'

Imelda snorted. 'Of course not. It's ridiculous. She's a very silly girl, spreading rumours and frightening people. Did she also try to convince you that you're a Wordsmith?'

'Yep. Which I told her wasn't possible.'

'Good! This world doesn't have the capacity for word shaping. I should know, I've been here long enough and I've seen nothing to show me I'm wrong.'

'You're the spy, aren't you?' Max said with distain. 'You're the one Jacob Carvallen sent here to keep an eye on us.'

'That's right, and I do a very good job.'

'You think letting girls kidnap people and suck them through a magic book into another dimension is good work, do you?'

Imelda deflated a bit. 'That was unfortunate, yes. But you're back now and it doesn't appear that my world is in any trouble from what you're saying?'

'No, it all looks fine. Only Merelie and Gandalf think anything's up. The Chapter Lands are cool. You can stop worrying and go back to the day job.' This led him to another point. 'You're a Wordsmith, then?' he asked.

'I am.'

'Any good, are you?'

'My skills are more than adequate for the task assigned to me.'

Max raised an eyebrow. The 'task assigned' seemed to be making sure the filing cards were in the right order and arranging primary school displays in the front window.

She noticed his expression. 'Oh alright, I'm not exactly called upon to be a Wordsmith much, but I can still word shape if I have to.'

In actual fact, it had been so many years since she'd been required to use the skills taught to her, she didn't know if she could still do it.

Imelda had no intention of telling Max Bloom that.

'Oh yeah, that's what it's called. *Word shaping*,' Max said, waggling his fingers around in the air, eyes rolling about in their sockets.

'Don't be flippant. I don't have to justify my people to you, boy.'

'And I don't have to stand here listening to you either.' Max picked up The Cornerstone. 'I should take this away and burn it.'

'You wouldn't dare!' Imelda was horrified.

'Wouldn't I?'

'It wouldn't burn anyway. It's no ordinary book.'

'I'm well aware of that, thanks.' He turned it over in his hands. 'Pity. I think I'd be doing us a favour. Shut us off from your world completely. Then you'd leave us alone.'

'That wouldn't happen. This world is linked to Chapter House Carvallen now. Permanently.'

'Great,' he said, throwing the book to her and getting up. 'Why don't you read yourself home and catch up on the latest gossip? I'm done here.'

Imelda watched Max Bloom storm out of the room and hoped it was the last time she'd be seeing him. She put The Cornerstone back on the coffee table and sighed with relief. It looked like all was well in The Chapter Lands and she could store the book back in the library shelves without worrying about unauthorised use any more.

Many strange thoughts rolled around in Max Bloom's head as he rode home. Most notably about this whole 'Wordcraft' thing. The idea that channelling the emotion and the conscious thought of thousands of people into some kind of physical power was enthralling - but sounded pretty unlikely, no matter how open minded you were. And if it was possible, the scientists would have worked out how to do it by now, surely?

The further Max went from the library, the more it felt like the whole escapade into The Chapter Lands had been a bad day-dream.

Max knew it *had* happened of course and his mind was merely trying to distance itself from such a patently absurd incident, but that didn't prevent him feeling like he'd been hijacked for a few hours and taken on a joy-ride through the fantasy section of Waterstones.

Chapter Houses and Custodians.

Cornerstones and Chapter Lords.

Monsters from the void and invisible guardians.

Different dimensions and damsels in distress.

It just needs a tetchy dragon on a pile of gold and it's complete.

Except that wasn't entirely accurate, was it?

The world he'd visited wasn't some medieval fantasy land with pixies and elves frolicking about in the trees, getting right up everyone's nose.

The Chapter House had looked and felt quite modern... like an Ikea showroom. The city outside had looked advanced as well. Nobody had talked in thees and thous, or flounced around in flowing gowns and shiny suits of armour. It had felt like a real, living place, not the product of some fevered hallucination.

Max rode up the drive to his house, feeling a deep sense of relief that he'd made it home. Being in another dimension was about as far away as you could go from the familiar, so making it back to the three-bed detached he lived in with his family was a blessing - and damn lucky in the circumstances.

It was late afternoon by now. The shadows lengthened on the ground and the chill October air was starting to bite.

Max shut the front door and walked into the kitchen.

'Afternoon bog breath,' said Monica Bloom from the breakfast bar, where she was munching a chocolate pop tart. Max was actually glad to see his little sister, underlining how bad a day he'd had.

'Alright sis. How's it going?' he said and smiled, which immediately made her suspicious.

'Where have you been then?' she asked.

'Why do you want to know?'

'Coz I do!' Monica was now half convinced that her brother had spent the whole day planning some horrible practical joke. He was never nice to her. Something must be up.

Max sighed. 'Ok, if you must know, I was sucked into another dimension by a magic book and spent the day being told I'm a powerful wizard. It sounded like a bad idea, so I came home.'

Monica screwed her face up. 'You're a right git,' she said and left the kitchen in a huff.

No pleasing some people.

Max rummaged around in the fridge, having realised how ravenous he was.

Once the hunger had been kept at bay with a large chicken and salad cream sandwich, he had chance to reflect that Merelie no doubt shared his little sister's feelings.

Max knew he'd done the right thing by leaving The Chapter Lands before getting more involved in Merelie's paranoid fantasy of brain sucking monstrosities laying waste to the populace - but that didn't stop him feeling just a tad guilty about deserting her.

He couldn't care less what the wizened old custodian thought of him, but Merelie had been very pretty and he couldn't stop re-living the hurt he'd seen in those glorious blue eyes as he'd buggered off across the dimensional void.

Alright, she had made him out to be something he wasn't... but she'd asked for his help and he'd snubbed her. The fact there was no evidence that purple void monsters were about to eat Merelie's brains didn't make him feel any better.

- 2 -

Three weeks passed and November's arrival was greeted without much enthusiasm. The weather outside went from cold and drizzly to *very* cold and *extremely* drizzly. This annoyed everyone, making them wish for the heady days of October, when you could go out of the house without three coats and a pair of thermal underpants.

Max got on with the business of being an idle teenager. Despite some strange dreams and a tendency to wince when somebody in purple walked past, the Chapter Lands experience hadn't had much of a negative effect of him.

He told no-one about his travels - not wanting to spend his remaining days locked in a room with padded walls. He almost let slip to Figgy one night while playing Call of Duty, but couldn't take the look of blank incomprehension and two hours with a flip chart and visual aids he'd have to employ to explain.

There was one bleak afternoon when boredom once again had him in its deadly embrace. He was sat in the lounge, staring at the motley collection of books his parent's owned, wondering if he could make one of them float in mid-air if he concentrated hard enough.

What followed was a feeble experiment that involved staring at several books, willing them to burst into song and start flashing like an epileptic fire-fly. He tried holding them open, closing them, standing on them, shoving them down his jeans, putting them on his head... and even head-butting one before giving up, having gotten not so much as a squeak.

This proved - if there were any doubt remaining - that the chances of him being a Wordsmith were zero.

Farefield library closed its doors to the public at 5.30pm most days, except on Thursday when it stayed open for the poorly attended book club, and on Friday when it shut early at 4.30pm - obeying the universal law that no bugger wants to do any work after 4pm at the start of the weekend.

To Imelda Warrington's immense relief today was indeed Friday. She was looking forward to closing early and going home for an evening in front of the soaps with a bottle of pinot grigio and a box of Maltesers.

While Imelda still felt like a Wordsmith of The Chapter Lands now and again, she'd be the first to admit to going native since being posted here twenty years ago. In a world of such comfort and distraction, maintaining your vigilance was difficult.

She did miss her homeland from time to time - especially the respect she'd enjoyed as a Wordsmith of Carvallen. Nobody there spoke to her like she was muck, as so many of the locals in this dreary little town tended to do on a regular basis.

Over the decades her word shaping skills had blunted. She'd vigorously practised the arts in the first few years, but after ten had passed, the desire to stay sharp had faded. No-one here could word shape, so what was the point?

The duels she used to have with the Wordsmiths of the other Houses were long behind her and blasting old Mr Lovetree across the library for returning a book late again would be overkill of the highest order.

She still did the job she'd been tasked with, though. No-one could say that Imelda hadn't provided many essays and interesting anecdotes about Earth, written in the pages of The Cornerstone - which whisked them back to be added to the Library's store of knowledge about the planet.

She'd also sent many books over to swell the ranks... though Paris Hilton's biography had probably been a mistake in hindsight.

Until three weeks ago her job had been easy, but then that damned boy had found Merelie's note and all hell had broken loose.

God knows how long the message had sat in that silly book, like a ticking bomb waiting to blow up in Imelda's face.

If only she'd found it first!

If it had appeared between the pages of a Catherine Cookson novel, she would have - having gone through the author's entire back catalogue twice. But no, it had to wind up in some stupid light weight piece of rubbish that nobody had picked up in years.

Even worse, it had come into the possession of a teenage boy with far too much back chat and enough curiosity to kill several nosy cats.

If one of her old ladies had discovered it - Mrs Blot for instance, who was as deaf as a post and happily senile - she could have explained it away with no problem.

Damn that Merelie and her silly ideas!

Imelda locked the front door, set the library alarm and walked back to the main desk, intent on tidying away some returned books.

This was a mindless task, but one she enjoyed. Her people were naturally inclined towards a passion for books anyway and she loved looking through the pile to see what people had been reading - and why.

Today's pile was a little anaemic when it came to classic prose, but was a fair representation of what the public liked: mass-market paperbacks with exciting covers and familiar storylines.

There were three Tom Clancys and a Robert Ludlum, borrowed by someone who probably thought the moon landings never happened. A couple of Mary Higgins Clarkes sat with a James Herbert, taken out by a person who wanted to believe in ghosts. Fahrenheit 451 and Slaughterhouse 5 had been hired by somebody trying to impress their friends - and the last book on the pile was a guide to dental health, indicating the reader's last trip to the dentist had come with a warning.

Imelda was sorting through these with an abstract smile on her face when The Cornerstone started to scream like a tortured cat.

She nearly fell out of her chair as the hideous high pitched bawling of a million people filled the library. Somebody had evidently got tired of the choir just *aaaahhhing* their way through life and decided to spice things up by tipping boiling oil over their heads. Flashes of silver light erupted from the book as it flew off the 50p shelf and started to flop around on the floor like a dying fish.

Imelda sprinted across the library, knowing she had to shut the thing up before somebody heard and came to investigate. Visions of police officers breaking the door down to find her holding a flashing, screaming book entered her head. Explaining it away in an interview would be next to impossible.

She shielded her eyes and tried to grab hold of the thing, but it was bouncing around so much she couldn't get a grip.

Imelda had a moment of inspiration. She tore off her jacket and held it out, ready to capture the maddened Cornerstone like a trout in a net. The book stopped flopping about for a split second and she threw the jacket over it, covering both with her body. The book continued to thrash, but at least the light wasn't getting out anymore. Now if only she could do something about the hideous screeching.

A massive pulse of energy exploded from the book, ripping her jacket to tatters and throwing her away violently, half blinded and deafened.

The Cornerstone flew upwards, smashed into the ceiling and fell back to the floor, face up and cover open, light burning from the pages.

Imelda struggled to her feet as the light grew more intense, casting a circle of radiance across the whole ceiling. The screaming got louder and became so unbearable Imelda had to cover her ears.

As if it were the most torturous birth in history, a limp body flew out of the book, putting an end to the screaming and light display as it dropped to the floor.

Imelda stumbled over on shaky legs to see who had been so forcibly pushed into this world.

It was Merelie Carvallen, unconscious and looking like she'd been through hell.

Twice.

Twenty minutes later, Merelie lay on the brown sofa in the staff room. Imelda sat dabbing a cool, damp tea towel on the girl's head and eyeing The Cornerstone on the coffee table with extreme suspicion.

It was under several large books, the microwave and a heavy pot plant.

Imelda couldn't rouse Merelie and was worried that the girl may have suffered serious injury. She had no visible signs of damage, but wouldn't stir at all. Her violent entry into this world and the book's hideous screaming indicated the trip had been very unpleasant.

Imelda thought about taking Merelie to hospital, but that would raise more questions than she was prepared to answer. If it came to it though, she supposed she'd have to and be damned with the consequences.

Travel from The Chapter Lands to Earth was a serious breach of the laws laid down by her House. It was bad enough that Max Bloom had used it to cross dimensions, but now Merelie being here on Earth?

Ten times worse.

Once more, Imelda found herself in the dark and waiting for somebody else to tell her what was going on.

Merelie's eyelids fluttered and she let out a low moan.

'Easy girl, you're safe,' Imelda said.

Merelie mumbled something about purple eyes and lapsed back into unconsciousness. Imelda ran the cool towel over the girl's face again, hoping she would come around properly sometime soon and explain herself.

At the same time Merelie Carvallen was making her painful entrance into Farefield library, Max Bloom was curled up on the floor of Steve Figson's bedroom with his hands pressed to his ears, trying to block out the screaming of a million choir members being covered in boiling oil.

He'd been thrashing Figgy at Halo when the sound had hit him like an auditory hammer and he'd collapsed, screaming his head off. Luckily, Figgy's mum was a nurse, and five minutes later Max was sat in her car being taken to A&E, wondering what the hell was going on.

Merelie's eyes opened and focused on Imelda Warrington's concerned face.

'Where am I?' she said in a weak voice.

'On Earth. In my library,' Imelda replied. 'How are you? In any pain?'

'No pain. It just feels like my head's been squeezed in a vice.'

'I'm not surprised. Travel by Cornerstone sometimes makes people groggy, and that didn't look like a normal trip.'

'Where is it? The Cornerstone?' Merelie said, her eyes darting around the room.

'It's under there.' Imelda pointed at the coffee table and the odd centre piece she'd recently built. 'It's not going anywhere.'

'I wonder how long it will take them?' she said, half to herself.

'To do what?'

'To figure out how to do it… to come through after me. They've got The Cornerstone on that side now.' Merelie was wide eyed with fear.

'Do you mean your father's men? Are they after you? What have you done girl?' Imelda demanded, taking on the tone of a school mistress.

'Nothing! And it's not my father's men.'

'Then who do you mean?' Imelda remembered what Merelie had whispered in her unconscious state. 'You mean people with purple eyes?'

This seemed to scare Merelie more than anything. 'Yes! They'll come for me like they did everybody else. I only got away because I made it to the Library with Borne and Garrowain - ' her eyes went wide with recollection. 'Poor Borne!' Merelie cried and lapsed into silence, wiping tears from her pale cheeks.

'Merelie? What happened?' Imelda said, placing a comforting hand on the girl's shoulder.

Merelie stared at her for a moment before answering. 'You're a Wordsmith, yes?'

'I am, but it's been a long time since I've word shaped,' Imelda admitted.

'You might get your chance tonight,' Merelie said, looking back at The Cornerstone.

'What's after you, Merelie? What do you think is coming through the book?'

The look Merelie gave Imelda was one part fear, one part anger - with a side order of grim satisfaction thrown in. 'I was *right.*'

'About what?'

'My dreams were real. They came through the doorway between worlds.'

Imelda's blood ran cold as Merelie's blue eyes shone with fear. 'What came through?' the librarian said in a hushed tone.

The Cornerstone started to glow.

'You're about to find out,' the girl said, a determined look on her face as she stood.

The Cornerstone glowed brighter and for the first time in years, Imelda Warrington regretted not keeping her word shaping skills in good order.

At that moment, Max was getting a light shined in his eyes by a doctor. In the next several minutes he'd fall prey to another massive seizure - this one ending with him screaming 'Merelie!' at the top of his voice before passing out.

The Cornerstone choir piped up again. Not screaming this time, but making a dreadful low pitched keening noise.

'It's fighting back,' Merelie said, from a defensive position behind the sofa. 'It's trying to block them.'

'That's a good thing, isn't it?' Imelda's voice had gone up an octave.

'It won't work.'

Imelda backed away from the coffee table as the book glowed like a miniature sun, continuing to wail in that horrible tone.

'The Cornerstone won't let anyone use it who shouldn't,' she replied, sounding more confident than she felt.

'These things aren't like us. They come from dark places,' Merelie told her. 'The Cornerstone's programming won't account for them. It won't know what to do. With Wordsmiths helping them, it doesn't stand a chance.'

The pot plant, microwave and books were blasted upwards, ricocheting off the ceiling. Imelda had to dodge shards of the terracotta pot as it exploded, sending the rubber plant spiralling over her head.

Merelie cried in pain as one of the heavy books hit her on the shoulder and she instinctively ducked behind the sofa to avoid more flying shrapnel.

The Cornerstone flew open, projecting a sick purple and black light that writhed and spun, bathing the room in a nightmarish glow. Somebody else burst from the book, but this person seemed more prepared for journey's end and hit the coffee table standing, legs bent to take the weight of impact.

The book slammed shut in an effort to stop anyone else following.

Imelda recognised the man who'd come through straight away. Having spent eight years of her life head over heels in love with him, this was no surprise.

'Elijah?' she said to Halia Carvallen's Arma.

Merelie came out from behind the sofa. 'That isn't Elijah, Wordsmith. Defend yourself.'

Merelie whispered words under her breath. The microwave, which lay broken by the staff room door, flew into the air, straight at the soldier's chest. He batted it out of the way and snarled at Merelie.

Imelda could see that Elijah's green eyes were now a seething mass of purple and black smoke. That, combined with the look of abject hate on his face, convinced her something dreadful had taken possession of her friend's body.

She'd heard all about Merelie Carvallen's dire warnings, dismissing them as the fancies of a girl with too much time on her hands. But here it was - in the flesh, coming to kill them - wearing the face of a man she'd once loved in her days at the Carvallen Academy.

Time to remember how the words work... and you'd better remember fast.

Imelda pointed at the door. 'Go!' she shouted at Merelie.

Merelie ignored her, whispered again, gestured with her hands and moved back as the sofa rose into the air in front of her.

'What did you do to my mother?!' she screamed, thrusting her arms out. The sofa shot towards the possessed Arma, fuelled by Merelie's rage.

He couldn't bat this away and both sofa and man smashed into the wall, knocking off shelves and smashing chairs.

'That won't keep it down for long,' Merelie said, heading toward the door.

'Long enough for us to get out and call the authorities!'

Imelda's desire to keep this beyond the attention of local law enforcement had disappeared. The minute a monster wearing the face of your ex-boyfriend shows up, it's time to call in reinforcements.

Both of them kept a wary eye on the sofa and the legs sticking out from under it as they hurried out of the mangled staff room.

'Somebody must have heard all of that,' Imelda said. 'They'll be coming to see what's going on.'

'They won't be able to help,' Merelie replied, speaking as someone who'd seen what those things were truly capable of in the last few days.

She was about to explain when the sofa came flying out of the staff room like a battering ram, straight at her head.

- 4 -

The events leading up to this dangerous situation began three weeks earlier, as Max Bloom winked out of existence in the Chapter House Library.

'I hate him!' Merelie exclaimed, as The Cornerstone drifted to the floor.

'That's a little harsh,' Garrowain said, scooping up the book and brushing dust from the spine. 'The boy has no reason to help us. Our opinion of his world isn't favourable, so his anger was justified.'

'That doesn't help us much though, does it?' Merelie replied and stamped off back to the Library Hub.

Garrowain shook his head, made a gesture with one finger that sent the huge guide to Earth sliding back into the shelf and followed after the incensed Merelie Carvallen, trying to think of something to say that might mollify her a bit.

As they returned to the comfortable surroundings of the waiting room, Borne looked down at his ward.

'You didn't expect this to be easy did you?' he said.

Merelie shot him a black look and slumped into one of the soft couches.

'Aah... you did, then.' He sat down next to her. 'That was a bit silly, don't you think?'

'He was supposed to be the one!' she said, pounding the arm of the couch.

'The one?' he replied, incredulous. 'You think fate is playing a part in this?'

'Isn't it?'

'Maybe... but it certainly won't show its hand to you, Merelie. You've got it in your head it has to be Max Bloom who saves us all, haven't you?'

'He seemed so nice!' This sounded a little pathetic, but it was all she could think to say.

'Looked nice too from your point of view, I expect.'

Merelie blushed at Borne's implication, but remained silent.

'Just because *you* like someone doesn't mean they're special to anybody else,' he told her, being as blunt as possible.

'That's unfair.'

'Is it? I don't think so. I was young once, I know how these things work.'

Garrowain, not wanting the discussion to veer into the finer points of teenage romance, interrupted. 'I think what your Arma is getting at is that hope is not lost, we just require another willing person from Earth to assist us.'

'But... but he seemed like the right one,' Merelie said, still trying to cling to an idea that had been well and truly blown out of the water. 'Do we start again from scratch then?' she said, looking downcast. 'Can you help this time, Garrowain?'

The custodian shook his head. 'As ever child, my actions are closely monitored. The other custodians and your father would know if I made contact with Earth for any reason.'

'Isn't there another way than just writing messages?' Borne said, frustrated.

'I don't know, let me think about it.' Garrowain looked up at an ornate clock on the wall. 'You should both be getting back. Your father will want to know Mr Bloom was safely dispatched.'

'He'll probably still ground me, you know that don't you?'

'Possibly. But you must do everything you can to keep him happy, Merelie.'

Merelie sighed and got up. 'Alright, I'll go and make nice. Come on Borne, let's not keeping father waiting.'

- 5 -

The next few days in the Carvallen lands were quiet. Business went on as usual across the districts, the citizens living their lives under the watchful gaze of their Chapter House.

Jacob Carvallen attempted diplomacy as best he could with his fellow Chapter Lords, travelling via League Book to the other houses.

League Books were smaller, simpler versions of The Cornerstone - allowing travel between points in The Chapter Lands only, rather than across dimensions. They were kept in a large chamber deep within the bowels of the Carvallen Library, guarded by Garrowain and his staff.

Each time Jacob would open the League Book, he would feel optimistic as he was transported instantly across thousands of miles. He would feel equally pessimistic when he came back, having failed to solve anything. Even the wise Garrowain could offer no words of comfort.

Bethan Falion was intent on teaching her people to read and write - going as far as to announce the building of new school houses in one of her largest cities. Lucas Morodai responded to this by sending an army eastwards, using a combination of Wordcraft powered airships and League Books that his spies had planted close to Falion's borders. The energy required to do this had killed several of his weaker Wordsmiths, but Morodai didn't have a problem with self-sacrifice - provided he wasn't the one being asked to do it.

He met Falion's assembled forces in one of the low, rolling foothills surrounding the sprawling city, in the shadow of Chapter House Falion. The battle was short and ugly, with the corpses of soldier and Wordsmith alike littering the field by day's end. Neither side came out on top, but the Morodai army lost more men.

Lucas would have been enraged at his lack of success, if he hadn't known the whole thing was a ruse designed to make the other Chapter Lord commit her forces at once. Even as his men fell, Osgood Draveli put the finishing touches to a pact struck with the creatures that dwelled in the void between worlds.

Morodai had done all the hard work and his obsequious servant only had to tie up a few loose ends, but it seemed to be taking an age. Draveli looked to be more interested in making sure everyone knew how important he was, rather than getting the job done properly.

Morodai chalked this up as yet another reason to do away with the fat man once the dust had settled. He only suffered his involvement at all because it had been seven Draveli Wordsmiths who'd stumbled on the Dwellers, during a botched trip to their House's dirty, depressing dimension.

Six had their minds devoured by the awful creatures, but one survived through sheer luck - and was able to describe the monsters living in the shifting purple void as vile beings that fed on thought, consuming every mind they touched. The fat Chapter Lord told Morodai everything and Lucas had put his own Wordsmiths to the task of making contact and convincing the Dwellers that a bargain of mutual advantage could be struck. Instead of eating the minds of the few unlucky enough to stumble across their nightmarish void, how would access to an entire race of people sound?

Once contact had been established and an agreement made, Morodai had set about determining a plan of attack with the horrific creatures.

The trade was simple: he would provide a way across the void into The Chapter Lands and in return they would do his bidding, attacking only those who opposed him.

He led, they fed. It was as straightforward as that.

As the dust settled on the battlefield and Bethan Falion started to plan her next attack, Morodai took over from Draveli to hasten things along. Using the Cornerstone from his own House, Morodai had several hundred Wordsmiths create a gateway big enough for the loathsome creatures of Merelie's nightmares to cross into The Chapter Lands.

They had no physical form in this plane of existence, so thousands of hapless citizens were press-ganged into being hosts - threatened with the death of their loved ones if they refused.

A purple and black river of inky, writhing smoke came bursting from the golden Morodai Cornerstone, separating into hundreds of tendrils. It targeted the screaming, shackled 'volunteers' as they were pushed forward onto the battlefield by Chapter Guards carrying sharp lances.

Lucas Morodai - being a canny negotiator as well as a power hungry lunatic - made sure that no more than a few thousand of the ravening, soulless creatures were allowed to come through, keeping their numbers more or less manageable. The gateway was snapped shut by his Wordsmiths before a deluge of Dwellers could swamp The Chapter Lands.

Those few thousand – marked by their smoke filled eyes and pallid faces - swarmed over Falion's army, invading the minds of all they came across, feeding and growing fat with every stolen memory and emotion.

It wasn't a pleasant process. The living purple and black smoke would erupt from the host's eyes and shoot into the eyes of the next victim, accompanied by loud screams and convulsions.

Some of the monsters would stay in the bodies they first entered, content with their new homes. Others would move from victim to victim, until they found one they felt more suited to their purposes. It was like test driving cars for sale - only with more excruciating pain and less checking for rust under the wheel arches.

Thousands upon thousands in Chapter House Falion felt the horrific touch of the Dwellers, their minds consumed in an instant. Human husks were left, devoid of all rational thought. They stared into space like zombies, occasionally letting out a quiet moan as they bounced gently off the walls.

It took roughly two days to subdue the Chapter House. With everyone in Falion's land possessed, catatonic or dead, Morodai and his supernatural army then turned their attention to the next House.

When the attack came to Wellhome in the south, they stood no chance and fell even quicker than Falion - Chapter Lord Aaron Wellhome one of the last to be turned.

Within the space of a fortnight, an army of possessed humans, Wordsmiths and Chapter Guards stood on the borders of Carvallen land, waiting to be unleashed on the last free House.

- 6 -

Merelie looked out of her bedroom window at the enormous army that now stood before the gates of the city.

It looked slightly odd, as armies go. Instead of the well armoured Chapter Guards being in the vanguard, thousands of bedraggled people stood in front, their smoky eyes fixed on the Chapter House and the city lying below it.

Why didn't they listen to me?

Everything Merelie had feared was happening. She'd heard the first few dispatches her father had received with mounting horror and certainty that her nightmares were coming true.

Jacob Carvallen had immediately locked down the whole Chapter House, allowing Merelie no contact with anyone other than Borne. There was no way to see Garrowain and no chance of recruiting someone from Earth before the evil hoard descended. She naturally blamed Max Bloom for the entire situation.

Merelie watched as her father's Wordsmiths and Chapter Guards went out to meet the enemy. A few minutes went by as some brief negotiations took place, before a command was given from the opposing forces, and the Dwellers swarmed over House Carvallen's finest like bees on a honey pot.

Merelie couldn't look anymore - she'd seen it too many times in her dreams – so lay back on her bed, listening to the sounds of the one-sided battle as it progressed from the walls of the city, through its streets and into the Chapter House itself. She wondered how long it would be until her father came lurching into her room, his eyes filled with Dweller smoke.

As it happened, it was Borne that smashed her bedroom doors open, scaring her as much as he had Max a few weeks previously. There was blood caked on one side of his face and he held his left arm close to his chest, a nasty gash running down his forearm.

'Borne!'

'We have to get you out of here, girl.'

'Where to? There's nowhere to run from those things,' she said with absolute defeat.

'You can quit that tone of voice for a start,' he ordered. 'We're not dead or possessed by those things yet.'

'Then what do we do?'

'If there's nowhere safe in this world, then maybe another will do. We have to get to the Library and use The Cornerstone.'

'But I'm not authorised - '

'When's that stopped you before?'

'But what good will it do?'

'You still believe somebody from that world can stop this?'

'Yes… yes I do.'

'Then come on!'

The massive Arma grabbed her hand and pulled her towards the door. Merelie gathered up a long dark green Carvallen coat and gave her room a last look. There was a small, scared part of her that thought she might never see it again.

The next fifteen minutes of Merelie's life were quite awful.

They passed groups of Carvallen Chapter Guards mounting a desperate attempt to stop the intruders. They failed, but did manage to hold the enemy back long enough for Borne and Merelie to work their way down to the Library. The screams of pain that echoed through the hallways were bad - the moans of pleasure that followed as minds and souls were devoured, were a thousand times worse.

Merelie word shaped as much as she could, sending smoke-eyed creatures, enemy soldiers and Wordsmiths flying in all directions. For his part, Borne wielded an antique cudgel ripped from a wall along one of the galleries, hitting anything he didn't like the look of with studied precision.

Down flights of stairs they ran, missing capture or conversion sometimes by mere inches. Arriving at the hallway leading to the Library came with a mixture of good and bad luck.

They'd reached their destination safely, but between them and the Library doors were several Chapter Guards fighting off multiple void creatures.

Merelie recognised one of them.

'Writer, *no!*' she cried.

'What is it, girl?'

'Look, Borne. It's Elijah! Mother's Arma has been possessed!'

Sure enough, Borne saw the lean and muscular form of his fellow Arma as he jumped onto a luckless Chapter Guard. The thing in his friend's shape gibbered and laughed insanely as it grasped the guard by his head. Thick purple-black smoke erupted from Elijah's eyes and entered the guard's. He twitched and screamed as it filled his head, the Dweller eating his mind with hideous glee.

The guard finally stopped shrieking and started to moan, gazing blankly at the ceiling, all trace of coherent thought wiped from his face.

Merelie felt tears prick her eyes.

Damn you Morodai. Damn you and your dog for unleashing this and damn me for not seeing your part in it.

Putting her rage to good use, she word shaped with as much power and control as she could, sending the Elijah-thing pin wheeling down the corridor. He smashed into his brethren, who'd been temporarily pushed back by the Carvallen Chapter Guards.

Merelie noticed for the first time there was a single Wordsmith amongst those defending the Library.

'Wordsmith!' she called.

The young man, no older than twenty, spun around. 'Lady Merelie!' he said. 'We had reports you'd been taken.'

'Not likely. What's your name?'

'Kelvin, Lady. Kelvin Holderness.'

'Related to Davina Holderness?'

'My mother!'

'Well Kelvin, I need your help.' Merelie looked down the corridor to see the Dwellers massing once again, blocking her way to the Library.

Borne had taken up position against the wall with the remaining Chapter Guards and had picked up a stray bow-gun, which he fired down the corridor.

'Anything, lady!' Kelvin said.

'I need your help forcing them back so I can get into the Library. Can you do that?'

'I can try Lady, but the Library doors wouldn't open for us. The custodians have barricaded themselves in.'

'I can fix that Kelvin, don't worry. Are you with me?'

Kelvin Holderness squared his shoulders.

'I am!'

'Then let's get to it.'

Both Wordsmiths threw themselves into the battle and with the combined effort of Borne and the Chapter Guards, the creatures were driven back, leaving the Library exposed.

'Keep it up!' Merelie shouted and placed her hand on the huge double doors. She whispered words under her breath that Garrowain had given to her - and her alone. No-one except the custodians and the Chapter Lord had free access to the Library. Garrowain had risked his job by telling her the passwords to get in. The words spoken, the doors swung open silently.

Beyond was the familiar well-appointed entrance lobby, this time filled with concerned looking old men dressed in the same garb as Garrowain.

'No!' one of them shouted, scuttling towards the door, 'you cannot come in here! The books must be protected!'

Behind, Merelie heard Kelvin Holderness scream. She turned to see him go down under a mass of Dwellers. More of the creatures started up the corridor towards her.

Borne smacked one of them square in the face so hard it took the thing off its feet, sending it crashing into the others.

'Merelie! Get inside!' he ordered.

She turned back as the old custodian reached her, trying to yank the massive door closed.

Oh, to hell with it.

She muttered under her breath, word shaped and the old man went flying backwards. This would normally have been a crime punishable by a lengthy sentence in the Chapter gaol, but right now Merelie didn't care.

Borne grabbed her round the waist, ran through the doorway and turned, slamming the door shut with his free hand. There was a whooshing noise as Wordcraft sealed the door.

Borne span round to address the custodians. 'How long will that hold?' he demanded.

One of the old men, who wasn't completely shell-shocked by all of this, stumbled forward. 'We don't know! We've never seen anything with their power!'

'No? I bloody have! Didn't believe me though, did you?' Merelie screeched. Borne had to hold her tight, otherwise she was liable to start whacking the frail old man around the head.

'Calm down, Merelie!' Garrowain demanded as he hurried across the hall, all signs of his advanced age gone. 'They couldn't see what was in the void any more than I could. Morodai did very well to block their existence from us.'

'I should have known that bastard was behind this!' Tears ran down her face. 'My mother's Arma is out there! He's one of them! It means she must be dead!'

Garrowain smacked Merelie across the cheek. This brought her to her senses immediately.

'You hit me,' she said in an incredulous voice.

'Indeed. I'll thank you to remain calm from now on, so I don't have to do it again.'

'How long will the door hold, Garrowain?' Borne asked again.

'Long enough to get you to The Cornerstone, which I trust is your reason for coming here?'

'Yes!' Merelie said. 'We have to find someone who can help.' A thought occurred to her. 'Will you come with us?'

'No. I would be no help over there. Besides, the books need protecting. Those things out there may have power, but we are not completely witless ourselves. But you must find someone who can be a Wordsmith from the other side, Merelie. You made the right decision in coming.'

'It was Borne's idea, actually. I was pretty much resigned to having my brains sucked out by purple void monsters.'

Garrowain tried to suppress a smile. 'It seems young Mr Bloom has rubbed off on you a bit.'

'Enough of this. Time is against us,' Borne snapped, ending the conversation. He walked through to the Main Hub, where the Codex sat on its pedestal.

'Your Arma is wise, child. We should go.' Garrowain addressed the other custodians. 'Try your best to prevent those fiends from getting in for as long as you can.' He put his arm around Merelie and they followed Borne through to the Library proper, sealing the doors to the Hub behind them.

Garrowain's staff lined up in front of the main doors and waited. They didn't have to wait long, as a scrabbling noise came from the other side almost immediately. The monsters were trying to get in.

- 7 -

Get in they did about a minute later, while Merelie, Garrowain and Borne hurried to where The Cornerstone lay at the heart of the Library.

The custodians fought bravely with their limited word shaping skills. They were used to moving books around and mollifying the incumbent guardian, not engaging in hand to hand combat with Dwellers in possession of the bodies of young, strong Chapter Guards. They were defeated in short order, leaving the Library open to abuse from the abhorrent creatures.

Led by the Dweller possessing Elijah, they swarmed through the entrance lobby, destroying the elegant furniture in an orgy of pointless destruction. It was but the work of a few minutes to get through the doors to the Main Hub, where the ancient Codex was treated to a horrible level of abuse, and would definitely require a good scrub once all this was over.

Sniffing out their prey, the Dwellers crowded around the door that separated them from the corridor Garrowain had led Merelie and Borne down mere minutes ago.

'They're right behind us!' Merelie said.

'They'll be through any minute,' Borne agreed as they hurried along the aisle.

'Stop!' Garrowain ordered. 'We have to slow them down.'

'And how exactly do we do that? There's too many to use Wordcraft,' Merelie said, her eyes locked on the doorway, now far enough away to be almost lost in the gloom.

'The guardian may wish to assist us.'

'What? That thing's as bad as they are!'

'Nonsense. It can be perfectly reasonable... as long you explain your point of view.' The old man looked up and spoke a few words under his breath. 'Observe.'

Merelie and Borne both felt it - a strong pressure against the temples, like having your head squeezed in a vice.

The guardian 'appeared' in front of them, its presence indicated by hardbacks and paperbacks flying off the shelves as it sped up the aisle.

Garrowain held out a hand. 'Stop!' he commanded.

Miraculously, it did.

The last book dropped to the ground as *something* hovered in front of the custodian's outstretched arm.

Merelie sort of knew what the guardian was. She could more or less understand the concept of so many dark thoughts being kept in one place that they manifested themselves physically in the form of a bad tempered invisible entity. The guardian had been around for years and while it had the potential to be lethal, it was treated like a vicious pet. One to be wary of at all times without a doubt, but also tolerated because it was unique and fascinating to study.

A custodian may get slightly mauled every now and again, and the hours it took to tidy away the books the guardian spat out in its wake were indeed tedious, but it was one of a kind and no other Chapter House had anything similar.

Bragging rights at the annual inter-House conferences were more than worth the occasional horrific injury, or week spent bent over picking up hardbacks.

Garrowain certainly exerted some control over it, which could prove useful. Especially as Merelie could now hear the hinges of the door at the end of the corridor beginning to squeal in protest as more weight was placed against them.

'Now, your help is required,' Garrowain began, in a tone any dog owner would recognise. 'There are creatures that would destroy this Library and the books it contains. Your home is under threat.'

The air swirled as the guardian reacted.

'I agree. It would be very bad.'

Several books flew off the shelves, bashing into one another before dropping in a heap. Garrowain winced, in the manner of someone who has seen this happen many times.

'My associates and I intend to stop said creatures by means too complicated to go into now, but we would appreciate it if you could hold them up while we proceed through the Library.'

The air shifted about.

'You understand me?'

'I don't think it does,' Merelie said, just as the door gave way and the host of monsters came storming up the corridor.

Borne stepped forward, gave the space where he assumed the guardian was a long hard stare, and pointed his finger back at the closing pack.

'Kill!' he commanded.

All three were blown aside as the guardian barged past them, speeding up the aisle, books flying in its wake.

It hit the pack of monsters coming towards them and Dwellers started flying in every direction.

Merelie was disturbed to note that not all of the ones that rocketed into the thick, soupy mist above their heads came back down again. She also fancied she could hear the sound of chewing for a couple of seconds after they disappeared.

'I think we should be leaving while we have the chance. The Cornerstone is close,' Garrowain said, as possessed folk continued to fly this way and that - the guardian having huge fun with its new toys.

It wasn't the smartest creature in the world however, so was unaware that two Dwellers, wearing the bodies of Elijah and Kelvin Holderness, had sneaked under its raging, invisible form.

Merelie took The Cornerstone from the shelf.

'It's not going to like this, you know,' she said. 'This is unauthorised use no matter what. It might not let Borne and I through.'

'We won't know until we try,' Garrowain pointed out.

'Put your arms around me Borne,' Merelie told her Arma, 'and hold on tigh - '

She was lifted violently off her feet as Elijah slammed into both of them.

Merelie was thrown forward and Borne crashed into the book shelf beside her, Kelvin Holderness leaping onto him like a rabid monkey.

The Arma was far bigger, but had been taken by surprise, so couldn't throw the smaller man off before the terrible purple-black smoke erupted from Kelvin's eyes.

'No!' Merelie screamed as the darkness took hold of Borne's mind.

'Go, girl! Get out of here!' Garrowain shouted, word shaping Elijah away.

Merelie saw her brave Arma's eyes consumed by the smoke, followed by his head snapping round to look at the custodian with blind hunger.

Kelvin's lifeless body slumped to the ground, the Dweller now transferred into Borne.

The Arma ran at Garrowain, who stumbled back, trying to get out of reach.

Merelie's attention was brought back to Elijah, who snarled at her. She desperately flung open The Cornerstone and began to read as the Arma attacked…

Merelie's attention was brought back to Elijah, who snarled at her. She desperately flung open The Cornerstone and began to read as the Arma attacked…

Merelie popped out of existence, while Garrowain ran deep into the bowels of the Library, the predatory Borne close behind.

Osgood Draveli stood in the Library's wrecked entrance hall, listening to the sounds of the guardian leaving the area, its playthings now still and offering no more entertainment.

'It's nearly gone,' he said to one of the Wordsmiths standing by him.

Draveli had entered the Carvallen Chapter House in triumph - once it had become clear that the creatures had disposed of any immediate threat - and had marched imperiously through the halls of the House, keen to see Jacob Carvallen and his snotty wife turned into Dwellers, ready and willing to serve.

He'd been diverted when word had come that Merelie Carvallen had escaped into the Library. The Chapter Lord had been forced to detour down here to take charge of her capture.

At this point, the fat little man was completely drunk on power, ordering the Dwellers around like slaves. Lucas Morodai treated them with more respect, knowing full well they could turn on him at any moment. But Osgood was - and let's be fair about this - a complete idiot. He didn't see any danger *whatsoever* in annoying incredibly powerful evil beings from another dimension.

Several possessed Carvallens stood at the doorway with him, keen to enter the Library and find more prey to feed on.

Had Osgood been blessed with any kind of backbone, they might have found some, but as he'd waited so long for the guardian to leave, by the time they discovered Elijah and the zombie-like Kelvin Holderness, all chances of a meal were long gone.

'What happened?' Osgood asked in his high pitched, nasal whine.

The thing inside Elijah snarled. 'The girl has escaped through that.' He pointed at The Cornerstone.

'Blast! Lucas won't be happy,' Draveli said, a note of panic interfering with his attempts to sound commanding.

He picked up The Cornerstone and mumbled a few words over it. The choir made a protesting squeal.

'No! You will do as I say!' he demanded.

Osgood may have been an idiot, but he was still a Chapter Lord and had enough skill in Wordcraft to tackle the book's defences - albeit briefly. He bombarded The Cornerstone with his will, until it capitulated and became quiet in his hands.

Draveli opened the book and stuck it in Elijah's face. 'Read this, creature. Be a good little dog... and go fetch!'

Elijah snarled once and looked at the page. He disappeared in a flash of silver light, the poor Cornerstone shrieking in protest.

Draveli tried to keep it open, but the book – now knowing the extent of Osgood's abilities - was having none of it, slamming shut with a last bright flare of light.

He passed it over to one of his Wordsmiths. 'Get this open again. Torture one of those old fools out front if you have to. I must go and report to Lord Morodai.'

Draveli went waddling back up the aisle, leaving the Library at the mercy of the Dwellers and The Cornerstone in the clutches of the enemy.

Part Four

Max Bloom loved attention. This especially held true when he was suffering from a debilitating illness, such as a mild head cold. He figured the more he told people how debilitating the mild head cold was, the better the chances were that they'd believe him and offer the requisite sympathy.

This never worked. What's more, on the one occasion he'd actually picked up proper influenza, the crying wolf factor kicked in and he was ignored by everyone until he threw up on the P.E teacher.

So you'd think he'd be more than happy with the little crowd of people gathered round him as a result of the two inexplicable seizures. He wasn't though... not by a long shot.

His mother was there, along with Monica. Max's little sister actually looked a bit worried, which hammered home the seriousness of the situation. Figgy and his mum were also in attendance. Her talking animatedly with Amanda Bloom, him picking his nose in the corner and trying to remain inconspicuous.

A rotund nurse took Max's temperature, while a doctor - who looked just about old enough to know what he was talking about - shone a torch into his eyes.

'I'm fine you know,' Max lied.

In fact his head was bursting and his stomach felt terrible, but he just wanted to get out of here as quickly as possible and make it back to that damn library. During the seizures he'd had visions of Merelie Carvallen in *big* trouble. He'd seen her enter this world and be followed by some big, scarred maniac who looked a bit like Lemmy from Motorhead.

A link had evidently been created between Max and The Cornerstone, meaning every time it got used, it sparked off one of these manic seizures. Unless he found the bloody thing and stopped it, he supposed he'd have one every time some idiot from The Chapter Lands popped across for a look about.

Max had sensed Merelie's state of mind as she'd breached the gap between worlds: absolutely terrified.

With the brief skim he'd also had of Lemmy's head as he crossed the endless gulf, the situation was clear. Merelie's dreams had come true. The monsters with smoke filled eyes had invaded her world and were now turning their attention to Earth.

Max had no idea what happened after Lemmy had burst out of The Cornerstone, but chances are he'd attacked Merelie - and Imelda Warrington, if she was there as well. He didn't think either would be able to put up much of a fight. He had to get out of this stupid hospital and over to the library.

'I have to get out of this stupid hospital,' he said to his mother, who broke off the conversation she was having with Figgy's mum.

'I don't think so young man. I want the doctor to check you over thoroughly.'

Max could see the tears of concern in her eyes and decided he had no chance of getting out of here any time soon.

- 2 -

When a citizen of The Chapter Lands displays a talent for Wordcrafting, they're immediately inducted into the training academy.

Only a dozen or so people a year are given the chance to develop their skills, graduating as Wordsmiths if they pass all the tests. The training is hard and most of those inducted fail - spending the rest of their lives in House sanctioned jobs, such as Library custodian or the Chapter Guard. Those who do pass can look forward to a privileged lifestyle acting as ambassadors for their House, defending it if necessary.

One defining aspect of a Wordsmith is their capability to think fast and use their craft without hesitation. Training becomes instinct, instinct becomes action.

This had been ingrained into Imelda Warrington.

Just as well, because years later, reflexes and skills not used for decades were required in an instant.

Imelda saw the brown sofa flying towards Merelie's head and her instincts kicked in. Her arms flew out and she word shaped.

It was weak and she was *very* rusty, but it was enough.

The sofa, instead of hitting Merelie square in the face and killing her, was knocked off course by Imelda's effort. It glanced off Merelie's shoulder, sending her spinning like a top, and flew past smashing into the library's horticulture section, knocking the entire stack over.

Merelie crashed into a nearby table, her head hitting the edge.

Elijah burst through the shattered staff room doorway and ran at Imelda, bellowing in rage, spittle flying from his lips. She tried to back pedal as he closed, but he grabbed her by the shoulders, his cold fingers digging painfully into her skin. The horrid smoke began to spin from his eyes and she knew she had to act or be damned where she stood.

Imelda shaped words into another blast of energy that sent the monster crashing into the astronomy section. She looked down at her hands with disbelief, amazed she was word shaping so effectively.

See? Being a Wordsmith still comes naturally. All it needs is a monster trying to kill you to get the ball rolling.

The library helped, of course.

A Wordsmith's power was enhanced by the presence of books, and here the weight of written thought and emotion was palpable. This made Imelda strong enough to bring the entire astronomy bookshelf down on Elijah, pinning him to the floor.

Watching him like a hawk, she made her way over to Merelie.

There was a trickle of blood coming from the girl's temple where she'd hit the table, but she wasn't unconscious, just heavily dazed.

'Are you alright?' Imelda said.

The girl put her hand to the wound, running an experimental finger over it. She flinched in pain and sucked blood off her finger. 'Where's Elijah?'

Imelda pointed to the fallen bookcase. One arm poked from under it. 'I think I've stopped him.'

'If that sofa had hit me dead on, I'd have been in real trouble. Thanks.'

'You're welcome.'

Merelie looked at Imelda for the first time with some respect. 'I thought you said you hadn't used your Wordcraft in a long time? You looked fine to me.'

'No-one is more surprised about it than me, Merelie.'

'You use my name like you know me.'

'I should do girl. I'm your aunt. Jacob Carvallen is my brother.' There was a trace of bitterness in Imelda's voice.

Merelie was absolutely stunned. 'My *aunt*? But... I've never heard of you!'

'Not a huge surprise. Your father and I had a falling out a long time ago. That's why I'm here. Jacob is the type to pretend somebody doesn't exist if they've displeased him. Out of sight, out of mind, as far as he's concerned.'

'Your name's Imelda Warrington, though.'

'In this world. In The Chapter Lands I'm Emerelda Carvallen.'

'What did you do? Why would father exile you?'

What Imelda did would have to wait, as Elijah now came bursting through the wreckage of the astronomy section, scaring them both.

'You cannot stop us,' he said, chewing down on the words as if the Dweller hadn't quite worked out how to use a tongue and lips properly. 'Your lands have fallen and this world will fall too. We will eat your mind and the minds of all who live here.'

'Oh, you think so?' Imelda said and strode forward, sending a blast of energy toward it. The Dweller was ready this time and raised Elijah's hands, making a gesture which sent Imelda's force harmlessly to both sides.

'Oh dear,' she said, strength draining from her voice.

'Little spells for a little mind,' the Dweller said with amusement.

Terror rose in Imelda's throat as he crossed the intervening space at frightening speed. An arm like an iron bar slammed into her chest and she flew backwards, hitting a free-standing rack of comic books.

The thing had brushed her aside like a minor irritation. His true target was obviously Merelie, still dazed from her fall... and easy pickings.

Imelda struggled to untangle herself from the rack. To distract the Dweller, she picked up the largest comic she could get her hands on. It was something called the Judge Dredd Archives, an inch thick book with a stone-jawed man in a helmet on the front cover.

She flung it at Elijah, assisting its flight path and speed with a bit of subtle Wordcraft. The book struck him on the head, sending the monster off course and giving Merelie enough time to dodge out of the way.

The girl tried to focus her power on the thing inhabiting her mother's Arma, but every time she tried to shape her words, a wave of nausea passed through her and her vision blurred due to the head injury. Merelie saw Imelda pinned by the comic rack and turned back to see the creature coming at her.

He grabbed her around the throat and started the terrifying process of claiming her. The living purple and black smoke burst from Elijah's eyes and covered her face. Merelie screamed, seeing into the monster's horrible mind as it began to engulf hers.

All it knows is silence… All it feels is emptiness...

As the darkness threatened to take her, Merelie remembered how Max had taken care of her possessed father in the dream she'd dragged him into. Concentrating as hard as she could, she set her feet, squared her shoulders and lashed out with her right leg, kicking Elijah in the crotch as hard as she could. The result was as satisfying for her in real life as it had been for Max in the dream.

The smoke cleared from Merelie's head.

Elijah made an '*oof*' noise, like a deflated football hitting a brick wall. His eyes crossed, his knees buckled and he slumped to the ground, hands cupping his groin.

It's one thing to possess a human body and control its voluntary functions. It's entirely another to control the involuntary ones. It doesn't matter how cruel and vicious a creature from the dark void you are, if you take a ride in a man's body and get kicked in the cobblers, you *will* be collapsed in a heap on the floor faster than you can say 'bad anatomical design'.

Looking at Elijah drop like a sack of potatoes, Merelie thought they had a fighting chance, providing he didn't start attacking them with his legs crossed.

Blood ran into her eyes from the cut, making it difficult to see. She stumbled over to where Imelda was extricating herself from the comic rack.

'Nicely done,' the librarian complimented.

'Thanks, but it's not going to keep it down for long,' Merelie replied. She ripped a strip from the bottom of the white top she wore and used it to dab away the blood from her face.

'I thought it had you.'

'It nearly did,' Merelie shuddered. 'I saw what it was, Imelda. I saw right into its mind.'

'And?'

'It's *hungry*. It comes from a place where there's nothing. No thought, no hope, no light, no life. It hates us for being alive in this universe - for having what it doesn't. It takes our bodies and devours our minds so it can feel what we feel... live how we live. No wonder they struck a bargain with Morodai. They'd have given anything to get into this world.'

'Then let's do all we can to send them back,' Imelda said, looking at the Dweller as it began to stir again. The Arma dragged himself to his feet, snarling with fury and pain.

Merelie and Imelda advanced. Both of them wove their hands in the air, drawing in the power of words as if it hung in space, a physical thing to be controlled and channelled.

Instead of unleashing individual attacks, they held back, getting closer to their quarry, scooping up every ounce of energy they could before unleashing it together at once.

The blast drove the Arma through six bookcases. Wood, paper and plastic flew in all directions with the force of Imelda and Merelie's Wordcraft.

'Bloody hell!' Imelda gasped, as the debris settled around her.

'I think we underestimated ourselves a bit,' Merelie said.

'It appears we've put a stop to that thing, though.' Imelda pointed at the mangled looking shape against the far wall, partially obscured by a pile of books and splintered wood.

They edged over to where Elijah lay.

He was unconscious, eyes rolled back into his head. Imelda poked him with her foot. There was no movement.

Merelie looked around at the mess. 'This is an awful thing to happen to a library,' she said.

'This is an awful thing to happen to my pension,' Imelda replied, drawing a confused look from Merelie. 'Don't worry, it'd take too long to explain and we have more pressing matters.' She gave Elijah another kick.

'He's out cold this time,' Merelie said, bending down to inspect the man's face. 'Looks like they're not invincible after all.'

'We were lucky - one of him and two of us. If they've overtaken The Chapter Lands, there's no way we can fight back.'

'Unless we find someone here who can help us,' Merelie said.

Imelda sighed at the combination of hope and excitement she could hear in the girl's voice. Her time with Max Bloom had apparently not convinced Merelie there wasn't a powerful Wordsmith waiting in the wings on Earth to jump in and save the day.

It was very frustrating.

Just because there were books everywhere and the population could read, it didn't mean Earth was a breeding ground for people with innate Wordcraft skills.

Imelda had been here for decades and knew what the place was like. The people of this world only cared about their annual bonus, BMI percentage, the two weeks in Benidorm they'd booked a year ago, and the acquisition of as much shiny plastic rubbish as possible. Books were just another aspect of day-to-day life - nowhere near as significant as in The Chapter Lands. In fact, a large percentage of the population didn't even bother to read. They were content watching soap operas and reality TV.

'I think you'd better concentrate on what *we* can do to stop this, Merelie. Relying on anyone else is never a good idea. It raises hopes and loses focus.'

'But there must be someone - '

Because this had been a trying day already and because Emerelda Carvallen had been forced into twenty years exile by an uncaring brother, Imelda lost her temper. 'For the love of God and the Writer!' she snapped. 'There is *no-one* here who can help Merelie! Nobody here can Wordcraft! This world isn't like ours or any others. Trust me, I've been here long enough to know! Yes, there is power here, but not like ours. They fight with guns... with bombs... with nasty weapons designed by nastier minds. There is *no-one here who can help!*'

The shocked look on the girl's face dashed cold water over her anger. Imelda took a deep breath and composed herself. 'I'm sorry Merelie, but I'm right. We stand and fight alone... for our loved ones and the Chapter House. And we'll die if necessary to defend them.'

'Spoken like a true Wordsmith.'

'That's what I am. Don't let the power suit and spectacles fool you, young lady.'

From in the distance they could both hear the sound of sirens.

'What's that noise?' asked Merelie, having not researched Earth society as much as she probably should have.

'That's the police, Merelie. This world's version of the Chapter Guards. What they lack in imagination, they make up for in sheer bloody mindedness. Explaining this mess away will be next to impossible, especially if they find you here.'

'What about Elijah?'

'I'll think of something... but you have to leave. Take The Cornerstone with you. I might be able to lie my way out of this and say this was a gas explosion or something, but trying to explain away a glowing, screaming book might be a bit of a stretch.'

'No-one else has come through.'

'And that's a saving grace. Go get it and leave through the fire exit over there. Hide somewhere until the dust settles... but don't go far, girl.'

Merelie ran back to the wrecked staff room, while Imelda put her mind to inventing a plausible story for why the library had apparently exploded and concussed a passing heavy metal fan.

Merelie found the book in the debris surrounded by bits of microwave and pot plant. She grabbed it, sprinted over to the fire exit, and headed out into the cold night air, looking for somewhere safe to hide.

- 3 -

Max had spent all night stuck in hospital, being poked, prodded and generally inconvenienced by white coats.

It was now eight in the morning and he'd just woken from a particularly disturbing dream which involved being chased through a library by a giant pair of scissors.

'Morning, love,' Amanda Bloom said in a cheery fashion from beside the bed. 'How are you?'

'Other than the fact I'm trapped in this hospital when I feel absolutely fine? Great, thanks. Any danger of a cup of tea?'

Amanda bustled off to track down a brew, giving him enough time to remember what had happened yesterday.

Seizures... Cornerstone... Lemmy from Motorhead... Merelie in danger... stuck in hospital.

He flung the bed sheets aside, jumped out and dressed in the clothes that had been folded in the cabinet beside him, including one of his favourite black hoodies. By the time Amanda came back, Max was lacing his Nike trainers and deciding on the best course of action.

Persuading his mother to drive him to the local library at eight in the morning for no apparent reason was top of the list.

'Why do you want to go there?' she asked when he told her.

'There's a book I really want to read that came back today. It's dead popular, so if I don't get down there now, somebody will get it before me.'

This, in Max's opinion, was *brilliant*. An on-the-fly piece of creative deceit any politician would be proud of.

'Well, the doctor says you don't appear to have any lasting effects from the seizures,' Amanda said, a bit unsure. 'First twitch I see though and you're back here sharpish. Got me?'

'Right.'

'Dad's got Monica this morning and I want to get home before he bores her to death.'

Twenty minutes later, Amanda's Ford Focus pulled into the road leading to the library.

'Bloody hell,' said Max, as they neared the disaster zone.

Police tape was strung across the road, blocking it off. Two bored looking coppers were turning traffic around and trying to ignore the morning drizzle. In the car park were several police cars, an ambulance and a fire engine, taking up every available space next to the grey library building.

It was clear something pretty catastrophic had happened. Max was willing to bet it had something to do with his seizures and that annoying book.

The image he'd had of Merelie – injured and scared – came back to him.

'Drive a bit closer, mum.'

Amanda did so and Max unwound his window, beckoning a bedraggled PC over.

'Can I help?' the officer asked, flashing them the quick smile he'd been trained to use in situations like this.

'What happened here, mate?' Max asked, showing a disregard for authority that would no doubt get him into trouble in later life.

'We're not sure... maybe a gas explosion. Can't say any more than that I'm afraid.' He looked at Amanda. 'I'll have to ask you to turn around and head back the way you came, miss.'

Amanda, who hadn't been a miss for eighteen years, gave the PC a winsome smile. 'Certainly officer, we'll get out of your way.'

She turned the car and headed back in the other direction, a half smile on her lips.

'Stop the car!' Max shouted.

Amanda braked and pulled the car over to the kerb, tyres squealing in protest. 'What? What!? Are you having a seizure?' She slapped a hand to his forehead, checking his temperature. Max batted it away.

'I'm fine!' he told her, looking through the rain streaked windscreen at the cold and lost looking figure of Merelie Carvallen.

- 4 -

'Wait here mum, there's somebody over there I know.'

Max got out of the car and jogged over to where Merelie was standing in the entrance to the local church. She was staring at the library, The Cornerstone clutched tightly to her chest.

Max didn't quite know how to handle this.

The girl looked tired and scared, so he supposed approaching her with care and consideration was the way to go. On the other hand, this was the person responsible for several smacks on the head, a couple of embarrassing seizures and the inability to walk past a book shop without feeling nauseous, so he didn't feel all that sympathetic.

He decided on a neutral approach.

'Hello Merelie.'

She spun around, eyes wide with shock. When she realised it was Max, shock turned to relief. 'Max! I'm so pleased to see you!' she cried, throwing her arms around him.

Mum's watching all of this like a hawk. I'm never going to live it down.

He extricated himself from the hug. 'What are you doing here Merelie?'

'It was the driest place to stand, underneath the trees,' she said, indicating the large oak growing nearby.

'Ok,' he wasn't sure she'd understood him. 'I meant... why are you *here*? In my world?' Then he remembered the seizure. 'They came didn't they? The monsters you were worried about.'

'Yes,' she said, her voice small and scared. 'Everybody's gone, Max.'

'You jumped over here to get away? Followed by that big bloke in the leather get up?'

Merelie looked surprised. 'How do you know about Elijah?'

He pointed at the book. 'That stupid thing. I saw you both come over. I had a fit every time the book got used and had to go to hospital.' The accusing tone in his voice probably wasn't fair, but he couldn't help himself.

'Your link to The Cornerstone must be very strong, Max,' Merelie said, curiosity momentarily overcoming her fear.

'Yeah. Any ideas why?'

'No. I've never heard of anything like it before. Maybe it's because of who you are.'

'You're not going to start that whole super wizard thing again, are you?' Max backed off and held his hands up.

'I'm too tired to think about anything right now.'

Max looked over at the library. 'What happened down there?'

'The thing that possessed Elijah came through The Cornerstone. We had to fight it.'

'What did you use? A cruise missile?'

'What?'

'Never mind. Can you get back?' His eyes flicked down to the book.

'It's not working,' she said, 'no power again. Anyway, I'm not sure if I should try, I don't know what's waiting on the other side.'

'Fair enough. Dropping into a crowd of those things wouldn't be a great idea, would it?'

Merelie shook her head and looked back at the library.

Max lapsed into thought.

On the one hand, the sensible part of his brain was ordering him to walk away and leave Merelie to her fate. He hadn't asked to get caught up in all this and now the police were involved it was likely to get even worse.

Then there were the hoards of void-dwelling, people-possessing monsters potentially lined up on the other side of the pages of The Cornerstone, waiting to suck his eyeballs out through his bottom.

While leaving well enough alone would be the sensible thing, Max was a teenage boy, and being sensible was generally to be avoided like the plague. Chuck in the hormones stirred up whenever the extremely pretty Merelie Carvallen was about and rationality stood no chance.

Dumb heroism was therefore the order of the day. Max didn't quite put his hands on his hips and look off into the middle distance, but he might as well have. 'You need to come home with me, Merelie. It's not safe here.'

'Imelda told me to stay here until she got rid of the Chapter Guards.'

'The what?'

'The ones in the armour.'

'The old bill, you mean? You standing here will grab their attention eventually. Besides, we can always come back later. No point you hanging round here getting wet and cold, eh?'

Merelie was exhausted from a night sleeping rough and would have traded The Cornerstone itself for a warm place to rest. 'Ok, Max, I'll come. This place scares me.'

'My mum's parked over there,' Max said and led the way over to the Ford Focus, dreading the next few minutes of his life.

When they reached the car, the grin on Amanda Bloom's face was so large it was a wonder the top of her head didn't fall off.

Max opened the back door and let Merelie in. She still clutched The Cornerstone close and looked wary as she lowered herself into the Focus.

Max got back in and steeled himself.

'Aren't you going to introduce us?' Amanda said, the amusement difficult to keep out of her voice.

'This is Merelie, mum... Merelie, this is my mum,' Max mumbled.

'Merelie? That's a very pretty name. Where does it come from? Ireland?'

'No ma'am. It was my great grandmother's name. She was Carvallen Chapter Lord for thirty years – and was famous for quelling unrest in the Borders and bringing them into the fold.'

'Aah. That sounds... lovely.' Amanda shot her son a bewildered look.

'She's... she's half Spanish,' Max made up on the spot, and immediately changed the subject. 'Can Merelie come back home with us for a bit? She was coming to see her aunt who works in the library, but obviously with what's going on she couldn't find her.'

Max's mastery of the convincing lie had reached new heights.

'Oh my goodness! Is she alright? Not hurt in the explosion I hope?'

'No ma'am,' Merelie said. 'She is well and talking to the *policies*.'

'See? Spanish!' Max threw in before his mother could comment on the girl's pronunciation.

Amanda knew something funny was going on here, but her son seemed to like this girl - she could tell by how red his face had gone - so let it go.

The rest of the journey home was carried out in silence, with Max biting his fingernails, Merelie gawping out of the window at the world around her and Amanda wondering what the hell a Chapter Lord was.

Amanda left Max and Merelie in the house while she went to pick up Monica - who was probably climbing the walls by now, having listened to her grandfather's stories about his bowel trouble for over an hour.

This came as something of a relief to Max. He was burning with curiosity about what had happened in Merelie's world and was pleased to get some peace and quiet.

He made Merelie a mug of hot sweet tea, which she sipped gratefully.

While the drizzle continued to stick to the windows outside - and while Imelda Warrington searched high and low for her - Merelie recounted the events of her life since Max had popped out of existence three weeks ago, ending with her escape as Imelda prepared for the arrival of the police.

- 5 -

'So, you were in your staff room making a cup of coffee,' the rather portly looking sergeant stated.

' ...and a curry flavoured Pot Noodle,' Imelda added, hoping she could throw him off balance with lots of trivial details. Slurping her tea couldn't hurt either.

' ...and a curry flavoured Pot Noodle, when you heard a massive explosion from outside.'

'Oh my yes. Huge, it was.' *Slurp.*

'Huge explosion from outside. You went out to investigate and that's when you heard another explosion from in here.'

'That's about the size of it.' *Slurp.*

'That was lucky, don't you think?' the sergeant said. He was beginning to regret coming out of the station to help with this one. There was a bacon sandwich with his name on it back at the yard and this woman was starting to get on his nerves.

'It would seem so.' *Slurp slurp.*

'This was the point at which you noticed the man dressed in black leather, lying in the wreckage?'

144

'Indeed. Very strange I thought that was.' Imelda's eyes went wide in a contrived effort to look scared. 'You think he's a terrorist, officer?'

'Um… I don't know, madam. I'd say this would be an odd target for a terrorist attack.'

'Yes. We haven't even got a copy of the Koran… or the Bible for that matter. Secularism is the watchword here at Farefield library!' Imelda remarked cheerfully, playing the part of the harmless and slightly befuddled librarian for all she was worth.

'Where is the young man? Is he alright?' she asked the copper.

If Elijah were to awaken and go on a rampage through the town…

'He's unconscious, but there aren't any obvious signs of trauma, which is incredible. There's something funny going on with his eyes, I'm led to believe. He's been taken to hospital for treatment.'

'Oh, that is *good* news,' Imelda lied.

'He' never made it to the hospital.

Five minutes drive from the library, on the hill leading out of town, the seemingly indestructible Dweller awoke and made short work of escaping the ambulance, leaving the paramedics the ones in need of extensive treatment.

Freed from the confinement of the shrieking metal box and spitting mad, the thing inside Elijah knew it had to reclaim the girl and get back to the safety of The Chapter Lands as quickly as possible. An echo of the brief link it had shared with Merelie's mind remained and the Dweller looked across the town, searching for her.

There was *something*… far away, but definitely there.

With a vague idea of where its target was - and a hunger so deep it hurt - the Dweller set off.

- 6 -

Back in Max's kitchen, Merelie had finished updating him on events.

'Christ on a bike. That sucks Merelie,' he said, biting into a bit of toast. 'I mean... your whole world taken over like that? And now one of them is here as well. Do you think it'll wake up again?'

'Hard to say. We hurt it, that's for certain, and it wasn't moving when I left.'

'Imelda can handle things,' he said, trying to sound positive.

'Maybe, though it sounded like she'd be with your policy people for a while.'

That actually gave Max some comfort. If this Elijah did spring up and start trying to suck some brains, Farefield Constabulary's finest would make a fight of it.

Would CS Gas work on denizens of the purple void?

Merelie sat in silence, her hands wrapped round a rapidly cooling second cup of tea.

Max stared out of the window.

What the hell do you say to someone who knows their world is doomed?

He didn't know what fate had befallen Merelie's friends and family, but he was sure it wasn't good. There was every chance they were dead... or sporting a new set of purple eyeballs.

He chose his next words carefully. 'Are you planning on going back?'

She looked at him and did her best not to cry. 'I suppose so. I can't do anything here. If nothing else, I can see if Garrowain got away. We can get out of the Chapter House and see if anybody else survived. Start a resistance or something.'

There wasn't much hope in her voice.

'That sounds... like a nice idea.' Max replied.

It wasn't his fault Merelie's dream of a saviour from Earth was just that... a dream. He still felt guilty he hadn't tried a bit harder to understand; maybe even giving this Wordcrafting thing a proper go if there'd been time. It wouldn't have worked, but at least he could have made a show of trying, for Merelie's sake.

She picked up The Cornerstone, which despite being knocked from pillar to post recently, displayed no new signs of wear and tear.

'At least no more have come through,' she pointed out. 'The Cornerstone's defences appear to be working again.'

Despite the fraught situation, Max was still curious about the strange book that had come into his life and made it so much more interesting.

'Who gave it defences?' he asked.

'The first Chapter Lord. When this world was discovered by Symon Carvallen, he wrote this Cornerstone to act as the gateway.'

'Was he powerful?'

'Yes, very. That type of Wordcrafting skill hasn't existed for a very long time, but back then there were enough powerful Wordsmiths to make The Chapter Lands a more exciting place to be.' Merelie sighed. 'They'd have stopped all this from happening.' She tossed the book down in disgust. 'I've wasted years thinking an off-world Wordsmith could save us. I should have been training harder to fight the monsters I knew were coming.'

'Don't have a go at yourself. You didn't know this Morodai bloke was working with them. After all, he's the one that let them in, yeah?'

'Yes.' There was a brittle look in her eyes that Max didn't like. 'I *will* go home... and if nothing else I'll see that bastard dead.'

'That's thinking positively,' he said, a response lamer than a three-legged horse. 'You're absolutely sure this is what you want to do?'

'What choice do I have? Imelda can't help, you can't help. *Nobody* in this world can help.'

'You could stay with me, where it's safe,' Max offered.

'I can't live here. This place is horrid. I'd rather die in The Chapter Lands.'

'It's not that bad,' Max said, feeling he should once again leap to the defence of his country, planet and universe.

Merelie realised she'd gone a bit far and gave him a wan smile. 'Not for you, Max. This is where you live. I'm sure there are things about this world that are lovely. But I'm lost here. It's such a strange place.'

She laid a hand on The Cornerstone. 'This is a pointless discussion anyway. I can't get back, The Cornerstone's dead. There's no charge in it to get me home.'

The thing did look a bit lifeless. There was normally a slight, imperceptible shimmer surrounding it, now conspicuous by its absence.

Max remembered that the last time it had been like this, Merelie had thrust it into a library bookshelf to recharge. Then he recalled the nearest library was currently surrounded by police and off limits.

There were other libraries in the area, but getting to them would be a pain. He guessed he'd have to take Merelie there on the bus or something. If she wasn't depressed enough already, a few minutes on British public transport should finish her off nicely.

Then, a better answer popped into his head.

Grandad.

Charlie Pearce's house, only twenty minutes walk away, was virtually a library itself, filled to the rafters with books. Surely there'd be enough power to charge The Cornerstone and send Merelie home?

He still wasn't sure this plan of action was advisable – one sixteen year old girl against a host of void dwelling monsters and dastardly Wordsmiths didn't give great odds – but she seemed determined, so who was he to argue?

He told Merelie about Charlie's wealth of books.

'That should work,' she agreed. 'Your grandfather sounds like a good man, Max. I'll look forward to meeting him.'

'If he gets talking about his haemorrhoids you might change your mind.'

'I just hope if I do get back, there's a reason for bothering. If Garrowain's dead and there's nobody else left…'

She left this hanging, not willing to put into words what they were both thinking.

- 7 -

Garrowain wasn't dead.
Far from it, in fact.

As Merelie had disappeared through The Cornerstone, he'd taken the sensible decision to run like buggery. Unfortunately, the freshly hijacked Borne had been in hot pursuit. The evil spirit that had invaded the Arma displayed a dogged determination and managed to stay right behind him as they twisted and turned along the stacks.

What went in Garrowain's favour was his total knowledge of every aisle, hallway and reading room of the massive Library. This kept him just far enough ahead of Borne to think about his next move.

Part of Garrowain's brain worked overtime on a solution, while the rest kept his feet pumping through the maze of bookshelves - the sound of grunting and growling close behind him.

Somewhere to keep him safely locked up.

That's what was needed right now.

The Library was not the type of place to offer immediate facilities for the imprisoning of possessed bodyguards, but one chamber sprang to mind that might serve the purpose. Garrowain had recently commissioned the construction of a new Library hub, meant to contain a selection of novels promised to him by his equivalent at the Falion Chapter House - a tall, whip-thin fellow named Hambrey. The chamber currently stood empty at the end of the classical art section and had only one doorway leading from it. It was the perfect place to store a maniacal monster - for the short term anyway.

The custodian made a few lefts and a couple of rights, finding himself in the correct corridor with the chamber at the end. Everything was going swimmingly until he saw that the door to the hub was missing.

A moment of panic overtook Garrowain as he sprinted down the aisle, desperately thinking of a way to salvage the situation.

The answer presented itself in the books he was running past. He'd have to build a barrier to keep the Arma contained, and he could make it with books.

Fortunately, the biggest, heaviest books in the Library were in the classical art section.

Garrowain ran down an aisle of books so big they'd need to sit on a coffee table reinforced with steel girders. He word shaped as he ran, using all that word energy to summon up a useful amount of power.

As he ran through the doorway into the empty hub, he dodged to one side just as Borne came crashing through, howling as he flew past. Garrowain spun gracefully, backed out and unleashed Wordcraft.

An entire shelf of gigantic books flew from their perches, forming a solid wall between Borne and the custodian, covering the open doorway completely. The Arma screamed and smashed into the barrier, the books giving way ever so slightly, but otherwise holding firm.

'Now, young man,' Garrowain said. 'I think that's just about enough of that.' He walked up to the newly created barrier and rapped his knuckles on it. 'This should hold you for a while. I'm aware the nasty little creature inside you is very strong, but I'll fancy it doesn't have the power to break free of this in hurry. This is my Library after all and I hold sway here.'

'You'll be my meal like the rest,' growled the Dweller.

'And a good meal I'd make, my boy! I've read many interesting things, and seen many fascinating sights. But I rather think I'll be keeping hold of my faculties a while longer.'

'I will break out of here and I will have you!'

'Well, let's just see about that, shall we?' Garrowain said, contemplating what to do next.

Holding a single possessed Arma captive was one thing; removing thousands of others, their Wordsmith masters and Lucas Morodai from Carvallen land was another problem entirely…

- 8 -

Speaking of problems, Imelda Warrington had a fairly major one. She'd lost Merelie.

The night before, the police had insisted on her going to hospital for a check-up, and had continued their interrogation while the doctors ran several pointless tests checking for gas poisoning. Imelda had done rather too good a job of pretending to be in deep shock and was dismayed to find herself ordered to spend the night in hospital. She'd done it, not wanting to attract any more suspicion, but had checked herself out early the next morning, desperate to find her niece.

Ironically, she missed seeing Max Bloom by seconds as they both crossed the hospital car park, the young girl from The Chapter Lands on both their minds.

Once at Farefield library - and trying to be as inconspicuous as possible given the amount of police - Imelda had hunted high and low for Merelie, with no success. She was now sat on a nearby bench, thinking about what to do.

If I were a scared sixteen year old girl, lost in another dimension and surrounded by strangers... where would I go?

Not being sixteen and having spent her teenage years on another planet, Imelda drew a blank.

A more constructive thought surfaced:

She does know someone here though, doesn't she? Max Bloom.

The one man sarcasm factory the girl had yanked across to The Chapter Lands without permission.

There was no way Merelie could know where Bloom lived and no way Bloom could know Merelie was here, but for some reason Imelda knew - *just bloody knew* - he was still involved in this somehow. The Cornerstone had almost adopted him, creating a connection she'd never seen it have with anyone else. He'd been over to The Chapter Lands - not once but twice - reappearing completely unharmed both times. Physically and mentally.

Nobody should be able to pop across dimensions, get chased by invisible monsters, enter the nightmares of another person and have their entire knowledge of existence turned upside down in one day, without demonstrating some kind of trauma.

Max Bloom was far from normal, and while it seemed he'd only got caught up in events by accident, Imelda was willing to bet vital parts of her anatomy that there was more going on here than met the eye. She was further willing to bet that if she found the boy, her chances of finding Merelie would rise significantly.

Having said all that, she had no idea where Bloom was either.

But you had him fill out his details the first time he came in, didn't you?

Bingo!

- 9 -

Jacob and Halia Carvallen were bound tightly in chairs in front of the massive desk in Jacob's study, behind which sat Lucas Morodai, flanked by two Dwellers.

'You're insane Lucas,' said Jacob, stating the obvious.

'Am I?' Morodai replied. 'From where I sit, I'd say I've planned and executed an operation that's brought every Chapter House to its knees. Not the work of an insane man in my book.'

'By allying yourself with these *things*,' Halia said with disgust.

One of them growled at her.

'Be careful what you say my dear. My colleague here would love nothing more than to eat every single last morsel of thought from your head.' Morodai flashed a reptilian smile. 'And then I'm sure Osgood would have fun with whatever was left.'

'You touch my wife - ' warned Jacob.

'Oh be quiet!' Morodai snapped. 'You're in no position to make threats.'

'Why do you let us live, Lucas?' Halia continued. 'Why are we spared?'

Morodai leaned forward, the smile returning. 'That's simple my lady. You have something I want.'

Jacob smiled bitterly. 'Of course we do. Compassion isn't your thing, is it Lucas?'

'Not really,' the Chapter Lord admitted, getting up and perching himself on the front of the desk. 'I will take what I want in exchange for the freedom of your people.'

'What's left of our people,' Halia said, sadness and hate in her voice.

152

Morodai waggled a finger at her. 'Tut tut. I've left many of your little citizens alive, Halia. Far more than Falion's, certainly. What's more, those... um... *borrowed* by my colleagues can be restored to their former selves.' He looked round at the two Dwellers behind him. 'As I understand it, when they're along for the ride, the mind of the host is shunted off to a corner somewhere, rather than being immediately devoured.' He lingered over that last word, making Halia shudder. 'Something to do with an active mind being needed for the body to function or some such... the details bore me.'

'What do you want, Lucas?' Jacob asked.

'Your adopted world! I want full access to that joyfully close-minded reality of yours, Jacob. Your Cornerstone is fighting my people and you need to re-write it. Hand over full control of The Carvallen Cornerstone and Earth to me and I let you, your family and this house survive.'

'Why?' asked Halia. 'You and the others all believe it's a soulless, pathetic place with no Wordcraft.'

'Who cares about *Wordcraft*?' Morodai laughed. 'I have more than enough of that here. Have you seen the resources that planet has to offer? The billions of people I can put to work? The technology so far in advance of our own, it could revolutionise The Chapter Lands? I only need Wordcraft to overpower their governments and bend the whole civilisation to my will!' He pointed at Jacob. 'You've wasted so many years studying them and fretting over their inability to word shape, when their true purpose was staring you in the face!' Spittle was flying from his lips now and his eyes blazed. 'Of all the worlds, yours has the most potential to be exploited. Wellhome's is full of meat-headed apes, Falion's is a self-righteous fantasy land and Draveli rules a planet so choked with pollutants it's impossible to breathe!'

'That's not how it works, Lucas,' Jacob argued, aghast at Morodai's greed. 'The relationship should be symbiotic. We shouldn't use our worlds, but work with them... nurture them'.

'Rubbish!' Morodai spat. 'My world needed no nurturing.'

'Yes, and look at it now... a planet of witless slaves with no freedom to express themselves. Your Library is pathetic... full of books borrowed or stolen from the rest of us. You've sucked the planet dry, you bloody fool!'

Morodai raised his fist to strike, but managed to bring himself under control. 'You think what you like, Lord Carvallen. But the fact remains, either you turn your world over to me and re-write your Cornerstone, or I will kill every single one of you. Starting with your wife.'

- 10 -

The Cornerstone - as has been established - is more than just a book. It can cross dimensions, defend itself against attack, and demonstrates a level of sentience that something made of pulped tree fibre really shouldn't possess... magical or not.

It likes Max, which indicates that while it's sentient, it might not be all that bright.

The Cornerstone has four brothers. All older, less intelligent and far less willing to be active participants in proceedings.

The golden Morodai Cornerstone has virtually no personality and the little it has is bitter and twisted. It's used - much like the people of Morodai's world - as a tool of labour, and nothing else. A mistreated tool at that, forced to ferry millions of luckless inhabitants across to The Chapter Lands. These people are put to work in the mines and factories - and in any other job the Morodai upper class finds too abhorrent for their own citizens to undertake.

Wellhome and Falion also have Cornerstones that lack much in the way of character, but are far happier with their lot in life. They're workhorses to be sure, but ones treated well and with respect.

Draveli's Cornerstone is a grotty blue hardback, covered in stains and worn heavily at the spine. It's as small minded, bigoted and uncaring as the people who travel through it.

The world it links to is a black, industrial nightmare, caused by generations of neglect and bad management. The book itself has developed a greasy, oily feel, having leeched dirt and muck from the minds of people it's been forced to transport.

The Carvallen Cornerstone connects with Earth - a place where billions of minds vie with each other for attention, and billions of voices struggle to make themselves heard over the din coming from everyone else. A world where the magic of books may be forgotten, but the magic of technology very much holds sway. A world where science and spiritualism are equals, and where feats of bravery and kindness are matched by acts of cruelty and vindictiveness every day. It was a wonder the thing hadn't gone stark raving bonkers.

Rather, the Carvallen Cornerstone had adopted a world-weary and cynical approach.

If it had a mouth, it would tut in contempt. If it had eyes, it would roll them in disgust. It had formulated this personality more or less on its own, having only ever been used sparingly to transport human beings - its power wasted due to how cautious the Carvallens were about visiting the planet.

Getting right down to it, The Cornerstone's personality was more or less that of a London cabbie.

It was also extremely stubborn, so there was *no way* it was taking anyone across the river at this time of night... metaphorically speaking.

- 11 -

The Wordsmiths were pulling their hair out.

No matter what they did, The Cornerstone remained resolutely closed.

Chapter Lord Draveli had left them with specific instructions to get the gateway open and find the Carvallen girl, but so far they'd had about as much joy as a vampire with gingivitis.

They stood in the Main Hub around The Cornerstone, where it sat on the pedestal usually reserved for the Codex - which had been chucked carelessly in one corner. They'd all taken turns to word shape at the book, trying to get the cover open, but had failed spectacularly so far.

All knew the punishment for failure would be having their minds sucked dry by the smoke-eyed monstrosities, so there was an understandable level of panic in the air. You could almost smell it.

One of the pensive Wordsmiths was a ratty looking fellow called Fergil.

He was an alumnus of the Draveli academy, so wasn't particularly talented, but did a nice line in invasive and cunningly constructed small-scale Wordcraft. This had earned him a lot of money in his homeland - carrying out petty acts of vengeance on unsuspecting targets for clients who paid very well.

It was all very dishonourable, but it was this seedy, below-the-belt magic that would eventually breach The Cornerstone's defence mechanisms.

While the other four Wordsmiths bombarded the book from all sides with flashy Wordcraft, Fergil stood back and waited, chewing his fingernail and watching intently for a sign of weakness.

He knew the book had a mind of its own and could be pushed into a mistake.

It was just a matter of time.

Garrowain could see this from the vantage point he'd set up above in the Library mists. He'd long ago become accustomed to the strange fog. Anything that might be lurking near the ceiling shrouded from sight knew better than to take a pop at him. Having watched events in the Library for decades, they knew what a clever little sod he was and weren't about to risk an embarrassing episode for the sake of a quick snack.

Garrowain thought about taking on all five Wordsmiths. If they got The Cornerstone open, it would spell trouble for Merelie and everyone else on the other side. He couldn't handle that many on his own though, he conceded. Better to watch developments and wait for the chance to do something constructive when the proper time came.

It was frustrating, but Garrowain was by nature a cautious man. This was probably why he'd lived for many years - and could even give indescribable monsters in the mist pause.

Part Five

Max thought about offering Merelie a 'backie' on his BMX, but this could be open to misinterpretation and the girl looked troubled enough as it was. Instead they walked to Charlie Pearce's house - a gothic looking monstrosity on one of the hills to the north of Farefield.

Charlie had lived there all his life, inheriting the place when both parents died in the mid-sixties. Max's mum had been raised there by Charlie and his wife Angela, who the old man had worshipped until her death eight years ago.

Charlie had always loved books, but since Angie's death this love had escalated to the point of good natured obsession. His life now consisted of tracking down as many novels as he could, putting them in his ever expanding collection that now threatened to overwhelm the entire house. His books kept him company, along with Nugget, the enormous but entirely friendly black Labrador that Amanda had bought for Charlie after Angela's death.

They reached the house and Max led Merelie up a weed infested driveway.

Charlie wasn't much of a gardener, so the weed theme continued all around the large plot of land the property stood in. The grass was three months past needing a cut and a couple of sad looking apple trees shed their leaves at a rapid rate, adding to the mess. Some of the detritus had been haphazardly piled onto the compost heap that leaned against the red brick garden wall.

From the rear garden, loud and excited barking could be heard.

Charlie's rusty Austin Montego sat outside a detached garage, which was itself only one or two years at most from complete collapse. The Montego's back seat was piled high with books.

This brought the first smile to Merelie's face in some time. 'He really does like books. That's nice,' she said.

'Yep. Looks like he's got a new load in for this week. I'll have to help him in with them later.'

They stepped into the broad front porch, which contained a large, grey stone gargoyle that for some reason was blowing a permanent raspberry, its stony tongue stuck out between its lips. Max rang the doorbell. It should have chimed sonorously to keep with the gothic look of the house, but instead played The Girl from Ipanema, ruining the ambience completely.

Merelie gave the gargoyle a look.

'Grandad's a bit eccentric sometimes,' Max offered by way of explanation. 'It can be a bit weird, but Christmas is always a giggle when he's around.'

'Christmas?' she asked.

Max thought about explaining, but the girl was probably out of her depth enough without being told an entire planet actively encouraged a fat man to break into their house once a year to leave them presents... and this was linked in some way that he'd never really understood to the birth of the little baby Jesus.

'Um, never mind,' he said. 'Maybe another time.'

The front door opened revealing Charlie Pearce, a classic grey-haired Grandad to his toes. Wearing black NHS glasses, a burgundy tank top over a blue shirt and brown slacks, the look was topped off by grey slippers with elastic bits on the side.

'Maxwell!' Charlie exclaimed with delight.

Max's full name is not Maxwell. Nobody else in the world calls him Maxwell and if they did they'd get a punch on the nose. Charlie can get away with it, because Grandad's always can.

'Wotcha, Grandad.' Max replied with equal pleasure.

If Amanda Bloom's reaction to seeing her son with a girl was melodramatic, Charlie's was positively Shakespearean. He bowed floridly at the waist, one arm raised to the side.

'My lady!' he cried. 'What have I done to deserve the pleasure of such beautiful company on this fine day?'

Merelie giggled. 'Hello sir.'

'And hello to you,' he said, giving Max a light thump on the arm and waggling his eyebrows in suggestive fashion. 'Maxwell! Introduce me to your new lady.'

'This is my friend, Merelie.' Max replied. 'Merelie, this is my Grandad Charlie. Please try not to take him seriously.'

Merelie curtsied and Max's heart stopped for a second.

'I'm honoured to meet you, sir,' she said, looking up at him with those glorious blue eyes.

'My word...' was all Charlie could offer in response.

The moment was broken by the arrival of Nugget.

He would have been on the scene earlier, but had been distracted by next door's cat Biff, a ginger tom with the personality of Reggie Kray and a penchant for terrorising anything with a heartbeat. Nugget had come off worse in two previous encounters, and was still smarting over the big scratch Biff had left on his snout last summer. Today, the cat had sat in the branches of one of the apple trees, watching Nugget bark himself into insensibility, before sloping off to torment the Jack Russell at number three.

Nugget saw Max, bounded over and started pawing at him, managing to hit his crotch at least twice. This was par for the course with Nugget.

'Nuggie! Down!' Charlie shouted and Nugget just about confined his excitement to finger licking and running between legs. Merelie even gave him a pat, wrinkling her nose as Nugget's doggie aroma rose to meet her.

'He reminds me of Ryder, one of father's mastiffs,' she said, while Nugget sniffed The Cornerstone in her hand, 'only chubbier.'

Nugget gave her a reproachful look.

Charlie noticed The Cornerstone and his eyes lit up.

'That looks like an interesting tome, Miss Merelie,' he said with obvious curiosity.

'Grandad,' Max said, 'You have absolutely no idea.'

- 2 -

Max and Merelie sat in the lounge on the old floral sofa Charlie refused to get rid of, with Nugget flopped between them. Merelie looked enchanted by the rows and rows of books covering every available wall space around her. More of them were stacked on the thick, oak coffee table in front of her, and she rested The Cornerstone on top of the pile.

Max thought his eyes might be playing tricks on him, but he could have sworn the thing looked slightly *thicker* since they'd brought it into the house.

The lounge was gloomy in the grey November light and smelled of musty wood and damp dog. A wide archway lead to a rustic looking kitchen, which held even more bookcases, in case Charlie fancied a bit of Dickens while he cooked.

The whole place had a cosy feel to it, as if all those books provided some kind of comfort and protection from the outside world.

It couldn't protect against the smell of dog... but nothing can when the dog's a big lad who's fond of eating out of the bin.

Nugget let out a silent doggie fart, adding more of his aroma to the room.

Charlie came in with a tea tray, loaded with mugs of coffee and a selection of biscuits the Queen would have been pleased to receive. He set the tray down and eased himself into a black leather armchair that looked older than dirt.

'So grandson of mine, what do I owe the pleasure? Your monthly visit isn't due for at least two weeks. I've already had the joy of your sibling's company this morning and now I find my cup runneth over with the offspring of my offspring.'

Max paused before replying. It was usually best when speaking to his grandfather, who could mangle a sentence until it was unrecognisable.

'Just thought I'd pop over and say hello, that's all,' he said, lying through his teeth.

'And you've brought the beautiful Miss Merelie along for what reason precisely?' He gave her a graceful smile. 'Not that your company is not the shining light in an otherwise mournful day, my dear.'

'She... er... likes books,' Max ventured, 'and you've got a lot of books.'

Charlie's smile broadened. 'Indeed I have, young man!' He turned to Merelie, who was munching on a garibaldi. 'Are there any specific genres of book you enjoy, my lady? Or are you a fan of all literary pursuits, broadly speaking?'

'Books are everything to me, sir,' Merelie replied, between mouthfuls of biscuit. 'Where I come from they govern our lives. Without them, the world is a flat and empty place.'

Charlie was delighted by this - and a little taken aback. 'Where do you hail from, for the written word to be so vital to your existence?'

'Spain!' Max leapt in. 'She's from Spain!' This lie really wasn't up there with the other whoppers he'd told recently.

Charlie's eyebrows arched like a cathedral roof. 'Spain, eh?'

Merelie, sensing this may lead them down a path that would take too long to navigate, changed the subject. 'Your collection is very good, sir. I'm sure there's enough power to work with.'

'Indeed... ' he agreed, looking perplexed.

'Like I said, Merelie loves the books!' Max laughed nervously and plunged onward. 'She... um... loves them so much, she'd like to put her book with yours for a bit. Just so it's... er... not lonely?' He made a face, knowing full well how stupid that sounded.

Charlie leaned forward.

'You'd like to put your book in with mine... on the shelf?' he said.

Merelie nodded.

'So it isn't... *lonely?*'

'Yes, sir.' Merelie said, deciding the next time she found herself in a situation like this, she'd do the talking.

Charlie remained sat forward, studying them both. Then, with lightning speed, he gathered up The Cornerstone, eliciting a sharp gasp.

He took in their shocked expressions.

'Expecting something to happen, were you?' he asked.

Both shook their heads quickly and gave him an awkward smile.

'Right then.' Charlie slotted The Cornerstone between Chaucer's Canterbury Tales and the memoirs of Winston Churchill. 'How long do you think your book would like to stay there? I mean, one can never tell just how lonely a book can get, being kept from its kind,' Charlie said as he sat back down.

'Oh, I dunno... not long,' Max guessed. 'What do you reckon Merelie?'

She didn't answer.

Merelie Carvallen was sizing things up. More specifically, Max Bloom's grandfather.

This was a man who surrounded himself with books. He showed a love of words she hadn't encountered in anyone else in her brief time here on Earth. He reminded her of Garrowain.

There might not be Wordcraft here, but apparently there were people who still knew and respected the power of words.

Knowing it was a massive risk, Merelie spoke. 'Drop it Max. Your grandfather isn't an idiot.'

'No, my dear. I rather fancy I'm not,' Charlie agreed. 'Would you or my grandson like to explain why you're actually here? I'm not buying the lonely book story one bit.'

'Er, Merelie,' Max said. 'You sure this is a good idea?'

'Yes, I am,' she said and gave Charlie a careful look. 'It's not just a book.' She got up, walked over to the charged Cornerstone and took it out. A single silver line of energy coursed down its spine.

Charlie's eyes widened.

'It's a doorway,' she told him, 'a means to travel to different worlds.'

Charlie laughed. 'You've just described every novel ever written as far as I'm concerned, my girl.'

'Yes, but with this book, the meaning is literal. This is The Cornerstone Book of Carvallen. Its purpose is to open a gateway between this world and mine. I am not from this place *Spain*.'

Max jumped up. 'Merelie! Too much information!'

'It's alright Max, your grandfather knows what books can do, for good or ill. He understands. And I need to know there's someone on this side of the doorway who does understand... who knows the power of words.'

'Maxwell? Has this fair maiden fallen foul of some affliction that befuddles her cognitive reasoning?' It was evident Charlie Pearce was trying to cover his shock with some verbal gymnastics. He couldn't take his eyes off The Cornerstone, which was now fat with power and glowed like an excited firefly.

Max gave up the pretence. 'Nope. She's as sane as you or me. The book does what she says. I should know; it's taken me to her world twice already.'

Charlie picked up a bourbon biscuit and sat back. 'Explain, please.'

Imelda got back into the library without much trouble. Only two PCs remained on scene guard at the entrance. Quite proud of the excuse she gave them - a sentimental attachment to the rolodex on the front counter, given to her by her wisened old mother, just days before her untimely death in a freak boating accident - Imelda made her way over to the main desk. She had to walk carefully around the splintered chunks of book shelf and the discarded leaves of paper that still blanketed the floor.

Whatever happens with The Chapter Lands, I'm probably out of a job here.

If by some miracle nobody blamed her for this, the library would be shut for months undergoing repairs.

Imelda rifled through the rolodex, looking up occasionally to make sure the coppers weren't watching. She found the card Max had filled in, popped it in the pocket of her slacks and headed back out into the late morning drizzle, offering the police an ingratiating smile as she passed.

Imelda then drove her Fiat Punto the two miles to Max's house. She parked up, went to the front door and rang the bell. If Max answered it was all to the good, if Merelie did even better.

If one of the boy's parents came to the door, she could always use an excuse about checking on overdue library books. This might seem like overkill, but promoting a robust response to the non-return of library property would set a good precedent - as well as covering her tracks in a believable manner.

She hadn't planned for *nobody* to answer the door.

Imelda walked round to the side of the house, checking to see if Max was hiding from her - she wouldn't put it past him - but couldn't see anyone through the windows or in the conservatory. The house was empty.

Heading back and wondering what to do next, her heart jumped into her throat when she saw Elijah standing in the front garden staring right at her.

Charlie Pearce picked up another bourbon biscuit and took a thoughtful bite.

It was, without doubt, a story worthy of the telling.

A land ruled by five great houses, founded on the discovery of other dimensions. Creatures of ill device from a dark, cold place between those worlds, yearning for the warmth of human existence. A power-mad dictator, striking a pact with the inhuman beasts to defeat and enslave his enemies. And behind it all, the idea that the beauty and magnificence of great writing could be harnessed as a physical force – as *magic*, no less.

'So, young Merelie, if I get this straight: you now intend to return to your world with no guarantee of survival and will try to overthrow this Morodai person? You think you stand much chance of success in this most dangerous of ventures?'

'I don't know, sir. But I've got no option.'

'The police, mayhap? They might render some assistance.'

'Grandad,' Max said with disbelief. 'She can't go to the old bill. They'd just spend six months filling out paperwork, then arrest her for wasting police time. Even if they did take it seriously, we can't let this world know about The Chapter Lands, it'd cause havoc!'

'For once, fruit of the fruit of my loins, you speak perfect sense. We'll have to rule out 'the man' as a source of help, then.' He gave Max a speculative look and turned back to Merelie. 'And what of this notion that young Maxwell here may well have powers secreted about his person, as yet undiscovered?'

Merelie sighed and her head dropped a little. 'That's what I believed for so long. But it isn't true. This world has no Wordcraft. None at all.'

'Imelda Warrington convinced you of this, I gather?'

Charlie was well aware who Farefield library's head of department was. He'd often spent an afternoon perusing the paltry library catalogue, tutting as he made his way through the fiction section, a deep frown on his face. A conversation would usually follow with Imelda, when he would complain there weren't enough books on offer.

'She did, yes,' said Merelie. 'Imelda said there was no Wordcraft in this world and I believe her now.'

'Don't be so quick to dismiss my species in general and my grandson in particular, Miss Carvallen.'

'Grandad,' Max spoke up, 'don't say things like that.'

'And why not?' he replied, raising his chin. 'If I wish to believe that untapped talents lie in that computer game addled brain of yours, I will. I can well believe the people of this world have become so enamoured with the sounds of their own voices that they've forgotten to stop and listen to what others might have to say. This planet is such a noisy place... no-one can hear themselves think! Maybe a little more silent reflection could lead to these Wordcrafting skills being unearthed.'

'Do you believe that sir?' Merelie said with renewed hope.

'Of course, my girl!'

Merelie looked at Max, the excitement back in her eyes.

'I am not a flaming wizard!' he yelled, scaring Nugget into another bout of flatulence.

Fergil the Draveli Wordsmith *was* a wizard - if a pretty weak one - and now saw an opportunity arise. Lashing out with a needle of Wordcraft at The Cornerstone's defences, he took the book completely by surprise.

While Charlie opened a window, Max got up and walked over to a bookshelf, getting away from Nugget's latest contribution to the discussion.

The Cornerstone continued to glow, illuminating the coffee table in an unearthly silver radiance. Max scanned the shelf and found what he was looking for. Charlie liked to keep things alphabetical and all the C's were in the same place.

Max pulled out his grandfather's copy of Call of the Wild and looked at the cover. The proud image of Buck, surrounded by white trees and mountains, was the same as his own copy. It was a picture that brought him great happiness.

If books had power, and power had weight... I wouldn't be able to pick this up.

He measured the book in his hand, but it didn't feel any heavier than the average paperback.

It was all nonsense. He was no Wordsmith.

His thoughts were broken by a low growl coming from Nugget's throat. Usually a placid and happy dog, hearing a noise like that, and seeing his jowls rise in a snarl, was quite disturbing.

'What's wrong, Nuggie?' Charlie asked, patting the dog's head.

Nugget now stood on the couch, hackles raised and the growl louder. He was staring at The Cornerstone.

'Max!' Merelie pointed at the book, which had begun to pulse with light. 'They're trying to get through again!'

'Grandad! Grab Nugget and get back!' Max shouted, as a sound like a thousand nails being scraped down a chalk board erupted from the glowing Cornerstone. He threw Call of the Wild onto the coffee table and grabbed Merelie's arm.

'What is it!?' Charlie shouted. 'Why is it doing that?' He held Nugget by the collar, who was still barking loud enough to be heard over the din.

'Bad people are coming Grandad! We have to leave!'

Charlie started to edge into the kitchen, Nugget straining at his collar.

Merelie was transfixed by The Cornerstone, which was now screaming and growling at the same time. It sounded like a malfunctioning Formula One car just about to explode. 'There's more than one this time!' she shouted.

'Then we need to get out of the hou - ' Max was cut off as a bomb exploded in his face.

- 5 -

Garrowain watched one of the enemy Wordsmiths - a small, skinny man with a long nose - pounce on The Cornerstone. His word shaping was subtle, and he'd obviously been building it for some time. Garrowain had to admire his skill, even though the result could be disastrous. The little Wordsmith let out the power at once. A scalpel cutting smoothly, rather than the sledge hammer approach the others had been using.

The custodian could almost feel the surprise and hatred coming from The Cornerstone as Fergil breached its defences, strode forward and ripped the cover open.

The other Wordsmiths crowded round, a couple of them letting out relieved whoops of joy.

Garrowain watched in dismay as Fergil disappeared, followed by three of his colleagues in quick succession. The fifth, a tall rangy looking fellow with bushy eyebrows and long straggly black hair, tried to access the doorway to Earth as well, but The Cornerstone looked like it had recovered from the sneak attack and was determined to make sure no-one else got through.

The tall Wordsmith was thrown away as if he'd been electrocuted, flying a good ten feet before hitting the wall and slumping unconscious to the floor. Some Dwellers, who'd been investigating the open doorways leading to the Library's stacks, sensed a fresh meal. They leapt on the hapless Wordsmith, fighting each other for the chance to feed.

Garrowain grimaced as they swarmed over him.

This was the opportunity he'd been waiting for, though. He couldn't prevent the Wordsmiths travelling to Earth, but with Dwellers distracted, now was the time to secure the Library. He mouthed a silent prayer to the Writer, drew the power of words around him like a mantle and dropped from his hiding place, eyes blazing and ready for a fight.

Max could have sympathised with the black haired Wordsmith. He was also thrown several feet from The Cornerstone, his fall broken by a hard and unyielding bookcase.

He looked up in a fog of pain to see Merelie lying unconscious and Charlie rushing forward to help her. His grandfather seemed to have avoided most of the explosion of energy that had erupted from the book.

Four men now stood around The Cornerstone, which still lay on the coffee table. Their arms were raised in preparation for attack. From the way they were dressed, Max thought they must be Wordsmiths. They all wore long coats: two coloured blue, the others in gold. Each had a House coat of arms on the left breast.

Draveli and Morodai. The bad guys.

One of the ones in blue, a small man with a face like a rat, looked around the room, orienting himself.

'Where's Binks?'

'Looks like the book stopped him,' one of the others said.

'Damn. We'll have to do this without him, then.' He saw Merelie. 'That's her! That's the Carvallen girl. Grab her!' he ordered and the other Wordsmith in blue walked forward, word shaping. An invisible hand picked up Charlie and Nugget, pushing them violently back. The old man slammed into the fridge freezer and Nugget skittered across the kitchen tiles, his hind quarters cracking the cooker's glass door as they made contact.

The rat-like Wordsmith ordered his companions in gold to grab Max and Charlie, earning him a look of utter contempt. He offered an ingratiating smile and asked them *nicely* if they wouldn't mind taking them prisoner. This got a better response, and one approached Max, the other going to secure his grandfather.

Nugget was now barking his head off, snarling and snapping at the intruders, trying to protect his master.

'Shut that thing up,' hissed the second Draveli Wordsmith as he picked up Merelie's unconscious body.

The Morodai looked down at the maddened dog, gave a small gesture with one hand and Nugget flew back across the kitchen, smashing through a set of doors and into the pantry, only stopping when he hit a large sack of potatoes with a dull, hard thud. He let out one loud yelp of pain and lay still.

'No!' Charlie and Max cried in unison.

An enraged Charlie Pearce punched the Morodai Wordsmith in the face as hard as he could. The man screamed in agony, blood streaming from his nose.

The skinny Wordsmith who fancied himself in charge, spun Wordcraft of his own and sent a barrage of paperbacks and hardbacks flying at Charlie. The old man threw his arms up in defence, but was hit several times, forcing him into submission. Max watched this as his own captor, the largest and meanest looking of the four, grabbed him by the hoodie and dragged him to his feet. This guy might not have been quite as big as Borne, but there was no way one hundred and fifty pounds of Max Bloom was getting away.

The Wordsmith pushed Max against the bookcase.

'No trouble from you, stupid monkey,' he growled.

Max might have been groggy from the fall and only half in control of his faculties, but he was also spitting mad. He lashed out with fists and feet, but the big Morodai man batted the blows away and yanked Max away from the bookshelf, throwing him onto the coffee table. Max, The Cornerstone, the tea tray and all the other books piled on the table went crashing to the floor. He screamed as broken china cut him in several places and his face mashed into the carpet.

'Don't kill him, Gormley!' the rat man shouted. 'He could be valuable if the girl doesn't co-operate.'

Gormley sneered and stalked over to Max, flipping him over with one massive foot. 'He'll live,' he grunted, grabbing Max's face and looking into his eyes.

The last thing Max saw before blacking out was the Wordsmith staring down at him, the sneer still plastered across his face.

- 6 -

Max came back to consciousness sat up against a bookshelf in the corner of the lounge, near where he'd been flung by Gormley. The big man stood over him, arms folded and watching his every move. The floor around him was littered with debris, including several smashed biscuits, broken bits of coffee cup and Charlie's copy of Call of the Wild - the cover half torn away. Max reached over and picked it up, not wanting it to incur any more damage. He looked at the torn cover, tears coming as he remembered what had happened to poor Nugget.

Charlie was sat in his leather chair, with the second Morodai beside him. A couple of large red welts had appeared on his forehead where he'd been struck by the books. He looked terribly sad and small. The guilt that raced through Max was almost too much to bear.

He'd brought this to his grandfather's doorstep. Had got him involved in this, and now Nugget was dead.

He looked up to see the ratty Wordsmith pacing, The Cornerstone clutched in his hands. Merelie was still unconscious, laid out on the sofa with her Draveli guard stood behind, gazing down with an expression Max didn't like one bit.

He turned back to Charlie. 'Are you ok Grandad?'

The old man looked up. 'Um... bruised a bit is all. But Nugget...'

'I know, Grandad.'

Max swallowed his grief. It was far better to be angry.

He looked back at the little Wordsmith.

'Blast it!' the rat man spat. 'This damn thing won't let us back through!'

'Are you working it right?' rumbled Gormley.

'Of course I am!' he bit back. 'It's just blocking us again.'

'It does that,' said Max. 'If it doesn't like someone it won't work. And it sure as hell doesn't like you, you rat faced bastard.'

The rat faced bastard leapt over. 'Call me that again and I'll crush you to death with a single word,' he hissed.

'Leave him alone and get on with it, Fergil,' the Wordsmith with Merelie said. 'We haven't got time to be threatening the local wildlife.'

Fergil shot him a black look, then spoke to Max again. 'You're the one the stupid Carvallen witch brought over, aren't you?'

'Kiss the boniest part of my arse,' Max threw back.

'Yes... yes it was you.' Fergil was starting to make some assumptions. 'You used it. The book let you through. It let a brain-dead, word-empty fool like you through.' He opened the pages at Max and thrust it toward him. 'Read it!'

'There's nothing there.'

Fergil looked at the blank pages and scowled. 'Maybe if you hold it,' he said and held the book out.

'Go suck pig balls,' Max told him.

Fergil pointed at Charlie. 'Do as I say boy, or I will twist the old man's head from his shoulders.'

Charlie looked at the Wordsmith with loathing.

'Don't listen to his mewling, son,' he said. 'A scabrous invertebrate like that isn't worth the sweat from a dromedary's hump.'

It took the scabrous invertebrate a moment to work out he'd been mortally insulted, then he word shaped. Charlie's head rocked backward as if he'd been punched.

'Stop!' cried Max.

The Cornerstone was thrust at him again. 'Open the doorway, boy... or more than your flea-bitten hound will die here today.'

Max took the book, dreading what would come next. He still held Call of the Wild in his left hand, clutched to his chest. When he took The Cornerstone in his right, a connection was made that changed Max Bloom on a fundamental level - forever.

A bolt of energy shot up his arm and the world around drained away. The Cornerstone's consciousness filled his head. It wasn't quite the same as a Dweller overwhelming the mind of its victim, but the process was just as invasive, and in some ways more traumatic. The Cornerstone wasn't subtle, after all.

The instant Max had taken the book, it had sensed Call of the Wild and the powerful love Max had for it.

It rummaged in his memories and saw the day he'd spent that Christmas, turning the pages in excitement, eager to see what happened next.

It felt the deep love he had for Buck, the heroic dog in the story, and by extension his grandfather's Labrador, Nugget. It also grieved with him that the happy dog had been killed moments before.

The Cornerstone revelled in the power the story had over Max and measured the weight of the words in his mind.

It meant for Max to understand this. Of how - at a deep and intrinsic level - every word Max had ever read went into shaping who he was as a person.

'**You see?**' it said in a dry, dusty voice, echoing in the vaults of his mind.

'*Yeah, I guess I do,*' Max responded through the fog of blinding light and pain.

'**The words make you who you are.**'

'*But I haven't read enough.*'

'**No?**'

'*Three books! That's all... the Montego manual doesn't count, does it?*'

173

'It only takes one to open the door, if you understand its power.'

A barrage of images from Call of the Wild flashed through Max's head. The last was of Buck, standing proud on a rock surrounded by icy tundra, his head turned upwards, howling at the sky.

A shiver ran down Max's spine. *'Alright, I get it!'*

'All books can have power like that, if you open your mind and see.'

The Cornerstone forced his head up so he could look at the bookshelves surrounding him. Sure enough, Max could now sense the books on another level, beyond what his eyes could show. It was as if they transmitted an invisible aura of power beyond their pages, out into physical space.

Some of these auras were weak, emanating from books without much strength to their words; either pot boiler novels written by average authors, or factual books where the information inside was dubiously researched at best. Other books - like the collection of classics Charlie had bought at the car boot sale - virtually *bled* the ephemeral energy into the world, warping it with their power.

Max felt this energy flowing into him, like a sponge soaking up water.

A memory of something Merelie had said bubbled to the surface, nearly making him throw up. He could picture her face, wide eyed and awe-struck: *'There are millions of books in your world, Max!'*

Millions of potential sources of the energy he was being bombarded with. The people of The Chapter Lands were born into a world where this power was like a thin seam of gold to be mined; where books were rare and literate citizens were rarer. But on Earth, Max had bathed in the stuff from birth, living in a world where thousands of books were printed every year.

This is what Merelie meant. This is why she thought a Wordsmith could come from here.

Is that what I am now? A Wordsmith?

If so, how did you make the energy - which he was now so full of, it was threatening to blow his head clean off his shoulders – work for you, like the Wordsmiths did?

'Use the words, Max. Turn them into your own.'

174

The Cornerstone showed him an image of a blacksmith crafting a sword from molten steel. It then created the image of Max standing in front of a bookshelf, the energy spilling from the books made visible, the same bright orange as the metal in the forge.

The book showed him reach out a hand, scoop up the energy and shape it into a ball.

Max let this idea roll around in his head, trying to get a proper grip on it. He was pleased to find it didn't take him that long to understand.

'It really is quite simple when you get down to it.'

'Yeah, it is I suppose. Let's see if it works.'

Max Bloom's eyes - shut tight during the whole exchange - snapped open.

- 7 -

Gormley, still standing guard over Max, found himself heading towards the ceiling at a hundred miles an hour.

He crashed through the artex like it was balsa wood, and was only spared instant death because the woodworm had been having a field day in the joists and they broke apart on impact. Gormley became wedged, his head and shoulders sticking up into Charlie's rather old fashioned bathroom, his legs dangling down into the lounge.

Fergil saw this happen and instinctively word shaped a barrier between him and the incensed Max.

Word shaping.

Max finally understood what that term meant. It was like pulling on a giant invisible ball of plasticine, breaking off what you needed and shaping it as you desired. He dragged power from the books around him, formed it into what approximated a long, heavy battering ram and lashed out at Fergil.

The rat faced little man was picked up and smashed through the large bay window behind, bursting into the front garden in a cloud of glass and wood. The other Wordsmiths, now terrified, attempted to push Max back with a storm of their own Wordcraft.

He erected a cocoon of energy and let their feeble blows bounce off. It felt like being tickled.

In response, Max dealt with Merelie's captor first, who followed his Morodai colleague ceiling-wards.

That left the one who'd killed Nugget...

This bastard was now escaping through the broken window in an effort to save his worthless hide. Max assisted his exit with a boot of Wordcraft that sped the escape attempt up considerably. The recently defenestrated Fergil was getting to his feet when the Wordsmith-shaped missile collided with him, sending them both flying into the large, extremely pungent compost heap.

Max surveyed his handiwork and looked down at Charlie Pearce, who was wide-eyed and clutching the arms of his chair.

'Bloody hell Maxwell!' he gasped.

'You alright Grandad?'

'I'll be ok... and judging from what I've just witnessed, you're more than ok, my boy.'

Max was surprised to find his grandfather was right. He couldn't see or feel any of the injuries he'd suffered at the hands of Gormley. He had a feeling that when this rush of power was over though, they might make their presence felt in spades.

He went over to Merelie and sat beside her. Her eyes fluttered open, focusing on Max.

'You know... we both need to stop getting knocked out all the time,' she said, sitting up.

'Agreed... how are you feeling?'

'Awful. But I'm sure I'll feel much worse later. What happened?'

'Some Wordsmiths came through The Cornerstone trying to get you.'

Merelie looked around. 'I don't see anyone.'

'Yeah... that might take a bit of explaining,' Max admitted.

A scream of rage came from outside. Fergil and the other battered Wordsmith were up, covered in compost. Max looked back at Merelie. 'Maybe it's better if I just show you.'

He got up and made his way over to the open window. Fergil and his friend saw Max coming and started to word shape.

'Max!' Merelie warned, coming up behind him. 'Get out of the way!'

He held up an arm. 'Leave this to me,' he said, trying to sound as calm as possible.

Max stepped out into the garden and sauntered towards the Wordsmiths. The blast wave of energy that came rolling at him rivalled the one Merelie and Imelda had used against Elijah. Merelie felt it coming and knew Max Bloom was dead.

However, Max smacked the blast to one side with a contemptuous flick of the wrist and gave her a cheeky wink.

This was so cool penguins could have mated on it.

Rather less cool was the fact the diverted energy wave hit Charlie's Austin Montego, driving it through the rotting garage doors. Inside, the car scraped along the concrete, sparks flying. This caused a leaky diesel canister to catch fire and explode. The Montego's half full petrol tank joined in on the act and the whole lot went skywards with an apocalyptic roar.

Max stared dumbfounded at the destruction he'd caused.

Mum's going to kill me.

In a poorly judged moment of hilarity, Fergil cackled out loud when he saw the look of horror on Max's face. This was noticed, digested and steps were taken.

Fergil and his companion were picked up by invisible hands, Max flexing his word shaping muscles to their fullest extent. He smartly knocked them together three times, rendering both completely insensible and let them drop to the ground.

Merelie, eyes wide and stunned, came to stand in front of him.

'Hi,' he said.

'You... you... ' She pointed at the comatose pair, the burning garage and back at Max.

'Yeah... looks like you were right,' he said, offering her an apologetic smile. 'Don't expect lightning bolts to start shooting out of my arse, though.'

- 8 -

Nugget wasn't dead.

As a massive *barrel* of a dog, built of hard muscle underneath all that fat, he'd been in many scrapes over his eight years and survived all of them. From falling down steep river banks to colliding with boys on pushbikes - Max had come off worse in that incident - he'd put his body through the mill on countless occasions, as any self respecting big slobbery dog should. Any animal that can survive mini-catastrophes like that and face down Biff the insane ginger tom must be as hard as nails. A little thing like being propelled across the kitchen floor by magic hasn't got a chance of killing him.

As Charlie staggered into the pantry, a dazed Nugget was quite contentedly munching on a mouldy potato.

Max ventured back into the kitchen, the shell-shocked Merelie in his wake.

'Nugget!' he shouted in delight, which made his head hurt. The rush of Wordcraft was leaving his body and many aches and pains were now making themselves known in no uncertain terms.

Nugget saw him, broke free of Charlie and trotted over on wobbly legs, planting a paw in Max's crotch. The pain was almost worth it.

'Never known a dog like it,' Charlie said, wiping his eyes. 'Good old Nuggie.'

Max patted the Labrador on the head and wiped masticated potato onto his jeans.

They all heard the sound of a car roaring up the driveway.

'Police?' Max said.

'Let's go see,' Charlie replied.

He opened the front door in time to see a lime green Fiat Punto come screeching to a halt in front of the porch. Slumped in the passenger seat was a man with a toilet bowl on his head.

Imelda Warrington - looking like she'd been on a date with The Terminator - got out of the driver's side and gave Max a long, hard look. Her hair was a tangled mess, her clothes were covered in grass stains and mud.

'What have you done now, Max Bloom?' she demanded.

While Charlie Pearce ate his chocolate bourbon, and just before all hell broke loose in his front room, Imelda Warrington was once again faced with the spectre of Elijah, still possessed and hungry for vengeance.

Only this time she was alone.

Bugger.

'Where's the girl?' he snarled.

'Your guess is as good as mine.'

'I will devour your mind.'

'Oh yes, yes,' she replied with contempt, and not a little bravado. 'What is it the children say? *What-evah.*'

Discretion being the better part of valour, Imelda turned tail and ran into the rear garden. Elijah gave chase. The librarian reached the middle of the lawn and shaped a bolt of power at the Arma.

If this had come from the newly appointed Wordsmith Max Bloom, Elijah might well have been occupying a different postcode, but Imelda had nowhere near that level of power, especially miles from the library.

Elijah shrugged off the attack and slammed into her, sending both sprawling into a nearby flower bed, his hands grasping at her throat. It fast became a one-sided fight. He was a two hundred pound battle hardened soldier and she was... well, a *librarian*, for heaven's sake.

As the air was choked out of her, Imelda desperately scrabbled around for something to defend herself with.

Peter Bloom liked gnomes.

This tells you virtually everything you need to know about his sense of humour. That and the fact he used toilet bowls to pot plants in.

Amanda Bloom was about as keen on gardening as a chronic hay fever sufferer, so the wide plot of land at the back of their house was all his to play with.

The gnome army had therefore built up over the years.

There were nineteen of them now.

Some were the old fashioned type: sitting on mushrooms, holding a fishing rod - you know the sort. Others were a lot stranger - including gnome versions of Darth Vader, Abraham Lincoln and Gene Simmonds, the bass player from Kiss.

Imelda grabbed the first heavy thing to hand and hit Elijah round the head with a surprisingly accurate gnome rendition of cartoon favourite Captain Caveman. The big man grunted and fell to one side, allowing her time to catch her breath.

She scrabbled away, getting to her feet as he launched at her again, blood pouring from where she'd belted him.

Putting the tall rotary washing line between her and Elijah, Imelda tried to gather enough Wordcraft to put him down for good. The weak bolt she sent hit the Dweller in the face, making him stumble into the washing line, where he became entangled.

Elijah floundered as his arms plunged into the line, the heavy leather ties on his tunic getting snagged in the nylon web. Backing away, Imelda noticed a dilapidated swing set sitting at the back of the garden, rusting itself into the earth.

She took a deep breath and began to pull in as much Wordcraft as she could muster in the brief time she had, while the Dweller struggled to get free. She focused on hooking the swing set with her mind, clenched her fist and attempted to send it flying at him.

It was a large and heavy contraption however, so 'flying' isn't quite what happened. It did meander like a happy drunk across the grass though, gathering just enough speed to clout Elijah, ripping the washing line from its concrete base as the whole lot crashed to the grass.

For a second it looked like this had done the trick. The indestructible creature lay still. Given the Dweller's resilience to everything that had been thrown at it so far though, it came as no surprise when it sat Elijah's body up and extricated itself from the tangle of metal with a series of grunts and growls.

'Oh for crying out loud,' groaned Imelda.

She hobbled towards to the house and had made it as far as the conservatory when the Arma caught up, spun her round and slammed her against the glass.

'Enough games,' it slobbered. 'Tell me where the girl is.'

'I have no idea!'

The thing grabbed her by the throat with one arm and studied her terrified expression.

'Then you're no use to me... time to eat.'

Thick, living smoke began pouring from his eyes.

Panic rose in Imelda's chest as she kicked fruitlessly against him. Despair swelled in her heart as the black smoke started to invade her mind. Complete surprise poked her in the ribs as a toilet bowl dropped onto the Dweller's head, finally ending the battle in her favour.

- 10 -

Shopping on a Saturday morning with an eleven year old girl is marginally more stressful than defusing a nuclear bomb.

The above statement would get wholehearted agreement from Amanda Bloom, who was at last returning home with her grumpy daughter from the hell that was the shopping precinct. Monica was in a mood because she'd once again been denied the joy of owning her own pair of Ugg boots, in favour of badly needed school shoes. She was also fed up because her mother had dragged her round Tesco for an hour, picking up a few much needed essentials – including some migraine tablets.

Monica was really living up to the nickname Moan-ica right about now.

'It's not fair, I never get what I want,' she pouted.

Amanda, who remembered the hundreds she'd spent on a Nintendo DS Lite for Monica's birthday, chose to remain silent and grind her teeth as the car turned into their road.

There was a puke green Fiat Punto parked outside the house. It was in the space Amanda favoured, the one closest to the front door - a godsend when loaded down with six Tesco shopping bags.

Guaranteeing a visit to the dentist in the near future, she ground her teeth more and parked further along. Monica leapt out of the car as soon as it came to a stop and flounced off towards the house.

'Thanks for the help, my little ray of sunshine,' Amanda said under her breath, lugging the shopping bags from the back seat.

As she locked the car Monica came back over, a scared look on her face.

'There's people in the garden, mum.'

'What?'

'People in the garden! A woman in a suit and a man dressed in leather. They look like they're fighting!'

Amanda heard a loud clatter of metal; the sound of a rusty swing set hitting a nylon washing line.

'Stay here,' she ordered Monica.

Amanda hurried across the front garden and down the side of the house, slowing when she saw a bedraggled woman running towards her being chased by a reject from Iron Maiden. Amanda winced as he slammed her into their conservatory.

Oh God, he's going to kill her.

She was absolutely sure of it.

There was a sex fiend in her garden about to do horrible things to a defenceless woman - just like in that video she'd watched the day the crime prevention man had come in to work. She had to do something!

The back garden didn't offer much in the way of weaponry - either melee based or ballistic - but what it did have were several old toilets Peter amused himself planting flowers in. Most of these were full of dying or dead plants, but there was one near her feet that Peter had emptied out just before flying to Malaysia.

Three years of obsessive gym attendance finally paid off in a few seconds as Amanda heaved the toilet bowl into her arms, staggered over to the conservatory and rammed it down onto the attacker's head, issuing a scream of sisterly rage as she did.

Imelda rubbed her throat and tried to catch her breath while Amanda stepped back to let the pole-axed Arma crash to the ground.

'Thank you,' Imelda gasped.

'Er... not a problem,' Amanda replied. 'Are you ok?'

'Oh yes, I should say so.' Imelda tried to tuck her errant hair back. 'Your timing was perfect.'

'Who is he?' Amanda looked back down at toilet head.

Imelda had told quite a few lies today to keep the locals in the dark and was ready for this one. 'I have no idea. I was merely walking along the road when this man jumped out from behind a bush and attacked me! I ran for dear life and ended up in your back garden.'

That sounded plausible.

'Did you hit him with my daughter's swings?' Amanda's eyes flicked over to the ruined metal swing set.

'Um… yes, yes I did. You know what they say… in times of crisis you get a surge of strength you never knew you had!' This was less plausible, but she was on a roll, so what the hell.

'I think we should call the police,' Amanda suggested.

'Yes! Good idea. Why don't you run in and give them a bell?'

'Will you be alright while I do it?'

'Me? Oh, I'll be fine. I'll watch this one until you get back. Wouldn't want him getting away now, would we?'

'No, of course not.' Amanda wasn't sure the sex fiend would be going anywhere, but went off to make the call anyway.

The second she was out of sight, Imelda jumped into action.

The police were the last people she wanted to see again today and another incident involving her and Elijah wouldn't look good, however much you tried to spin it. She had to get away from here as quickly as possible. Dragging a large man with a toilet on his head is not an easy thing to do, especially when you're a fifty two year old woman who's been on the go for a while now, and could really do with a nice sit down and a cup of tea. She managed it though, weaving what limited Wordcraft she could to lighten the load and help pull Elijah over to her Punto.

As she was ramming him into the passenger seat, Amanda re-appeared.

'What are you doing? The police are on their way.'

'Excellent! Good work.'

'What are you doing with him?'

It would have taken a couple of hours to manufacture a believable lie for this one, so Imelda didn't bother. 'Look Mrs Bloom - ' she began, then cursed herself.

'How do you know my name?'

'I know your son.'

'Max? How do you know him?'

'Look, I don't have time to explain, but this man isn't someone the police can deal with and I have to leave right now before they get here. I promise to pay for the damage to your garden.'

Amanda looked worried. 'What's my son got to do with this? Is he alright? Do you know where he is? I haven't seen him all day. Have you seen him today? Is he alright?'

Imelda put her hands on the woman's shoulders. 'Max is fine, my dear, I have no doubt of that,' she said. 'I'm sorry I can't tell you more but I really do have to be going.'

She moved round to the driver's side, jumped in the car and started the engine. 'I promise I'll get Max to ring you once I see him!'

Amanda didn't answer, just stood there in shock.

A small girl that Imelda supposed was Max's sister joined her by the kerb. 'Why has that man got a loo on his head, mummy?'

Imelda didn't wait to hear the answer.

She stuck the Punto in gear and drove away, holding her arm out to stop the top heavy Arma whacking her on the shoulder with his new porcelain headpiece.

If I were a teenager with a clever mouth and a knack for getting into trouble, where would I be?

Imelda turned onto the main road and saw a column of smoke rising to the north above the suburban tree line, a mile or so away.

Ah ha!

- 11 -

'None of this is my fault!' Max protested.

Imelda glared at him, indicating she didn't believe a word of it.

'Aunt Emerelda, are you ok?' Merelie asked.

'*Aunt Emerelda?*' Max said.

'Yes, Mr Bloom, Merelie and I are related. I got this thankless job because her father doesn't like it when his little sister argues with him.'

'You're going to have to explain that to me at some point,' Merelie told her.

Charlie Pearce had been staring at Imelda for a few moments, trying to work out where he knew her from. It dropped into place when he'd mentally rearranged her hair into a neat bun and removed the mud and grass from her face.

'Miss Warrington?' he said in amazement.

Imelda studied him for a moment. 'That copy of Catcher in the Rye is a week overdue, Charles.'

This was getting too much for Max. 'Do you *know her*?' he said to his grandfather.

'Oh yes, we've had several stimulating verbal battles about the literature on offer in her place of employment,' the old man said, with fond recollection in his eyes.

Max looked back at Imelda, who was scowling at him again. 'I can do magic!' he said with pride, feeling the need to add his own revelation to proceedings.

They were all aware of quite a crowd forming at the bottom of the driveway - pointing and staring at the house with its new flaming garage feature.

'I think you should all retire from sight,' Charlie said. 'I'll go and speak with yonder crowd and hopefully get them to disperse. I get the feeling we could do without any more attention right now.'

'Good idea. Make sure no-one calls the fire brigade yet.' Imelda said and went to the passenger door. 'Max, help me with this one, we can't leave him here.'

The newly appointed Wordsmith started to protest, but saw the look in her eyes, and did as he was told.

'I'll go make sure The Cornerstone is charged,' Merelie said.

Imelda opened the car door and Elijah's toilet covered head flopped out, followed by the rest of him.

'I can float him in, if you like,' Max offered, waggling his fingers.

'Max, if you have developed Wordcraft somehow in the brief time since I saw you last, for once I'm very pleased to be proved wrong. If Merelie was right then maybe we do stand a chance here. But do you think it would be a good idea for you to start messing around with it in sight of that lot?' Imelda pointed at the rapidly increasing size of the crowd.

He couldn't argue with that. 'Alright... you grab his legs, I'll get his head.'

Between them they managed to get the unconscious man into the house and onto the sofa. As they did, Max filled Imelda in on recent events, including how he discovered his new found abilities. By the time they'd added the lifeless forms of the four Wordsmiths to the long couch, Charlie had come back, having done a great deal of fast talking in the street. He'd managed to convince the crowd that everything was fine, and that he'd already called the fire brigade, so there was no need for anyone else to worry. Nobody had been hurt and he'd been meaning to demolish that garage for a while now anyway, so it was probably lucky in the long run.

'That'll give us a few minutes,' he said. 'But that much disturbance is bound to have the police here in double quick time I'd imagine, so whatever you're planning on doing, I suggest some unseemly haste before this house is crawling with curious bobbies.'

'We have to go back,' Merelie said. 'Use The Cornerstone to return home.'

'To what girl?' Imelda asked, cleaning muck off her face with a towel Charlie had supplied. 'From what you say, the place is crawling with the enemy and we've no got idea what they've done with The Cornerstone on that side. We could pop out right into the arms of Lucas Morodai.'

'Good!' snarled Max. 'I fancy having a crack at him as soon as I can.' He waved his hands around in the air, trying to look as menacing as possible.

'Calm down, Rambo,' Imelda said. 'You may have developed some power, but your common sense hasn't improved much. Even if you have the strength to take on Morodai and his servants - and that's by no means certain - we've got Merelie's parents to think about.'

'They're probably dead,' the girl said, in a resigned manner.

'You don't know that, so less of the doom and gloom, young lady. Your father's a resourceful man, so there's still hope. But if they are still alive and we go blundering in, Morodai will kill them for certain.'

'Well, we can't just sit here,' Max said, still hand waving.

'Do cease that infernal mime show, Maxwell,' Charlie scolded, gratefully sinking back into his armchair. 'You look as if you've lost control of your faculties.'

'We have to know what's happening on the other side,' Imelda continued.

'A reccy!' Max piped up, eager to contribute something other than exaggerated hand waving.

'What?' Imelda said.

'A reccy. You know... a reconnaissance mission? We have a nose about, see what's up and pop back here if there's any sign of trouble.'

'Great idea, Max,' Merelie told him, eliciting a smile. She took The Cornerstone from the bookshelf and held it out. 'We should be able to do that with The Cornerstone, if it'll let us.'

Imelda shrugged. 'Don't ask me to do it, that thing's never liked me. It won't listen to a damn word I say.'

'I'll do it,' Max volunteered. 'It likes me. It showed me how to do Wordcraft, so it'll help me do this, no problem.'

'It *showed* you?' Merelie looked incredulous.

'Yep. It spoke to me too.'

'It's a book, boy. It doesn't speak.' Imelda scoffed.

'Oh yes it does!' He felt a bit ridiculous defending a book - but this was a ridiculous situation when you got right down to it. 'It told me how to find the words and use them. It's all quite easy once you get the gist of it.'

'Quite *easy*?' Imelda seethed. 'I spent fifteen years of my life learning how to word shape. Merelie's been taught since she was a child! It is not *easy*.'

'I hate to interrupt,' Charlie butted in, 'but I fear the incipient sound of a two-tone siren. Perhaps this discussion can be delayed until later?'

'He's right... enough chit chat.' Imelda took The Cornerstone from Merelie and gave it to Max. 'Get to it then. Have a word with your friend and find out what's going on over there.'

Max took The Cornerstone.

'Right then you,' he began, 'we've got an understanding by now, I reckon. It looks like you want to help us and I need to pop over and check out what's going on in the Chapter House. But if it's all kicking off, you've got to pull me back here before someone noodles my doodle. That good with you?'

Imelda rolled her eyes.

She was taken aback when The Cornerstone gave a brief but bright flash of silver, apparently indicating agreement.

Max grinned, opened The Cornerstone and began to read:

Imelda rolled her eyes.

She was taken aback when The Cornerstone gave a brief but bright flash of silver, apparently indicating agreement.

Max grinned, opened The Cornerstone and began to read:

The light faded and Max found himself back in the Carvallen Library's Main Hub - and about to be impaled on an enormous spike, carried by a smoke eyed monster running headlong at him, gibbering insanely.

He word shaped in a panic and the Dweller rocketed upwards, disappearing into the mist. There was a loud thump as the creature came into contact with a buttress or two, and it dropped back out of the mist, getting its cloak caught on one of the sconces where it hung like a badly mistreated Halloween decoration.

Max turned and saw Garrowain leaning against the wall, looking at him with disbelief.

'How's that for dramatic timing?' Max said, grinning from ear to ear.

Part Six

Just after The Cornerstone had reluctantly transported Fergil and his cohorts to Earth, Garrowain had dropped to the ground next to the pedestal on which the rapidly cooling book sat. The Dwellers didn't see him - they were still fighting over the fallen Wordsmith, giving Garrowain the chance to run through to the empty entrance hall.

He hurried over to the main door, still open from the earlier invasion, glanced outside to see the corridor empty and pushed the door shut as quietly as possible. Placing a hand on the lock, he muttered a few well chosen words, the mechanism activating with a loud clank. These were the strongest security passwords he could summon. They should prevent anyone from outside causing him trouble – for a while, at least.

Running back to the Hub, he saw that the Dwellers had finished draining the luckless Wordsmith. This was unfortunate, as Garrowain was outnumbered and up against enemies who now gave him their full attention. What's more, they stood between him and The Cornerstone. Assessing the odds and realising the value of a tactical withdrawal, he sprinted for the nearest open Library door, hoping the remarkable book could fend for itself. The Codex had been flung into a corner, so Garrowain had no idea where he'd end up, but anywhere was better than surrounded by Dwellers. The monsters gave chase, smelling the opportunity for the best meal they'd come across since entering this world.

Garrowain ran through the Library and more of the creatures, who'd been wasting their time defacing books, joined in the hunt.

Before long, the custodian started to get short of breath and was beginning to think this whole gambit might have been a bad idea. This was the second time in as many hours he'd been forced into an unseemly sprint through the Library and it was becoming irritating in the extreme.

Unlike the Dweller hitching a ride in Borne's mind, these ones didn't have much knowledge of the Library and couldn't keep up with the old custodian for long. Many got lost as they scrambled after him - and would remain so until well after the events of this story. That still left too many for Garrowain to deal with at once though – more than twenty - all ravenously hungry for a taste of his mind.

The Guardian of the Stacks wouldn't be able to offer him any help. With the Codex damaged, the section of the library the invisible creature lived in was temporarily cut off – which was dreadfully inconvenient, as an angry, invisible monster would be just the thing to deal with the pack of ravening Dwellers that were rapidly hunting him down. Garrowain found himself heading towards the hub room that contained the Carvallen League Books and offered up a prayer of thanks to the Writer.

That was the answer!

Simply open a League Book of his choice and transport to some far-flung corner of the planet.

But that wouldn't do, would it? He'd leave these monsters the run of his Library and virtually hand The Cornerstone over to Morodai. He'd need to help Merelie when she came back and couldn't render any assistance a thousand miles away, hidden under a rock.

Maybe the League Books could still help, though.

Garrowain word shaped, throwing books in the way of his pursuers, slowing them down enough to give him a bit of time once he reached the hub room. The League Books – eight in total – were on a book shelf sat in the centre of the circular room. The place each one went to was written on the cover.

Four connected with the other Chapter Houses - though all had been blocked by Morodai as a security measure during the invasion. The other four would transport you across the Carvallen owned Chapter Lands. Garrowain sought out the League Book that went to Tamera Falls.

Six months prior, the League Book at the other end had been placed on a Carvallen ship, bound for its new home in Merving, a town in the Borderlands. The ship had struck trouble in the rough sea crossing from the Falls and had sunk off the coast. At the time, Garrowain had been outraged that a League Book had been lost in such a fashion. Now though, that mistake could prove extremely useful.

He picked up the Tamera Falls book, spun around and held it open as the crowd of Dwellers pushed their way through the bottleneck created by the narrow doorway. Garrowain muttered over the League Book and bright blue light flooded from its pages as the doorway opened.

The first three Dwellers were sucked through to a watery grave before they'd had chance to register what was happening. The next couple realised something was wrong and tried to stop, but were tumbled into the doorway by the creatures behind them.

Garrowain walked forward, holding onto the book for dear life as it shook in his hands, trying to cope with the influx of bodies. The last three Dwellers disappeared into the halo of blue light, catapulted across the miles to a fast and unpleasant drowning.

This was all the League Book could take. As soon as the last possessed creature had gone through, it tore itself apart in Garrowain's hands. 'No way to treat a book,' he muttered, as the flakes of paper drifted to the floor.

Having dispatched the immediate threat, Garrowain took a short breather and considered his next move. He knew his only real course of action was to make his way back to the Main Hub and secure The Cornerstone. It had measures of protection built into it, but he wasn't sure how long those defences would stop the void creatures from tearing it to pieces.

Steeling himself for more unwanted exercise, the custodian crept back towards the Library entrance, trying not to attract the attention of any Dwellers left in the area. This succeeded nearly all the way there, right up to the point he crossed the threshold back into the Main Hub.

As he did, a lone Dweller appeared from one of the other doorways. It was wearing the body of a tall, muscular Morodai Chapter Guard - though the armour had become ragged and dented in several places, and covered in a mixture of dirt and blood. The creature was tearing out pages from a slim volume of poetry, eating them in a methodical manner. It saw Garrowain mid-creep and let out a hungry howl.

'That is no way to treat a book!' the custodian scolded and sent Wordcraft lashing out.

The Dweller was used to attacks like this, having been in the vanguard of all Morodai's assault formations, so it neatly side-stepped the blast of energy with practised ease and charged at Garrowain. It was then the old man's turn to display some fast feet, dodging out of the way of the howling creature.

The Dweller slammed into the wall, breaking one of the long metal sconces. The orb of blue light toppled from its perch and smashed into a thousand pieces on the flagstones. In a rage, the creature grabbed at one of the intricate wrought iron bars the sconce was constructed with, prying it off.

Wonderful, now it has a weapon.

Garrowain dropped back to the opposite side of the room, trying to keep out of range. The monster ran at him, the bar held out like a lance. This was when Max Bloom popped into existence, blasting the Dweller into the ether, and taking the custodian completely by surprise.

- 2 -

'A wonderful piece of dramatic timing, young man,' Garrowain replied, 'and some formidable Wordcraft, if I'm not mistaken.'

'Yep. Turns out Merelie was right,' Max conceded. He thrust his chin out and affected a heroic pose. 'I'm a Wordsmith!' He thought for a second. 'I'm a mega-Wordsmith!' He paused again. 'I'm a MEGA-SMITH!'

'How did this happen, Mr Bloom?' Garrowain said, fearing the boy might explode any minute from sheer ego. 'The last time I saw you, you wanted no part of this and referred to me as being *bloody bonkers*, if I recall.'

'Things have changed a bit, chief.' Max replied, once again proving a gift for understatement. 'There'll be time to explain later, but right now… is this gaff safe? Only there's a load of people on the other side who have to leave my Grandad's house before po-po shows up.'

Garrowain only understood about thirty percent of that sentence, but just about got Max's meaning. 'There are a few possessed unfortunates still milling about, but I've sealed the main doors to the outside world, so no-one else can threaten us for the time being.'

Max sucked in air through his teeth, digesting this. 'Good enough,' he said, sticking his head back in The Cornerstone and disappearing in the customary flare of silver light.

'Looks like we're alright,' Max said as soon as he'd reappeared in Charlie's lounge. 'The old fella's blocked off the Library from the rest of the Chapter House.'

'Good!' said Imelda with considerable relief.

'What do we do with them?' Merelie pointed at the five unconscious bodies they'd collected. 'We can't leave them here for the… *po-leese* to find.' She seemed quite proud of her pronunciation.

'I'll tell The Cornerstone it's got some heavy lifting to do,' said Max.

He spoke to the book, marvelling at the fact he no longer felt like a complete moron talking to an inanimate object. It didn't seem to have any objections to the plan.

Nor did it mind when Imelda took hold and attempted to transport back to The Chapter Lands. It seemed the grudge The Cornerstone had against her had been forgotten - for the moment at least. Imelda offered Charlie Pearce a polite goodbye and read the last few moments of her life as they wrote themselves across The Cornerstone's pages.

Max's grandfather had seen a lot in his sixty five years on the planet, but was entirely unprepared for seeing a tall, middle-aged woman blink out of existence.

'Bloody hellfire!' he exclaimed, as The Cornerstone stopped glowing and started to float to the floor. Merelie plucked it out of the air before it finished its descent.

'Disconcerting, isn't it?' Max said, a bit shocked himself, having never seen the book used from this perspective.

Merelie walked up to Charlie and gave him a gentle kiss on the cheek. 'Thank you for all your help, sir.'

'Call me Charlie,' he replied, in a trembling voice.

'Thank you, Charlie,' she smiled. 'I hope I'll see you again soon.'

'And I you, my dear. Take good care of my errant grandson for me, won't you?'

'I will,' she promised, giving Max an indecipherable look, before leaving the lounge in a flash.

Max grabbed The Cornerstone and looked over at the unconscious bodies, propped up on the sofa.

'Right then. Let's get this lot sorted,' he said, looking down at the book. 'You up for this, Corny?'

The book did nothing for a moment, unsure of what to make of this new nickname. It then glowed briefly in assent.

'Cracking.'

Max turned the book away and opened it towards the sofa.

On the other side of the doorway, Garrowain was having a joyful reunion with Merelie when they were both forced to get out of the way as a floral patterned sofa from the 1970s appeared in mid-air and crashed to the flagstones, unceremoniously dumping all five of its passengers onto the ground. The toilet on Elijah's head finally gave way as it connected with the hard stone floor, sending shards of white porcelain everywhere. The Main Hub was definitely going to need a good vacuum when all this was over.

Max looked at the space where the sofa used to be with horror, and gave his grandfather a deeply apologetic look.

'Never mind boy,' Charlie said, a wry smile on his face. 'I probably needed a new one anyway. The ratty thing was more Nugget's than mine these days.'

Nugget gave Max a disgruntled look - not happy about having his favourite sleeping place transported to another dimension.

'Sorry Nuggie,' Max apologised.

The sound of far off police sirens drifted into the lounge.

'Better be going Max,' Charlie warned.

'Will you be ok?'

'Oh yes. I'm sure I'll be able to render a believable explanation for all this carnage in the minute or so I have before they come bursting in through the door.'

'I should be back soon, with any luck. But if I'm not, can you tell mum... ' He stopped, not knowing what to say.

Charlie patted his shoulder. 'I'll think of something, lad. Just make sure you do come back safe. Don't try anything stupid - and ensure that beautiful young lady comes to no harm.' He smiled. 'I don't think you'll have any trouble with the last part.'

Max went bright red and tickled Nugget behind the ear.

'Bye, Nuggie,' he said, grimacing as the dog ran a sticky tongue over the back of his hand. 'Grandad... when I'm gone, just stick The Cornerstone in the bookshelf. No one will know what it is.'

The sirens got louder.

'Go my boy!' Charlie repeated.

Max looked down into The Cornerstone, read the last few seconds of his life and followed the others over to The Chapter Lands. His grandfather then awkwardly took hold of the glowing book and slid it into the nearest book shelf. He sat down in the armchair and let out a deep sigh. Nugget, now bereft of a decent place to rest, flopped his head into Charlie's lap.

'Well Nuggie, this has been a day we won't forget for quite some time. About as exciting as it gets... a story worth recounting to the best of acquaintances, don't you think?'

In response, Nugget let out a long, sonorous fart.

Everyone's a critic.

- 3 -

Imelda Warrington looked around the Carvallen Library for the first time in over twenty years and had to fight back the tears. She'd become accustomed to the idea of never seeing her homeland again.

'As I live and breathe… Emerelda Carvallen.' Garrowain said. 'It's good to see you again, my lady.'

'Hello, old man,' she replied, shaking off the wave of emotion. 'To tell the truth, I'm surprised you're happy I've come back.'

'It was never my idea to exile you, Emerelda. Your brother's temper was always short, especially as a young man.'

'No reason to banish your sister,' Imelda said, her eyes flashing, 'simply due to a difference of opinion!'

Garrowain sighed. 'Slightly more than a difference of opinion, Emerelda. You threatened centuries of tradition and custom.'

'Yes I know… and I hear Bethan Falion's doing the same thing now, with a much higher cost to her people.'

'Indeed.'

'I'm amazed Jacob hasn't sided with Morodai.'

Garrowain looked genuinely angered by this. 'Your brother is nothing like Lucas Morodai. He put his own feelings aside to act as negotiator - trying to prevent more bloodshed. He would never take part in atrocities like this!'

Imelda was suitably chastened. 'I'm sorry Garrowain. You're right. My brother can be a stubborn fool, but he's no murderer.'

Merelie popped into existence next to them.

'Merelie!' Garrowain cried and threw his arms round her.

'It's so good to see you!' she told him.

'I feared for you so much when that monster followed you through The Cornerstone. You'll have to tell me how you eluded him.'

'Max and Imelda saved me!'

One librarian looked at the other. 'Imelda?'

'It seemed more appropriate over there,' she explained.

'Where is Elijah?' the custodian asked, 'and the Wordsmiths that went after you?'

The Cornerstone started to shake on the pedestal, making a deep rumbling noise. It didn't sound like it was protesting, merely shouldering a heavier load than usual. In an explosion of light and sound, the sofa coughed into existence, forcing them to jump out of the way.

'It must've got a bit carried away,' said Merelie.

'That'd be the boy's unwholesome influence on it,' Imelda pointed out.

'Before we go much further, I would appreciate an explanation as to what went on over there. I trust it's a fascinating tale?' said Garrowain, studying Elijah and his broken porcelain crown.

'Looks like things haven't exactly been boring over here,' Merelie remarked, glancing at the zombified Wordsmith and trampled Codex.

Max popped into the room and breathed a sigh of relief. 'That was too close. The fuzz were almost on top of me.'

'Fuzz?' asked Garrowain. 'Is this some kind of malevolent entity from your world?'

'Depends if your car insurance has expired, chief.'

Merelie took Garrowain's hand in hers. 'Where's Borne? What happened to him?' she asked.

'He's safe, my girl. Though still under the influence of one of those creatures, I'm afraid. I will take you to him, but we should decide on our next course of action first.'

Garrowain used a subtle form of Wordcraft to ensure their prisoners stayed unconscious. Max studied what he did carefully, as the idea of knocking Monica out for a few hours when she was being annoying appealed to him immensely.

After that, he helped bind the five men with ripped bits of clothing for extra security, before using a bit of light Wordcraft to move the sofa over into the corner with a flourish, neatening the place up a bit. He also floated the Codex back over to its pedestal, giving it a quick buff with one sleeve as it drifted into place.

Stuffing The Cornerstone unceremoniously into his jeans at the small of his back, he clapped his hands together, indicating a job well done. Tidying up was so much easier when you could do magic. Garrowain looked on in disbelief.

'It's incredible,' he said, in an incredulous tone. 'No training. No apparent need to focus his power. No verbalising of words to assist in shaping. No real effort being made at all.'

'Sickening, isn't it?' Imelda stood at his side. 'We spend our lives scrabbling around for a tiny amount of the word source here, while he basks in the stuff all his life and doesn't even know it.'

'It's like feeding a hundred weight of fertiliser to a flower,' Garrowain observed. 'Only it doesn't bud for years, until one day...' he drifted off for a second, thinking about the implications. 'With more like him, you could build an army that would shake the universe,' he finished in an awed voice.

Imelda looked aghast. The idea of millions of people from Earth wielding Wordcraft chilled her to the bone. There was enough death and destruction over there without introducing that kind of power into the equation. It'd threaten The Chapter Lands in the long run as well. She told Garrowain as much.

'Yes... I see your point,' he conceded. 'Perhaps the universe should remain resolutely unshaken. One Max Bloom is quite enough.'

A loud booming noise coming from the other side of the main Library doors interrupted the conversation.

'What's that?' Max said, hurrying through to the entrance hall.

'Our enemy, I would say,' Garrowain answered and followed. 'They've no doubt discovered that entry to the Library is blocked. I'd say their efforts to get in using Wordcraft have failed and they've fallen back on more prosaic methods.'

Another loud boom echoed through the hall.

'I think we'd better find somewhere to hide,' warned Imelda. 'Those doors look sturdy enough, but I wouldn't want to be standing here if they break.'

'I bloody would!' growled Max, rolling up his sleeves.

'Don't be stupid, boy. You have no idea what's on the other side of that door and besides... remember what I said about Merelie's parents? Right now, you're only useful as long as they don't know what you're capable of.' Imelda turned to Garrowain. 'Can you conjure up a safe place for us to hide for a while?'

'I should think so. The Codex won't function, so we're restricted to the areas we can access, but there's an empty area of the Library we can reach. Through the first door on the left.'

'Right, let's get out of here,' Imelda said and marched back through to the Hub as another blow landed on the heavy double doors, making them rattle on their massive hinges.

'Um... there is just one slight problem with my idea,' Garrowain admitted, thinking of Borne still held behind the wall of books.

'We'll worry about that when we get there, whatever it is it can't be worse than what's about to come through those doors,' Imelda pointed out. 'Come on all of you, let's go!'

Max remained in the entrance hall for a moment, studying the doors as another loud boom indicated whoever was outside wasn't giving up in a hurry.

He turned and followed his companions back into the Library, somewhat annoyed he wasn't getting the chance to get stuck into a fight. He needn't have worried. The fight would shortly be coming to him.

- 4 -

Osgood Draveli was not at peace with his world. Everything had been going well when he'd left his Wordsmiths with what should have been the simple task of cracking the Carvallen Cornerstone and retrieving that annoying girl.

He'd waddled up to Jacob Carvallen's study in the heights of the Chapter House and had a good gloat at Carvallen and his wife, enjoying the experience with almost child-like glee.

He'd always hated Jacob - with his strong voice, piercing eyes and commanding good looks. Osgood's voice was whiny, his eyes were pig-like and his looks couldn't command a fish to breathe underwater. Therefore, seeing Jacob reduced to the status of prisoner was *glorious*.

After that he'd gone to find his master.

Lucas Morodai had set up camp in the Carvallen Great Hall. From there, he managed the destruction of those few forces still holding out against him across The Chapter Lands.

Pockets of resistance were attempting to fight off his army, but were crushed at every turn. Morodai knew that very soon everywhere would be under his control, and he could turn his attention to stripping the other worlds of whatever assets he desired - Carvallen's being the prime target.

Both men had been as happy as the proverbial pigs in muck, but their moods had soured at the unwelcome news that the Library had been barred from them, with the Carvallen Cornerstone on the other side of the door.

Morodai raged at Draveli. The fat little toad had been given one job to do and he'd still managed to make a mess of it.

'How could you leave those idiots alone knowing the custodian was still free?' Morodai yelled, face red with anger.

'I thought they could handle it, Lucas!' Draveli simpered.

'*You* should've handled it, you idiot!' Morodai grabbed the front of Draveli's robe and pulled him closer. 'Get down there, get that door open and get me that Cornerstone. Otherwise, I will feed you to the nearest Dweller!'

A terrified Osgood Draveli now stood in front of the Library doors, sweating heavily and screaming at the Wordsmiths he'd corralled into helping. 'Get those doors open now! Your lord commands it!' he squealed.

His men had uprooted a massive stone column from a nearby courtyard and were smashing it into the doors with their combined Wordcraft. It wasn't subtle, but was having the desired effect.

The doors splintered, looking like they could give way at any moment. Several Dwellers waited beside the Wordsmiths, champing at the bit to get in. With a final surge of effort, the stone column rammed right through, shattering the doorframe as it breached the Library.

The Dwellers were first in, clambering over the shattered remains of door and column, ready to suck the life out of anything they encountered inside. The first people they came across were the unconscious Wordsmiths left behind by Max's group, so they got a decent meal for their efforts.

They left Elijah alone, recognising that he carried one of their brethren around in his head. The Dweller inside had still not reanimated Elijah's body and had no intention of doing so until someone could guarantee it there were no toilets or gnomes in the vicinity.

Draveli's Wordsmiths cleared away the larger chucks of debris and Osgood walked in, his eyes darting everywhere. Making his way through to the Hub, he saw the creatures swarming over the Wordsmiths he'd left in charge of breaking The Cornerstone and knew something had gone horribly wrong.

'Find The Cornerstone! Kill anyone you see!' he ordered.

His troops fanned out through the open doorways as commanded, and Osgood Draveli gratefully lowered his enormous behind onto the floral sofa that sat nearby - wondering where in the world the thing had come from.

- 5 -

'He's behind this?' Max said to Garrowain, tapping on the barrier of books the custodian had created.

'Yes and still under the control of a Dweller, I'm afraid,' the old man replied, walking up to his hastily constructed barrier. 'Are you alive in there?' The book wall bulged outwards as the Arma slammed into it, roaring with anger. 'I'll take that as an unequivocal yes.'

They all heard a crash from far behind as the Library doors gave way.

'We'd better hurry up and do something!' Merelie said. 'It sounds like they're in. They'll be on top of us any minute!'

'Right then, chuckles,' Max said to Garrowain. 'You get rid of the wall and I'll make sure Captain Steroids doesn't get too fist happy.'

The custodian had now been around Max Bloom long enough to have a rough idea what he was talking about and dispelled the Wordcraft holding the books in place. As Borne came barrelling out with murder in his eyes, Max picked him up with a deft turn of the wrist and pushed him back into the empty hub room, pinning the Arma against the far wall. They all went in and Garrowain re-established the barrier.

'How long will it take them to find us?' Imelda asked.

'A little while, I shouldn't wonder,' he said. 'I'm not sure how long this barrier will last when they do though.'

203

'We'll worry about it when the time comes,' she replied. 'In the meantime, we could all do with a rest. I haven't stopped since this morning and my ankles are killing me.'

'Poor Borne.' Merelie walked over to where he was trapped against the wall, snarling and staring at her with those hideous smoke filled eyes. 'What should we do with you?'

'If there was a way to extricate the thing inside, it could restore Borne's faculties and he'd be able to assist us,' Garrowain said.

'We could try ripping it out,' Max suggested.

'Do... and this mortal dies,' the monster spoke from Borne's lips.

'Oh, Mister Talkative now, are we?' said Max. 'Got yourself caught and fancy a little chat, eh?'

'I will eat your mind!' it screamed.

'Good grief, talk about a broken record... haven't you got any other threats? That one's pretty bloody lame when you get right down to it.' He thought for a second. 'Maybe you could tell me you're going to rip my head off and crap down my neck? That's a good one!' Max was warming up now. 'Or how about threatening to kill my pets? ...use my lungs as punch bags? ...my skull as a fruit bowl? ...have my balls for breakfast?'

'Is this accomplishing anything?' Imelda asked.

'No, it just irritates me when people aren't original. It's a sign of laziness,' said Max, a boy who could waste an entire day playing Resident Evil given half the chance.

'These are monsters from the void between worlds, Mr Bloom,' Garrowain said. 'I don't believe where they come from offers much of an atmosphere for creative thought.'

'Tell me about it, I've been there.'

This was met with universal looks of dumb-founded surprise.

'You... you've *been there*?' Garrowain said in a strangled voice.

'Yeah. First time Corny brought me over. Hasn't happened again. It was pretty weird and scary though, so I'm not fussed.'

'Are you trying to tell us that The Cornerstone showed you where they come from?' Merelie said, pointing at Borne.

'I guess so. Why, is that unusual?'

'Of course it's bloody unusual!' Imelda snapped. 'It should just transport you between dimensions, not show you the bits in between! Why didn't you tell us this earlier?'

'I didn't think it was important!'

'I think we should concern ourselves less with when this piece of information came to light and more with what it means,' Garrowain said. 'The Cornerstone took Max somewhere it has taken no-one else. It must be significant.'

'It *knew*,' Merelie said with awe. 'It knew Max had the power in him and wanted him to know what he'd be up against.'

'Possibly,' the custodian conceded. 'We're discovering more and more that The Cornerstone has its own agenda in all of this. I'd go so far as to say it's been manipulating us all for its own ends... especially you, Merelie.'

The girl thought for a second. 'The dreams you mean? The nightmares? That was The Cornerstone warning me?'

'I'd hazard a guess,' Garrowain smiled, '...correctly, I believe.'

'Why didn't it warn her dad?' Max argued. 'Why tell just Merelie about it?'

'I imagine it thought it far easier to manipulate a young girl than a Chapter Lord,' the custodian said. 'She was far more likely to do its bidding.' He patted Max on the shoulder. 'You're here my boy, because The Cornerstone wanted you here.'

'Why me?' Max moaned.

'Why not you?'

There really was no answer to that.

Max held the book up. 'Cheers, buddy,' he told it in a mournful voice.

'This is all very well, but we've got one of those things in here with us and a lot more out there,' Imelda reminded them.

Max walked over to Borne. 'If Corny's got the power to take me to where these things live... maybe it can send this one back.'

Borne's head snapped up. 'Never! We will stay and we will eat all your mind!'

Max smacked him on the forehead with The Cornerstone. 'Give it a rest, you're giving me a headache.'

'Mr Bloom may be on to something,' said Garrowain. 'The Dwellers were allowed access to this world using the Morodai Cornerstone. Perhaps another can be used to force them back?'

'Worth a pop,' said Max and opened the book in Borne's face. 'Do your stuff, Corny!'

At first nothing happened.

'I will not leave this host. It is mine!' the thing inside Borne shrieked.

'Nobody likes a gloater.'

Then, the Cornerstone choir piped up in a clear and vibrant *aaaahhh*. They'd been forced into some pretty graceless caterwauling recently and were more than happy to knock out their classic number. The look of terror on Borne's face was a picture.

'Oh look, Mister Gloaty's not so happy now, eh?' Max said, looking smug. 'When you get home, tell your little buddies to stay exactly where they are, or me and Corny here will be paying a visit.' Max leant forward, affecting the meanest scowl he could, '...and you won't like the way I redecorate your living room.'

This was officially the *twenty third* worst threat made in human history.

It had the desired effect though, as the monster screamed in a satisfying manner and purple-black smoke started to billow from Borne's eyes, pulled towards the pages of The Cornerstone. The Arma's wailing was matched by the rising tone of the choir as one battled the other. Max had to hold his other hand over his eyes as the book started to glow brighter than he could stand to look at.

As quickly as it had started, the extraction was over and the last tendril of smoke disappeared, the choir ending their performance on an abrupt note.

Borne let out a very human groan of pain and slid slowly to the floor. Merelie put her arms round him, tears wetting her cheeks.

'Well done buddy,' Max said, closing The Cornerstone and giving it a pat.

Garrowain knelt and gave Borne a thorough examination.

'He appears to have suffered no ill effects physically from his time in captivity,' he concluded, snapping his fingers in front of Borne's face. 'Arma? Can you understand me?'

Borne looked up, his eyes clear. 'Yes, old man... and you don't have to shout.'

It didn't take long to explain the situation to Borne. He was a man of action and used to taking orders. He didn't need all the blanks filling in.

He did raise one bushy eyebrow when told of Max's new found Wordsmith status and raised the other one when Max floated in mid-air for a couple of minutes by way of demonstration.

Eventually though, it all came down to some simple problems.

Chapter House over-run... Carvallen's imprisoned or dead... Dwellers everywhere... Morodai in charge.

Thirty seconds later, one final and immediate problem was added to the list: hiding place found, book barrier about to give way...

- 6 -

Garrowain flinched every time the wall shuddered. Imelda and Merelie helped sustain it while Max was busy in the corner whittling his own power into a giant mental fist, ready to smash the enemy once the others let the barrier down.

After a few anxious moments Max told the others he was ready and they lowered the wall. The second it was gone Max word shaped, sending a dozen Wordsmiths and Dwellers barrelling back down the aisle to land in a heap at the other end.

What followed then could only be described as a rampage through a hoard of Wordsmiths and Dwellers that were completely unprepared to deal with Max Bloom and his new found power. Most of them were thrown like rag dolls in a variety of directions as Max led the group back towards the Main Hub. Unfortunately, a few minutes into his charge through the Library, Max got a bit too carried away with the whole thing and ran off up the aisle screaming like a banshee, ignoring the protests from his friends.

An important question was therefore answered at this point, as Max found himself completely surrounded in an unfamiliar part of the Library. Just how many Wordsmiths and Dwellers could he defeat before being overwhelmed and taken prisoner?

It turns out the answer was 42 - though it did take one sneaky little sod creeping up and walloping him across the back of the head with a book to finish him off. It would have come as no surprise to Max that the book in question was the Haynes Manual for the Austin Montego.

Thanks to him keeping their enemies busy though, Merelie and the others were able to sneak back over to the Main Hub unmolested, while Max was getting carted off unconscious. Hiding in a small, gloomy vestibule just off the main corridor, they could see Osgood Draveli taking delivery of his unconscious form.

'He'll kill him,' fretted Merelie.

'Perhaps,' said Borne. 'But it would serve Draveli better to hold him hostage.'

Sure enough, the Chapter Lord's voice augmented with Wordcraft boomed across the Library. 'I know you're here, Merelie Carvallen! You and your friends show yourself, or this fool dies!'

'Well, that's put a crimp in things,' Imelda stated dryly. 'We can't give ourselves up, you know.'

'But Max... ' Merelie looked back at the limp form lying at Draveli's feet.

'Max will be fine, girl. Draveli's not dumb enough to actually kill his bargaining chip.'

'I wouldn't be so sure,' Garrowain disagreed. 'Osgood Draveli is just stupid enough not to realise what Max means to us.'

Merelie groaned.

'This situation gets worse by the minute,' said Borne.

'By the second, I would say,' rasped Elijah, standing in the dark behind them.

- 7 -

'So nobody saw him in there before we hid?' Imelda enquired, as she was pushed to her knees in front of Draveli.

'Other things on my mind,' apologised Borne, who wasn't entirely over his lengthy period of possession just yet. 'You should have killed him when you had the chance.'

'We hit him on the head with a toilet, what more do you want?'

Max came round to a tableau of disapproving looks from his companions and an evil, self-satisfied grin on Osgood Draveli's face. He held The Cornerstone in one chubby hand. Five Chapter Guards stood over them, with Draveli's remaining servants stood behind their master.

'Excellent,' he said. 'So nice of you to join me... and hand over this most precious of items.'

'Hands off my book, fatso,' snarled Max, more out of habit than anything.

He got a clout round the head from a Chapter Guard for his troubles and started to draw in power to retaliate.

'Stop that right now,' Osgood warned, 'or I crush the girl's heart in her chest.' He looked at Merelie, made a fist and she screamed in agony.

Max immediately stopped, letting the gathered energy dissipate.

Draveli sneered. 'I have no idea how a monkey like you managed to learn Wordcraft, but I'd advise you to keep it in check.'

'You want to hope I never get you alone, fat boy,' Max said in a black voice.

'Hah! I am a Chapter Lord! You couldn't match me. I would grind your face in the dirt.'

'Whatever, chunky.'

'To think... you thought you could outwit us,' Draveli began, obviously gearing up for a speech.

Max leant over to Merelie. 'Are you ok?' he whispered.

'I think so,' she replied weakly. 'Just feel a bit giddy.'

'We have control of your land,' Draveli waffled on, 'and control of your city. There's nothing you can do to stop us.'

'This bloke's a walking cliché,' Max said with contempt. 'He's probably going to say he underestimated us in a minute.'

'Yet you continue to defy us!' Draveli cried. 'Scurrying away like rats escaping from their cages.' The fat man drew himself up and looked down his podgy nose at them. 'I never thought you could be so bothersome, but it appears I underestimated you.' Max rolled his eyes. 'But no matter! The Carvallen Cornerstone is now ours! The last of the five to come under our control. The gateway to every dimension is now within our grasp.'

'The Cornerstone will never allow you free access,' said Garrowain.

'It will if Jacob Carvallen tells it to... and I have his daughter's heart in my hand, so he'd better!' He clenched his podgy fist again and Merelie screamed.

'Pffft.'

Draveli looked at Max. 'What?'

'Pffft,' Max repeated. 'You're not in charge here, you're just Morodai's little poodle. He says jump, you say how high.'

Draveli went an alarming shade of red, which on a fat man is never a pretty sight. 'We are equals! We rule together!' he squealed.

'Pffft.' Max had known bullies like this before. They loved riding on the coat tails of their bigger, nastier friends, but hated being reminded of the fact. 'Yeah right... you say that, but once we've all been taken care of, he'll be nicking your lunch money and giving you a wedgie in no time at all, I bet.' Max lent forward, appraising Draveli carefully. 'You can't do anything without running it by him first, can you? Or are you just too stupid to get The Cornerstone working by yourself, tubby?'

Imelda Warrington was at this point forced to readjust her opinion of Max Bloom. She knew he was too big for his own boots and had a smart mouth, but he was also a very clever boy when you got right down to it.

'Is that true, Osgood?' she joined in. 'You need Lucas to do everything for you? That's a little sad isn't it? Max here can use The Cornerstone and he's not even from The Chapter Lands.'

'Shut up! I don't need anyone!' Draveli raved. 'You think your miserable book can stand against me?'

The Chapter Lord ripped open The Cornerstone - which was pretty quick on the uptake, and had begun storing up a nasty surprise for Draveli the second Max had started going *pfft*.

The choir made a noise that sounded like *Gah*! and an incandescent bolt of lightning erupted from the book's pages, turning the whole room behind Draveli silver. He was instantly blinded and deafened. The Wordsmiths and Dwellers standing behind him were also stunned, leaving only the five behind Max with their faculties intact.

Intact for about five seconds that is, because Borne, Garrowain and Imelda simultaneously took advantage of the distraction to deal with them.

Max got up and walked over to where Draveli was groping around on the floor and picked up The Cornerstone before the Chapter Lord could put his chubby digits on it.

'Now then, lard butt,' Max said. 'What was that about grinding my face in the dirt?'

Osgood Draveli might have put up a decent fight if he wasn't partially blind and dazed from The Cornerstone's attack. As it was, Max got bored of using him as a human pinball after a minute or so and cast him aside. He then turned his attention to bouncing the rest of the Wordsmiths and Dwellers off the walls, until Imelda told him to stop, as it looked like he was enjoying himself too much.

The ones Max missed were taken care of by Garrowain with Wordcraft and Borne with his fists. In short order, all resistance had been dealt with.

Max rubbed his hands together as he surveyed the scene. 'Good stuff,' he said, pleased with his work.

'Don't let it go to your head,' said Imelda. 'We've done alright here, but there's still Morodai to take care of… and the Dwellers.'

'There'll be hundreds, if not thousands of them out there,' said Garrowain. 'Most of them more powerful than these, I'd wager. Morodai would want his strongest allies closest to him.'

'Then we'd better figure out how to get rid of them,' Max said, walking over to where Elijah lay, out for the count again after being pole-axed by a nasty smack to the head from Borne. 'Starting with this one, I reckon.'

- 8 -

Max pulled The Cornerstone away from Elijah's face as the choir died away. The look of gratitude the Arma gave him made him feel quite embarrassed.

'Thank you!' Elijah cried with relief, tears in his eyes.

Garrowain took The Cornerstone from Max and began ridding the others of their possession. Borne gave Elijah a bear hug and laughed. 'Good to have you back, my friend!'

'How are you, Elijah?' asked Imelda, knowing what the man had been through.

'As well as could be expected, Emmy,' Elijah replied. Merelie's eyebrow shot up at the use of the nickname.

'Thank goodness. I thought you'd be damaged for good with everything we threw at you.'

'That thing kept me protected from harm for the most part. I wouldn't have been much good to it broken into pieces,' the Arma said, touching his head and remembering the toilet incident.

'My parents?' asked Merelie. 'Are they alive?'

'Your mother still lived the last time I saw her. I tried to fight off the intruders when they ambushed us in her quarters, but they were too strong. As that thing took hold of me, your mother was being tied up. I heard one of them mention she was not to be hurt, by order of Lucas Morodai.'

'And my father?'

'I'm sorry, I know nothing of his fate.'

Merelie's look of anguish nearly broke Max's heart. 'We're not going to find out what happened to them standing here,' he said, putting his arm round her.

'We still need a plan,' Imelda reminded him.

From the corner of the room where Garrowain was attempting to free another luckless victim of the Dwellers, there was a loud cry. They all turned to see the custodian backing away from the book, which he'd dropped to the ground. From it, a monstrous figure of black and purple smoke rose, lunging toward the old man, one clawed hand outstretched. Garrowain fell, arms raised to ward off the spectre.

It thrust an amorphous claw into the old man's chest and he let out a blood curdling scream. Max word shaped, sending a blast towards the shadowy creature. The Wordcraft struck and the thing exploded into tattered ribbons of smoke. Garrowain slumped back, his head hitting the flagstones, body spasming in pain.

They hurried over and Borne lifted him gently to the sofa, where the old man settled and came out of the seizure.

'You alright?' Max asked.

Garrowain gave him a grateful look. 'I think so. Thank you, my boy. That's the second time today I owe you my life.'

'What happened?' Imelda said.

'I was trying to release that man from his bondage. All was going well until that creature erupted from The Cornerstone.'

Max examined the book, which seemed no worse for wear. 'I think that's the last time we'll be sending a Dweller home using this.'

'What we were doing must have been noticed and steps taken to stop it,' Garrowain agreed, his face as white as chalk.

'What was it?' Merelie asked, sitting at Garrowain's side, taking his hand in hers.

'I don't know, child. Another Dweller I suppose. One powerful enough to breach The Cornerstone and enter our world in its true form.'

'What did it feel like?'

'Very cold and very *angry*,' Garrowain said and winced, clutching his chest where the claw had entered.

'Let's not give it another chance to kill one of us,' said Borne. 'Max is right, we can't free any more people using The Cornerstone.'

'Then they're doomed,' Elijah said, as he bent down to look at one of the fallen men. 'We should slit their throats now to make sure they can't cause any more trouble.'

'Don't be so hasty, Arma,' Garrowain said, struggling for breath. 'You'd be in your grave if we'd taken that attitude. This Cornerstone can't help anymore, but Morodai's might. He used it to free them all from the void... maybe we can reverse the process.'

'Stealing the Morodai Cornerstone so you can test that theory will be impossible,' Elijah replied. 'Lucas keeps it close by and well protected.'

Max stepped in. 'Which is why - as I said before - we should stop talking and start moving. Corny's brother is with Morodai and Merelie's parents will be floating about in the same vicinity.'

'What makes you say that, boy?' Borne asked.

'Gloating. What's the point in vanquishing your foes and taking over the world if you can't have a good old fashioned gloat, eh?'

Borne didn't look too sure about that explanation.

'If we just go running out into the Chapter House, we'll be overwhelmed,' Imelda said.

Max looked at the unconscious bulk of Osgood Draveli. 'I've got an idea.'

- 9 -

Elijah woke the fat man with a few slaps to the face.

'Get away from me!' he squealed, backing against the nearest wall.

'Now look here Porks-a-lot, the situation's simple,' Max said. 'You're going to help us get through the Chapter House without a fight, or this day's going to get a lot worse for you.'

'Never! I will never help you and your worthless gang, boy!' Draveli spat back.

Max leant forward, the rest of the worthless gang crowded round him. 'Really? What if I promise to pull your head out through your arse if you don't?' he said, supplying Draveli with the nastiest grin he could muster.

Five minutes later, a white faced Osgood Draveli walked along the corridor leading to the upper floors of the Chapter House. He couldn't even begin to picture what having one's head pulled out through one's bottom would look or feel like, but was determined not to find out.

The Chapter Lord walked in front with Borne, who was trying his hardest to still look under Dweller influence. He'd picked up a guard's helmet to cover his eyes, so they didn't give away the fact the smoke had disappeared. Max and Merelie were behind, apparently in chains, as was Imelda a step further back. Elijah brought up the rear, similarly attired to Borne. They'd left Garrowain recuperating in the Main Hub.

'I would slow you down given my condition,' he'd rationalised. 'Besides, somebody has to make sure the Library isn't damaged further. I can do that, at least.'

The con they were employing probably wouldn't stand up to much scrutiny, but it would get them far enough with any luck.

'Where are my parents being held, Osgood?' Merelie asked.

214

'I'm not entirely sure… '

'Head – arse – pull through,' reminded Max.

'They're being held in your father's study!'

'Then that's where we're headed,' Borne hissed, prodding Draveli with the bow gun he'd found hanging from the belt of a zombified Chapter Guard.

They encountered few people down in the bowels of the House, but as they ascended several flights of stairs, they started to see Dwellers lurking in the shadows. None of the creatures seemed interested in a confrontation, but Max still held his breath every time they went past. The procession also came across more people unfortunate enough to have been fed on by the Dwellers. These victims wandered the hallways - mouths hung open, eyes unfocused. Merelie waved her hand in the face of one and got no reaction at all.

'You and your master will pay for this,' Borne whispered to Osgood, making the fat coward go even whiter.

The first people to actually stop them were three Wordsmiths standing in a sunny courtyard. Max recognised this as the place where he'd popped into existence the second time he'd come to The Chapter Lands.

All three Wordsmiths were of Morodai ilk and could barely contain their contempt when they saw Osgood Draveli. Contempt gave way to surprise as they realised he'd taken Merelie Carvallen prisoner.

'You actually managed it then, Lord Draveli?' one of them asked.

'Yes,' squeaked Osgood, aware of Max's eyes boring into his back.

'Lord Morodai will be pleased,' the Wordsmith smirked and went up to Merelie, taking her chin in his hand.

'Pretty little bitch, aren't you?'

Max coughed politely. The Morodai looked at him.

'What's your problem boy?'

'That would be you, pal. Say nighty night.'

'What are you talk - '

The Wordsmith went sideways across the courtyard and through a window. Borne and Elijah took care of the other two as they stood there in stunned horror.

'If it all goes as easily as that, we're laughing,' Max said, poking Draveli in the back. 'Keep walking, tubby.'

They continued along the same corridors Merelie had dragged Max through three weeks ago. He was dismayed to find that the pleasant vista he'd seen out of the tall windows had been replaced by a scene of utter destruction. The city surrounding the Chapter House was now a disaster zone. Buildings burned and debris littered the streets. Max could see Dwellers teeming through the broad avenues, clambering onto overturned trams and sniffing their way through the rubble of broken buildings.

In the harbour to the south were several large vessels - long grey things that looked like ships from the Second World War - the gold symbol of the Morodai household on their prows. Golden airships were tethered to the highest Carvallen buildings and Max could see troops disembarking using long metal gantries.

I'm not even from this world and that makes me bloody angry.

Continuing their journey through the Chapter House, a few more Wordsmiths - all Draveli's kin - came up to speak to him, and when they did, Max's heart went into his mouth thinking the fat man would give them away.

He didn't though, and after four of these tense exchanges they encountered no-one else, eventually reaching the door to the hallway where the enormous wooden staircase led to the upper chambers. So far, the whole House had been relatively empty, but when Borne opened the door to the hall, they saw it was full of Dwellers.

'Don't try anything,' Max warned Draveli. 'Unless you want to bet these things can save you before I pull your head out through your backside.' The idea was even beginning to turn Max's stomach a bit, but it was a useful, effective threat.

'I won't try anything, just please don't hurt me,' Draveli moaned.

'Clear us a path,' Borne ordered.

Draveli nodded and addressed the Dwellers. 'Remove yourselves from here. I command you!' he shouted, voice cracking with fear.

The Dwellers didn't budge.

'I said I command you!' Draveli shouted again.

'Think of something, otherwise you know what's going to happen,' Max threatened.

'I speak for Lord Morodai and he commands you to leave!' Draveli tried.

This had the desired effect. Morodai's name carried far more weight. One by one, the Dwellers sloped out of the room through several doors that led away from the hall.

As the last one left, Borne let out an explosive breath. 'That was unpleasant.'

'Could have been a lot worse,' Elijah noted.

'Let's keep going,' said Imelda, starting to climb the staircase.

Max followed, once again noting the massive portraits of Carvallens past hanging on the walls, and the gigantic tapestry of the world that hung above the staircase.

What the hell?

He stopped. Merelie bumped into him.

It's the world.

'What's the hold up boy?' Imelda said.

It's the bloody world.

Max pointed at the tapestry.

The first time he'd seen it, Merelie had rushed him past so quickly it hadn't registered. All he'd noticed was a large tapestry depicting the Earth, with the continents picked out in heavy stitching. Nothing odd about that, at all. Unless you were on a totally different planet, that is.

'The tapestry…' he said in a quiet voice.

Imelda looked at it, frowning.

'What about it?'

'It's the world.'

'Yes. It's a tapestry of The Chapter Lands, so what?'

'No… it's *Earth*.'

And it was.

It was a map of Earth, just like you'd find in any atlas.

'It's The Chapter Lands, Max,' Merelie said, pointing at one part in the middle that was quite blatantly England. 'Look, that's where we are, in the Carvallen lands.'

Sure enough, right on the spot where the cities of southern England should be was a picture of a tall building with 'Chapter House of Carvallen' written under it in flowery script.

The other four Houses were also on the map. Morodai's was where Moscow should exist, Draveli's was just about where Delhi in India was. The Falion Chapter House stood where New York ought to be, and Wellhome's looked like it was slap bang in the middle of the Brazilian rainforest.

Names of a thousand other towns and cities were dotted across the tapestry, some similar to their counterparts in our world and some wildly different.

Several things clanged into place in Max's head.

'This is Earth,' he said. 'Well… it's not, but it is.'

'Hadn't you figured that out?' said Elijah. 'Your world is a parallel version of ours, like every other one discovered by the Chapter Houses.'

'Oh my! That is rich,' Draveli cackled, forgetting for a second how precarious his situation was. 'The monkey with the Wordcraft didn't even know that?'

Borne clipped the fat man round the ear like an errant schoolchild. 'Shut up or I'll knock your teeth out,' he warned.

Merelie took Max's hand. 'I can't believe no one explained it to you Max. I can't believe *I* didn't… We both live on the same planet, just different versions of it. Yours is called Earth, ours is The Chapter Lands.'

'And all the others are Earth too?'

'Yes, of course. Same planet, different universe.'

Max looked back up at where the Carvallen Chapter House was positioned. 'That explains why The Cornerstone was in my town. It's the same place, isn't it?'

'Geographically, yes. The Carvallen lands incorporate the country you call England and a majority of the land mass known as Europe.'

Max let this sink in.

I'm still in Farefield. At least where Farefield would be back home.

'Fascinating as this revelation is,' Imelda spoke up, 'we still have the small matter of defeating a power-mad Chapter Lord and his demonic underlings… in case anyone had forgotten.'

'No need to be sarcastic,' said Max, who knew the tone when he heard it.

'We'll have plenty of time for geography lessons if we survive this,' Borne said, 'but right now, I feel decidedly exposed and in need of stout walls between me and any Dwellers that might be lurking hereabouts.'

He poked Draveli into movement and they trooped up the stairs.

Max was lost in thought as they hurried along the long galleries and staircases that would eventually bring them to the door of Jacob Carvallen's study, in the uppermost floor of the Chapter House.

It all made sense, he had to confess.

A series of Earths in parallel universes.

The same world, but different.

He could imagine a stone-age civilisation being overrun by Morodai's bunch of maniacs thousands of years ago, or Falion's people coming across a more advanced society in the Middle Ages. He guessed that by the time Symon Carvallen had made contact with our version of Earth, we were far too set in our ways to believe in stuff like magic, or books that could open doorways to other worlds.

The revelation threw The Chapter Lands in sharper focus as well. He could now get a grip on how large they were and how much power each Chapter House wielded.

Garrowain had said there were several hundred million people in The Chapter Lands – most of who could not read or write – and Max thought this was just as well. Millions of people with the ability to Wordcraft sat on Earth's proverbial doorstep would be dangerous.

And never mind all that… what if the nations of his planet - stocked to the eyeballs with all manner of horrifying weaponry - discovered these parallel worlds and had designs on them?

Max decided that if he did wade his way successfully through this mess, he'd have a lengthy conversation with Merelie and Garrowain – and try to persuade them that the link to his world should be closed forever. He didn't want to be the cause of inter-dimensional warfare, and convincing them that The Cornerstone should be closed once and for all was the best way to prevent it.

Borne broke his train of thought as he ordered them to stop. They'd reached the lobby leading to Jacob's study.

'We're nearly there and I don't trust this fat fool to get us in without giving us away. So do we plan what we intend to do, or just jump in and take our chances?'

Max would have leapt at the second option, but fortunately wiser heads prevailed.

- 10 -

When given the onerous task of guarding a door, there are several survival mechanisms that can be employed to ensure boredom doesn't turn your brain to soup. Daydreaming is a favourite - if you're unlucky enough to be on your own.

Subjects of the daydream should be as distracting as possible. If you're a man, boobs are always a popular choice, and if you're a woman, shoes usually have much the same effect.

If you're lucky enough to have a companion, you have a whole plethora of entertaining options to choose from when whiling away the hours between shift changes. You might share a witty and somewhat exaggerated anecdote about your last romantic conquest or shoe shopping trip. You might discuss important philosophical topics, such as the nature of existence, or what a bunch of lying toe rags politicians are.

If you're a bit hard up for good anecdotes, or lacking somewhat in the intellect department, a good game of I-Spy is recommended by bored guards across the multi-verse.

The two unfortunates outside the door to Jacob Carvallen's study are engaged in a game right now.

It's a tense one.

Mumford - on the left - is leading four rounds to Terski's three. Both are part of Lucas Morodai's personal bodyguard and could probably kill you just by looking at you, if they so desired. Neither has had an original thought in their lives and couldn't comment on the nature of existence if you dangled them over a pit of exploding scorpions and threatened to cut the rope.

They do play a mean game of I-Spy though. It's Terski's turn and he's determined to pick something hard to fox his colleague and draw the game level.

'C' for ceiling is too easy, as is 'S' for sandwich. Then there was 'H' for helmet... which was quite cunning, Terski thought.

Another option then presented itself for consideration.

'F' for fat man flying down the corridor, screaming his head off.

Borne and Elijah were up and running the minute Max sent Draveli cannon-balling into the two guards. The luckless Mumford and Terski were suitably stunned by the ballistic Chapter Lord and made short work of by the two Armas, who could kill you without even bothering to look.

By the time the rest made it to the study door, it was being unlocked by someone inside, no doubt wanting to know what all the fuss was about. This wasn't the wisest move as the fuss was two angry soldiers, backed up by an over-enthusiastic teenager with newly discovered magic powers.

Two more Chapter Guards were helped into unconsciousness by Borne and Elijah, while Max took care of a single Morodai Wordsmith - introducing him to a nearby wall at some speed, in what was fast becoming his favourite manoeuvre.

'That was easy,' said Borne.

'Obviously not expecting much opposition,' Elijah rumbled. 'Morodai is over confident and that could be to our advantage.'

Merelie let out a cry of joy and ran over to where her mother and father were tied to their chairs, still very much alive.

'Merelie!' her father said, with relief.

Jacob Carvallen looked drawn and pale, but happy to see his daughter. Halia looked as tired as her husband, but she too smiled as Merelie threw her arms around her. Elijah and Borne cut their bonds, while Max and Imelda tidied up the fresh selection of limp bodies, piling them safely in one corner.

Osgood Draveli also lay dribbling by the door, out for the count again. If he survived this, he'd be so covered in bruises he'd resemble a ripe plum if stripped naked.

Max tried his level best to remove that particular image from his head as he kicked a guard's helmet under a chair. He turned round to see Imelda frowning at Jacob Carvallen. He remembered the nature of their relationship and decided this could be an interesting conversation.

'Emerelda,' Jacob said with no trace of emotion.

'Jacob,' she replied at sub-zero temperature.

Silence followed.

And followed a bit more.

'There's nothing like a warm family reunion is there?' Max noted.

'The last time I saw you,' Jacob said to him, 'you were slung over Borne's shoulder and being sent back to Earth.' He looked at his daughter. 'I assume this didn't occur?'

Merelie began to answer, but Max interrupted.

'I did go back as it happens, but had a think about it and decided to come back here and face extreme danger to save you and your entire civilisation.'

'Indeed?' The Chapter Lord clearly didn't believe a word of it.

'He's telling the truth, Jacob,' Imelda sighed. 'Merelie was right about Max. The Cornerstone showed him how to use Wordcraft and since then he's been more insufferable than ever. But he is telling the truth, you owe him your freedom.'

'Er... he owes us *all* his freedom,' Max objected, not wanting to take all the credit.

'And we're very grateful,' said Halia, touching her wrists, which had been rubbed raw by the rope. 'Morodai was beginning to make some unpleasant threats.'

'Such as?' Elijah said, his eyes narrowing.

'He threatened to kill Halia if I didn't allow him the full use of our Cornerstone,' Jacob supplied. 'He knows that to conquer Mr Bloom's world he needs its co-operation.'

'Conquer my world? Why?'

'Resources, Mr Bloom. Your people made into slaves and your technology bent to his purpose. You'd provide many meals for his Dwellers as well, I'd imagine.'

'Oh, spectacular,' Max said. 'I'd best be doing something about that, then.'

'*We* will Max,' Merelie said. 'If you help save us, we'll do the same for you... won't we father?'

'Agreed. But right now, I fail to see how either can be accomplished.'

'Garrowain thinks the Morodai Cornerstone can be used to suck back the Dwellers infesting our world,' Imelda said, 'the same way it brought them here in the first place.'

'It's possible, I suppose,' he conceded. He then noticed that Garrowain was missing. 'Where is my head custodian?'

'Injured, sir,' Elijah spoke up. 'A void creature reached through The Cornerstone in an attempt to kill him. Max here prevented it. We left him guarding the Library.'

Jacob looked at Max again. 'You're proving more useful that I thought you would, boy.'

Max was getting really sick of being called boy all the time.

'Thanks,' he said and counted to ten in his head, trying to keep cool.

Imelda, knowing the danger signs, changed the subject. 'If we're going to make this plan work, we need to find Morodai. Where is he Jacob?

'Close by. He lurks in the Great Hall, commanding his minions. When he's bored, he likes to come up here and threaten us.'

'See?' said Max. 'Nobody likes a good gloat more than your main villain.'

'So he could appear any second then?' Merelie said, standing close to her mother.

'Potentially,' her father said. 'The last I heard he was dealing with some resistance near Tamera Falls. I don't know how long that will take.'

'If he's busy, we can take him by surprise,' Borne suggested, getting an approving nod from Elijah.

'It's the best plan of attack,' he said. 'Surprise is our main advantage... along with Max of course.'

'Is there no way we can do this without risking ourselves?' Halia objected. 'There's been too much killing already. Can't Lucas be reasoned with?'

'The time has passed for negotiations,' Jacob told her, a bleak look on his face.

'Couldn't agree more,' said Max, raising his fists.

Imelda tutted.

'What? Merelie's mum and dad are ok, so what's stopping us from getting in there and having a proper go at him?' Max said and shook a fist in melodramatic fashion.

'What do think, gentlemen?' Jacob asked Borne and Elijah.

'The opportunity to nip this situation in the bud is tempting,' Elijah offered.

'Time to take the house back,' Borne agreed.

'Very well… Halia and Merelie, you will stay here,' Jacob commanded his wife and daughter. They both protested vigorously. 'I will not have you in harm's way!' he told them. 'The stakes are too high already without risking my family again. You'll stay hidden here, with the door barricaded.'

Max gave Merelie a sympathetic look, knowing how much she'd hate to be kept out of the fight.

'Now,' the Chapter Lord continued, 'does anyone have a suggestion on how we get in front of Lucas without confrontation beforehand?'

Max gave dribbly Draveli a speculative look.

'If a plan ain't broke…'

- 11 -

Lucas Morodai listened to his chief Chapter Guard Selroy relaying information about the rebels in Tamera Falls with increasing impatience. What should have been a simple sweep and clear of Carvallen's remaining forces had become a troublesome side conflict. One that even the Dwellers seemed unable to quell.

The Carvallen people had provided more resistance than the other Chapter folk. Falion and Wellhome's citizens had given up the fight once they knew the Chapter House was taken, but this lot seemed determined to fight on until there was no-one left standing. Which there wouldn't be, if Lucas Morodai had his way.

Other than these pockets of resistance, the plan to conquer The Chapter Lands had gone more or less without a hitch. He'd lost men for sure, but his Dweller allies had proved their usefulness time and time again, making short work of those standing in his way.

He looked forward to setting them loose on the other versions of Earth he now had at his disposal – including that fat idiot Draveli's.

Osgood had come to the end of his usefulness.

Morodai would let the Dwellers have him soon. He might even watch while they ate his mind, just for the fun of it.

This pleasant daydream was ruined by the sibilant hiss of the Dweller who now occupied Bethan Falion's slim frame. 'You should allow more of my kind through the gateway, Lucas. They could overturn these insects at the Falls and secure complete victory for us.' It languished in one of the chairs at the Carvallen centre table, eyes flicking over to the Morodai Cornerstone, sat within its master's reach.

'I don't think so, my friend,' Lucas replied, looking over a dispatch from southern Carvallen. 'It won't take my forces long to overwhelm what's left of their resistance.'

The thing inside Falion hissed in disapproval.

'Calm yourself,' Morodai said, resting his hand on the golden Cornerstone book, its metallic cover reflecting the light that struck it from the wide skylight above. 'Once this is resolved, I will open the gateway again and unleash more of you on the other worlds. You can have your fill of humans then.' He gave a thin smile. 'Never think me a fool, though. I won't allow too many of you into The Chapter Lands. I don't trust you *that* much.'

The dweller let out a rasping cackle. 'Your wisdom does you credit, my Lord.'

'As does your cunning, my friend.' He turned back to the Chapter Guard. 'Return to the Falls and impress upon the army there that if they don't secure the place within twenty four hours, I will allow the Dwellers a free meal. Do I make myself *clear*?'

'Perfectly, my Lord,' Selroy replied, knowing which side his bread was buttered. He snapped off a salute, turned and marched out, wishing he'd chosen that career in dentistry like his father had told him to.

The large doors at the rear of the hall then banged open and another Morodai Chapter Guard came clanking over to where Lucas sat, brewing up some unpleasant things to do to Halia Carvallen if Jacob didn't start co-operating.

'What do want?' he asked the guard.

'Chapter Lord Draveli wishes to see you, my Lord.'

'Why?'

'He has successfully taken Merelie Carvallen hostage, my Lord. She must have put up a real fight. He's black and blue.'

'Aah... good! Send him in, please.'

The Chapter Guard clanked back to the door.

A few seconds later, Osgood Draveli entered, followed by two Chapter Guards, Jacob Carvallen, a tall woman in a strange looking suit and a young man dressed in even odder attire.

Morodai stood, as did the Dweller disguised as Bethan Falion. 'What's the meaning of this, Osgood? I gave no orders for Carvallen to be brought down here. Where is his infernal daughter?'

'I thought it fitting that he come down here and grovel for his daughter's life!' Draveli squeaked, making this up on the spot.

Max groaned. A lie that made no sense was as bad as the truth in circumstances like this.

'I see,' Morodai replied, looking closely at the entire party. 'You know, you really are a worm, Osgood. Allowing yourself to be captured by the enemy and bullied into betraying me. What did they say they'd do to you?'

'I said I'd pull his head out through his arse,' Max piped up, knowing damn well Morodai hadn't fallen for their ploy at all.

He stepped forward and slowly started to draw in what energy he could.

'Colourful,' Morodai said. 'I can understand that working on him. Personally, I think you could have just threatened to make him jog a mile - that would have done it.'

This almost made Max smile, but he remembered who he was talking to.

'You must be the boy from Earth who thinks he's a Wordsmith,' Morodai stated, showing that he'd been privy to far more information than anyone had guessed.

'And you're the nut job who let these purple eyed tossers out of the box.'

The Falion Dweller hissed.

'That's correct,' Morodai raised an eyebrow, '*Max*, is it?'

'Yep, that's me. Guess you knew what we were up to all along, eh?'

The Chapter Lord flashed his patented thin smile. 'Enough to make necessary preparations, should the need arise,' he said. 'So now I think it's time to stop this little attempt at rebellion going any further.'

Morodai clapped his hands together twice and things got a lot trickier for our heroes very quickly.

Dwellers of all shapes and sizes came flooding in through the four sets of large double doors on each wall of the Great Hall, surrounding Max and company. They snarled and growled, salivating at the prospect of another feeding.

'My... this is going extremely well,' Imelda remarked.

Jacob Carvallen put his hands out to Morodai. 'Please Lucas, you don't have to do this.'

'Yes he does,' Max said, starting to draw in more power, which felt disturbingly limited in this high chamber. 'He'd like nothing better than to watch this lot rip us apart.'

'For a shaved ape, you exhibit some sense boy,' the amused Chapter Lord told him.

There it was again:

Boy.

'And for a loony from the Chapter Lands, you exhibit a desire to get your head pulled out through your backside, mate,' Max responded, having real trouble letting go of that particular threat.

'Try anything and our new arrivals will regret it.' Morodai pointed over to the entrance behind the crowd of Dwellers.

Max groaned as two Wordsmiths appeared, holding Halia and Merelie captive. The girl gave him an apologetic look.

'As I said, I am always prepared,' Morodai gloated and looked up, addressing Merelie's mother. 'My dearest Halia, I had hoped your husband would be more co-operative and I could allow you all to live, but it seems he has other ideas. Now you get to watch him die in front of you... won't that be nice?' He looked round at the thing in Bethan Falion's body. 'Would you and your friends like a meal, my dear? Please feel free.'

Falion snarled with ravenous glee and leapt towards the surrounded group, the other Dwellers taking this as their cue to attack.

Part Seven

While Lucas Morodai had been in mid-gloat, Max had started crafting a barrier in his mind that could protect the whole group. As soon as the Dwellers advanced, he threw this up, hoping it would hold the monsters back.

It worked. The Dwellers began to run into the barricade, howling as they smashed into the invisible dome Max had erected, bloodying noses and breaking bones.

'Lucas!' shouted Osgood Draveli, standing just inside the barrier. 'Let me through, for Writer's sake!'

Lucas Morodai said perhaps the most predictable thing he could have at this point. 'You've failed me one too many times, Osgood. I promised my colleagues a meal and you'll make a fine one no doubt... once that boy's power fails.'

'Bite me!' Max shouted.

The barrier was holding, but the Dwellers were packed four or five deep in some places, all of them pushing against the hastily constructed umbrella of energy Max maintained. A few had begun pushing their arms through as the pressure began to weaken it.

'Max?' Imelda yelled, backing away from the flailing limbs.

'I know, I know! '

'You see? Talent isn't everything... you need training!'

'Oh... and what an *excellent* time you've chosen to point that out!' he bit back, as one Dweller pushed all the way through the invisible shield and ran at Borne.

The Arma set his feet, bent forward as the creature reached him and hoisted it over his shoulder, back through the barrier.

'We'd better think of something!' he shouted.

'There's nothing we can do! We're doomed!' squealed Draveli.

'That's looking on the bright side, you bloody coward!' Max shouted. 'Why don't you stop complaining and help me with this shield?'

The Chapter Lord looked at him with distain. 'You really know nothing, boy! I can't help you! A Wordsmith casts his own craft. No one else can intervene or assist!' Draveli told him, sending a bolt of Wordcraft at a Dweller nearly through the wall, knocking it back into the crowd.

In his periphery vision, Max could see Halia and Merelie being dragged up into the highest level of seats that circled the great table. Morodai obviously wanted them to have a clear view as they watched their loved ones being ripped to pieces. One Wordsmith slapped Halia when she tried to look away, tears coursing down her face.

Her Arma saw this too. Elijah called out to Borne as he snapped the wrist of an insistent Dweller grabbing at him. 'Can you help me over the crowd?' He pointed at where Halia and Merelie stood.

Borne turned to look at where his mistress and her mother were being held and nodded in agreement. The big man squatted and laced his hands together. Elijah sprinted across, jammed one foot in Borne's hands and was catapulted over the throng of Dwellers, Borne's massive arms driving him upward.

Elijah somersaulted gracefully and landed like a cat just beyond the creatures. He clambered up the rows of seats screaming a hideous battle cry and crashed into the Wordsmiths holding the Carvallens captive.

'Run!' he shouted at Merelie and her mother, pounding on their terrified captors as he did.

Lucas Morodai, now stood on the huge centre table conducting this symphony of destruction, saw Elijah's efforts, snarled in fury and sent a spear of Wordcraft arcing towards the Arma. It struck him in the chest, piercing the tough leather waistcoat he wore, neatly skewering him with a precision born of years of practise.

Blood ran from Elijah's mouth as he doubled over and fell between two rows of seats. A group of Dwellers, whipped into a frenzy, swarmed over him.

'No!' screamed Halia.

'Elijah!!' Borne roared and began battering his way through the barrier and the ranks of Dwellers, in an apocalyptic fury so absolute it even shocked Lucas Morodai into immobility for a moment. The huge Arma steam rollered over anyone stupid enough to get in his way and such was the ferocity of his attack, he made it to Halia and Merelie before any Dweller was able to stop him. He glanced down briefly at where the monsters still crowded over his dead friend, but shook off the grief, knowing it would do him no good. Halia was in floods of tears and Merelie's face was ashen.

'We're leaving this hall... now!' Borne told them.

'No!' Merelie shouted. She started back down to where Max was now sweating with the effort of maintaining the barrier, and Draveli and Imelda were still fighting off the Dwellers. 'We can't leave them... and we have to get that Cornerstone!'

The book in question lay at Morodai's feet as he shaped more spears of power at Max, trying to pierce the rapidly disintegrating force field.

'Stay behind me, then!' the Arma demanded and began wading his way back toward the Chapter Lord. Merelie came after, Wordcrafting away Dwellers as she did.

Morodai saw the attack coming and span round to meet it.

As he prepared another lance of power aimed at Borne's heart, he was rugby tackled to the table's polished surface by the rotund and extremely angry form of Osgood Draveli. Morodai squawked in surprise.

Osgood had watched Morodai standing exultant as the very monsters Draveli had helped bring into this world threatened to suck his mind dry. He'd been utterly betrayed. Despite everything he'd done - all the insults he'd taken, all the injuries he'd sustained - Morodai had thrown him to the wolves in an instant.

Anger had propelled him through Max's barricade, the mass of Dwellers, and up onto the table within reach of his former ally. Draveli wasn't much of a fighter, but did do a nice line in vicious hand slapping and shrieking like a little girl. It certainly distracted Morodai long enough for Merelie to reach in and grab the golden Cornerstone.

'Borne! Get me through to Max!' she screamed, ducking below the grasping arms of a Dweller.

Borne ripped out one of the plush high-backed chairs from its place at the table and swatted the creatures away until there was a clear path for Merelie to run through.

'Get back with mother Borne! There's nothing more you can do. Max will protect me!' She put her head down and sprinted at the barrier. 'Max! Let me in!' she yelled.

Max saw her coming and let that side of the barrier drop. Merelie ran in and he slammed the invisible wall back up before the Dwellers could follow. Borne ran back up to where Halia still sat, intent on protecting his dead friend's mistress.

Osgood Draveli was still doing a good job of keeping Morodai overpowered, slapping and shrieking so much that his ex-master couldn't concentrate enough to muster any Wordcraft. Morodai may have been a powerful Wordsmith, but he was a hundred and seventy pounds to Draveli's two ninety.

'Merelie! I told you to get to safety!' Jacob grabbed her by the arm as she went to Max.

'We need to send them back, father! Otherwise we're all dead anyway!' She held up the Morodai Cornerstone to Max. 'You need to send them back!'

'Er... kinda busy here, Merelie!' he replied, grimacing as another wave of Dwellers rebounded off the unstable force field.

'But you're the only one who can stop them!' she wailed.

'For crying out loud Merelie, I'm not the answer to everything! If I let this down, the Dwellers will be over us in seconds!'

'Then what do I do?' she pleaded.

He looked at her with panicked frustration. 'I don't know!'

'Send them back, Merelie,' her father said in a calm voice as he knelt beside her. 'You don't need Max to do this. They're your nightmares, not his. You can send them away.'

Merelie looked desperate. 'No! That's not how it should work. That's not what The Cornerstone wants!'

'The Cornerstone chose Max... but it also chose *you*, Merelie,' Jacob said. 'Your strength made all this possible - your connection with the words on the page. So use them. Use Morodai's book. Send the monsters away.'

Merelie looked down for a moment, then into her father's eyes. She nodded and rose to her feet, opening the Morodai Cornerstone.

'Open the gateway and send them back,' she said to it in a firm tone.

The golden book glowed briefly with a sickly purple light, but otherwise did nothing.

Merelie took a deep breath. 'Send them back, now.'

It still refused to do anything.

'It's no good. It won't listen to me, I'm not a Morodai,' she said, dejected.

'Maybe it'll listen to its own kind!' Imelda called over from the other side of the shrinking barrier, where she was holding back several snarling Dwellers. 'Give her our Cornerstone, Max!'

One of the monsters - Bethan Falion no less - broke completely through the invisible wall and ran at Imelda, screeching in fury. Both women went tumbling to the ground, the Dweller's teeth snapping at Imelda's face, smoke starting to spill from her eyes.

'It's down my pants!' Max shouted.

'What?' Merelie looked horrified.

Max saw the expression not just on her face, but her father's as well. 'The Cornerstone, I mean! It's in my jeans... at the back!'

Merelie understood and lifted his hoodie, snatching the Carvallen Cornerstone from where he'd stuck it for safe keeping. She put both books on the ground, opened them, rested her hands on their pages and begged her Cornerstone to help.

Please! Please make it send those things back!

The Cornerstone heard her plea... and the great choir began to sing.

- 2 -

Back at the big prize fight, Morodai was finally getting the upper hand against his chubby counterpart. He smacked Draveli twice in the face, stunning him, giving the thin Chapter Lord time to get to his feet.

'You little weasel! How dare you attack me!' Morodai spat and pointed at the nearest Dwellers. 'Kill him! Rip him to shreds! Take his mind and destroy his body!'

Several of the creatures broke off from the pack trying to get at Max and swarmed over Osgood Draveli. He screamed once and was lost from view as living smoke engulfed his corpulent body.

Morodai turned his head away in disgust.

It was then he heard the unearthly sound of the Carvallen Cornerstone above the howling of the Dwellers. Morodai looked down to see that his own Cornerstone had gone and realised what was happening.

'No!' he screamed, jumping from the table and fighting his way past the throng of Dwellers in an attempt to reach Merelie.

The choir grew louder and The Cornerstone glowed like a silver sun. Max could see the bones in Merelie's hand like an x-ray, as the light from the book grew more intense.

Its Morodai counterpart started to shake and twist under Merelie's other hand, protesting against the bullying it was getting from its brother.

'Send them back!' Merelie screamed one last time.

She was blasted away from the books as lightning flashes of pure Wordcraft exploded from both. The lightning arced back and forth between Cornerstones as they tried to overpower one another. The battle was even, neither able to dominate.

Max looked up from the light show. More and more Dwellers were almost through the barrier – and Lucas Morodai was right behind them.

If this goes on much longer, we're dead.

He made a split second decision and let the force field drop completely. At the same time he reached out, snatching a bolt of lightning in his hand as it crackled from one book to the other.

'Here,' he said to his Cornerstone, 'let me give you a hand, buddy.' Max slammed his fist, sizzling with pure Wordcraft, into the centre of the Morodai Cornerstone.

That seemed to do the trick.

He was thrown away as a vortex of sickening purple light started to spin up from Morodai's book where his fist had struck. The cyclone blossomed upwards, spinning faster and faster as it grew in size and speed. Fingers of lightning erupted from the core of the vortex, the whip-crack of energy echoing through the cavernous hall.

Max, knowing how a vacuum cleaner worked, had a fairly good idea what was coming next.

'Er... we may all want to take cover!' he shouted, grabbing the Carvallen Cornerstone before it got caught up in the maelstrom.

He dropped flat on his face, hoping a Dweller wasn't about to jump on his back. They were in no position to attack however, the vortex was seeing to that.

The creature inhabiting Bethan Falion's body was the first to be pulled into the seething mass. She looked up from the fight with Imelda, saw the tornado of dark energy whirling from the golden Cornerstone and tried to crawl away, moaning in terror.

Living smoke started to boil from the Chapter Lord's eyes, pulled inexorably towards the spiralling light. With one last reluctant howl, the Dweller inside Falion was ripped from its host and sucked into the ever expanding cyclone.

In fact, all the Dwellers were now being drawn from their hosts in the same way. The cacophony of howling monsters was almost too much to bear as each tried to escape the pull exerted by the whirlpool of purple light. Long, thick tendrils of smoke whipped and writhed in the air as the disembodied creatures were sucked back into the cold, dark void they'd come from.

As each Dweller was extracted, the victim's body bucked and thrashed, collapsing when it was freed from bondage, the smoke gone. The vortex continued to grow to a huge size as it ate more and more Dwellers, reaching the high ceiling of the Great Hall. The Morodai Cornerstone swelled and rippled, trying to cope with the influx of smoke creatures.

Finally, the last monster was dragged from its human host and sucked into the vortex. Max stood, expecting to see the golden Cornerstone snap shut, its job done.

'Um... it's not stopping,' he said to no-one in particular.

'I rather think that's because it isn't finished yet,' Jacob warned, indicating a build up of living smoke at one of the high, plate glass windows in the domed ceiling above.

'What the hell?'

'Oh Writer,' moaned Merelie.

Imelda grabbed Max's arm. 'We should probably get back before - '

The glass dome shattered, sending razor sharp shards raining down on them. Max was forced to erect the force field again to prevent everyone being cut to pieces.

'It's drawing them all back!' Merelie screamed, 'from across the whole Chapter Lands!'

'How long is that likely to take?' growled Max, getting sick of being the magic shield boy.

'Not long by the look of it,' said Jacob.

A flood of Dweller smoke streamed through the broken ceiling into the Great Hall. Even that hole wasn't big enough. The smoke started to build up against the side of the Chapter House.

Part of the building gave way as the flood became a torrent - cracks in the stonework widening and splitting as the spirits of thousands of Dwellers flowed toward the vortex. The entire room was now a whirling hurricane of smoke and debris. Everyone had to seek cover as huge chunks of stone and glass were caught in the maelstrom - the Chapter House around them disintegrating under the stress exerted by the cyclone of energy.

Imelda was lucky not to be crushed by a section of wall about ten feet across as it hurtled past her head and slammed into the floor, tearing a massive hole through to the lower levels. In the tumult, all Max and his friends could do was hold on and hope to come out the other side unscathed.

- 3 -

It didn't happen quite that way. Max suffered a rather painful blow to his shoulder from a piece of masonry, and Jacob would wear a long scar down the left side of his face for the rest of his life from a splinter of glass whipped up in the storm.

The vortex started to slow, having completed its task of returning every Dweller to the void they'd erupted from. The spinning tornado dissipated entirely and the Morodai Cornerstone slammed shut in an appropriately dramatic fashion, smoking slightly from the torment it had been subjected to. Silence descended as those left alive and intact took stock.

Lucas Morodai was the first to act.

The Chapter Lord had hidden himself under the marble centre table. With a howl of rage, he leapt over to his golden Cornerstone and gathered it up, letting out another howl - this time of pain as his hand burned on the scorching hot book.

'This doesn't end here!' he snarled at all of them, tucking the book into his robes.

'You're right about that, you raving psycho!' roared Max. 'It's about time somebody took you down a peg or two.' He gathered his power, as did Imelda, Merelie and her father.

Morodai then did what any self respecting villain would do in such a situation: he legged it.

Pulling another book from beneath his long coat, he gave Max one last look of utter hate before flicking the small volume open and disappearing from sight.

'He's got a League Book!' Merelie cried.

'A what?!' said Max, running to where the Chapter Lord had stood. All that remained was the League Book, lying on a pile of rubble. It had 'The Library of Chapter House Morodai' written on the cover.

'Where the hell did he get that?' Max ranted.

'He must have had it on him the whole time,' Jacob said, joining his wife as she climbed from her refuge underneath a row of seats. Borne followed, brushing grit and dust from his massive shoulders.

'Well... that's just not fair!' Max yelled, not quite going so far as to stamp his feet. He picked up the League Book and opened it. 'Take me where he went!' he ordered.

Nothing happened.

'Fabulous, we've let him get away!' he groaned, smacking the League Book against an overturned chair a couple of times in impotent fury.

'See if The Cornerstone can make it work,' Merelie suggested. 'It seems to like bullying its own kind around.'

Max nodded and took The Cornerstone. He put the League Book on the ground, holding it open with a couple of handy rocks and placed the opened Cornerstone next to it, putting his hands on both. 'Corny?' The book gave an eager silver flash. 'Can you make this thing transport me to wherever Morodai's gone?'

Corny flashed in assent.

Max's universe hadn't exploded for quite a while, so it really enjoyed the chance to do it one more time.

- 4 -

The light dimmed and Max found himself in a dark, square room. Rather than stone, it was constructed of iron and looked like the inside of a battleship. Red fingers of rust ran down the dark grey walls and there was a dry, metallic taste in the air.

The Cornerstone had also made the trip and the League Book they'd used was sat on an iron shelf to one side. Next to it were several others, going to places with names Max either couldn't pronounce or didn't like the sound of. He picked up the League Book going back to Carvallen, tucked it into his waistband and crept over to the only doorway out of this strange little room.

He peeked out cautiously.

It was different to the Carvallen Library. There were bookshelves of course, heaving with many volumes, but these were constructed from the same rusting iron as the room Max stood in.

He didn't know it, but Morodai Wordsmiths thought metal was a better conductor for word power than wood. Whether this was true or not was debatable, but they believed it, so did everything they could to incorporate metal into their Wordcraft. They even went as far as coating the books themselves in it.

This was why Morodai Wordsmiths tended to be more muscular than their counterparts in other Chapter Houses; having to lug heavy, iron-clad books around all the time is a good work-out, if nothing else.

There was no mist hanging above Max's head - that must be a peculiarity of Carvallen's Chapter House. In fact, he could clearly see the ceiling, which continued the lovely rusting iron aesthetic. A sickly orange light permeated the racks, coming from an unidentifiable source.

Word shaping should be easier here with all these books.

Max walked out along the aisle, watching for any signs of ambush and peering down through the metal grating at more levels of the Library below. It looked like he was on the top floor of a building that extended at least five or six floors down. He fancied he could see movement below - dark shapes moving between the racks, partially hidden in the tangle of corroded iron.

It's hard to creep about on big, clanking metal grates, so it wasn't too long before Max's presence was discovered.

When attack did come it wasn't from Lucas Morodai, but rather his Library custodians - the equivalent of Garrowain and his ilk. Unlike the wise old men of Carvallen, these custodians were a bunch of evil, dribbling midgets. They wore thick black overalls and round gold metal helmets. Piggy eyes stared out from smooth, round faces and an almost constant stream of spittle clung to their pointy little chins. Max decided he could make short work of the six nasty little dwarves dashing towards him and tried to spin up some Wordcraft before they had a chance to bite his ankles.

There wasn't any… not one drop of power to be pulled from the ranks of books around him. He desperately trawled the area with his mind, but couldn't detect a hint of the stuff anywhere.

The Morodai custodians reached him and started smacking him as hard as they could with their tiny fists. He could have probably fought one off, but six of the nightmarish little goblins had no trouble subduing him with a few well timed slaps across the face and kicks to the shins.

'Stop it! Stop it! Ow! You little sod!' he shouted in pain, dropping to one knee.

They grabbed both his arms and held him down. The dwarves may have been small, but they were also phenomenally strong. Max was stuck fast. Dozens more of the evil critters swarmed onto the walkway, eager to get a front row seat for the upcoming show.

One of the custodians wrenched The Cornerstone from Max and sprinted over to where Lucas Morodai had appeared at the end of the aisle. He took the book from his little servant, the reptilian grin reappearing on his face.

'What's wrong, boy? No power to draw from?' Morodai ambled forward, once again enjoying the chance for a good gloat. 'I wouldn't imagine there would be. This is my Library and I say who gets to tap its power and who doesn't.'

The Chapter Lord bent down and hit Max across the face with The Cornerstone.

'Maybe I should have planned this better,' Max said, spitting blood onto the grating below.

'Yes, maybe you should have.'

Morodai hit him across the face again, droplets of blood splashing The Cornerstone's cover as a fresh cut opened in Max's bottom lip.

'You and your friends ruined a carefully constructed plan. I was very close to having The Chapter Lands in my power forever,' Morodai told him, a scowl on his face.

Max chuckled. 'Yeah well, I'm happy to have screwed up your plans.'

Another smack across the face rocked Max's head to the left, wiping the smile from his face. Morodai then held The Cornerstone out like it was a rotting piece of fish.

'This thing is at the centre of all my problems, isn't it?' he said. 'Carvallen's damned Cornerstone.'

He dropped it, and in a childish display of temper, stamped on the book three times, sending loud echoes through the Library. He kicked it to one side - where it came to rest against a book shelf with the cover open - a large, black boot print stamped across the page.

'I'll think of a way to destroy that filthy thing later, but first... I do believe I'd like to take some of my understandable frustration out on you, Mr Bloom.'

Morodai lifted Max into the air with Wordcraft and held him in place a foot off the ground.

'Now then, of all the Chapter Houses, do you know what makes mine unique?' he asked in a conversational tone.

'Small genitals and a lack of personal hygiene?' Max suggested.

Morodai didn't rise to this. 'What makes it different is that we are the only Chapter House to actively pursue Wordcraft skills that can be used against a human being... and I don't mean the rather uncouth method of throwing word power around until it crashes into a hapless bystander.' Morodai's eyes narrowed as he focused on Max's left arm. 'I mean the far neater and more demanding skill of manipulating the human body to one's will. Once you are skilled at this, it's quite marvellous what can be achieved.'

Morodai's eyes narrowed and the little finger on Max's left hand snapped with an audible crack. He screamed, pain shooting up his arm.

'You see?!' Morodai exulted. 'Such a small effort leads to such a satisfying response! Why batter an opponent with a wall of energy when one can simply snap the bones in his body using far less power? Economy is the key, Mr Bloom!'

To demonstrate again, he broke the ring finger on the same hand. The resulting scream made the Morodai custodians chitter with excitement.

Max swallowed, trying to stop his gorge rising.

'My first mistake was not killing that stupid girl when I had the chance,' Morodai said, standing eye to eye with Max. 'Maybe that would have been better for you as well, yes? You would have lived your life in blissful ignorance, instead of being tortured to death in this far away place.' He leaned right in so his nose almost touched Max. ' ...and make no mistake, you *are* going to die here.'

Max's entire left wrist snapped. The pain was now so intense he blacked out for a second.

'It's not only bone breaking we teach,' Morodai continued. 'The ability to suck the breath from someone's lungs is also a valuable weapon.'

He gestured again and a tight band of pain spread across Max's chest. It was like the first encounter with The Cornerstone's defence mechanism in Farefield library, only much worse. The life was being crushed out of him. Finding a breath was impossible. His ears started to ring with the pressure and in the cloud of agony, it sounded almost like the singing of The Cornerstone choir - accompanying him off this mortal coil with one last rendition of their signature song.

Morodai let go.

The relief was indescribable.

'Not too much, I think,' the Chapter Lord said. 'We don't want the fun spoiled too early.' He tapped his chin thoughtfully. 'Perhaps when I'm done with you, a visit to young Merelie Carvallen won't go amiss. I'd imagine I could have even more fun with her.'

Max tried to struggle free, eliciting a delighted chuckle from his torturer. The band of pain returned, worse this time. Max wanted to scream, but there was no air in his lungs to give it life.

He realised he could hear the choir again… and even through the fog of pain he could tell it really *was* them, not just ringing in his ears. He could hear the cadence in their voices, the harmonies embracing one another as The Cornerstone, still lying trampled on the floor, sang to him as he died.

Max turned his head away from the piercing glare of Morodai's green eyes toward the book. It was pulsing with light now, as if willing him into action.

'No books,' he told it. *'No power with no books.'*

Morodai misinterpreted the gesture.

'Giving up are we, boy?' he said.

Boy.

He wished he'd had the time to do something about that.

'No books though, Corny. Can't be a Wordsmith without books, can I? Nope, I'm just a stupid boy having the life squeezed out of him by a homicidal maniac.'

'I am a book Max, a very special one,' The Cornerstone reminded him in its dry voice.

'I don't think one book will do it, Corny.'

'Correct,' the book agreed. **'But I'm also a doorway, remember? And I can lead you home Max. I can lead you here…'**

The Cornerstone burst into a supernova of silver light, the choir sang their hearts out and the gateway to Earth opened.

Drizzly, cold, boring old Earth.

A world full of books. *Millions* of books, all bursting at the seams with the dreams, hopes and fears of an entire human race. An immense ocean of energy that The Cornerstone had just provided a convenient conduit to.

Glorious power filled Max Bloom from the tips of his aching toes to the top of his bruised head. He swam in the river of Wordcraft The Cornerstone pumped into the library, feeling the pain draining away as the magic sunk into every pore.

Max raised his head slowly, his eyes fixed on the Chapter Lord.

Morodai saw the change, sensed the energy flood into Max Bloom and tried to snap the boy's neck. This had no chance, but Max did feel a slight itching sensation for a fleeting moment. He broke Morodai's hold and dropped to the floor with hands curled into fists.

'Now then, Lucas,' Max spoke in a voice so calm and controlled, Morodai's knees went weak with fear, 'about that boy business...'

The hammer blow that struck Morodai would have crushed every bone in his body to a fine powder if he hadn't already erected a field of protective energy. As it was, he was sent flying back down the metal walkway, bouncing off the book shelves like a pinball.

Max glanced at the crowd of custodians. The bullet headed midgets were propelled at high velocity in a variety of directions, shrieking in terror. They ricocheted off one another and the metal walls surrounding them, creating an almighty din.

All this didn't quite seem enough for Max. He therefore decided to pull the whole Library down around him.

Taking in a deep breath, he let the energy spouting from The Cornerstone soak into every pore of his body, until he could hold out his hands to see silver light flowing and twinkling under the skin. In a scream of rage the Incredible Hulk would have been proud of, Max unleashed a colossal shockwave that billowed out across the ironwork Morodai Library.

The rusting metal book shelves tore and shattered, sending books shooting through the air. The metal walkway ripped apart, buckling and twisting like it was made of tin foil. The iron columns that held one level of the Library above the other warped and crumpled in on themselves, causing the floors to collapse into one another.

Max floated in mid-air on a wave of word power. The walkway beneath him disappeared, joining the rest of the crumbling metalwork in its descent.

This was all stupendously noisy of course, but The Cornerstone choir could still be heard over the cacophony, having apparently bought a stack of Marshall amplifiers for just such an occasion - turned up to 11.

Max then decided it felt a bit stuffy and that he could do with some air. As if somebody had taken a giant, invisible can opener to the ceiling, it ripped open with a shrieking of metal that could be heard a hundred miles away.

Glancing up through the jagged gash he'd created, Max got his first view of the Morodai city beyond the library and saw that he was surrounded by a series of tall, dark towers.

The skies above were leaden grey. He could feel sticky drizzle hitting his face and getting under his hoodie, making his neck wet.

For some reason, he found this quite appropriate.

- 6 -

The teenage Wordsmith glided forward, eyes blazing with silver light, in search of Lucas Morodai. The Cornerstone bobbed along behind him, still supplying energy by the bucket load.

He found his quarry near the back of the cavernous hall, blubbering in terror as his world fell down around him. Morodai cowered behind a barrier of Wordcraft thrown up against the falling wreckage. He hadn't put it up quick enough to prevent one long iron spike pinning him to the floor at the shoulder.

Max drifted down to where the Chapter Lord lay.

'I could destroy you with a glance. You know that, don't you?' he said.

Morodai tried to pull out the shard, but gave up when his remaining strength ran out.

'After all, you'd do that to me, wouldn't you?' Max continued, 'because you think power must be used. I mean, what's the point in having it if you don't *use* it, right? If you don't punish people weaker than you?' He shook his head. 'I'm a seventeen year old kid from a crappy town where nothing ever happens and even I can see that's a bloody stupid way to live. You're nothing but a bully, Morodai.' He crouched and looked the Chapter Lord right in the eye. 'You know what? The problem with being a bastard and showing off how strong you are is that sooner or later someone comes along who's stronger than *you*.'

'Just kill me,' Morodai said, in a weak voice.

'I'm not going to kill you, you idiot. Didn't you hear what I just said? Just because I could turn you into a smear against that wall, doesn't mean I want to.'

'Then what do you intend to do?'

'I'll take you back to Jacob Carvallen. He can decide what to do with you. I'm sure you have courts and trials over here.'

'We do,' Morodai agreed, bowing his head in submission.

'Good. Now, hold still and try not to scream too much.'

Max concentrated on the metal spike, which slowly slid out of the ground and Morodai's shoulder. The Chapter Lord didn't scream, but did go a few shades whiter.

'Thank you,' he gasped as Max tossed it aside.

'Yeah, whatever. I'm just too bloody nice, that's my problem.'

Max took out the League Book that was still tucked into his jeans, ready to transport them both back.

As he did, Morodai – who had been playing possum - whipped out the golden Morodai Cornerstone. 'I won't be standing trial anywhere… *boy!*' he snarled, ripping the book open. Max covered his eyes as light erupted from it.

Lucas Morodai disappeared from existence, leaving Max stunned.

- 7 -

With great care and respect, Borne laid out Elijah's body on the centre table in what remained of the Carvallen Great Hall. He placed a hand on his comrade's chest and offered up a silent prayer to the Writer that he would find peace.

Osgood Draveli's body – his face frozen in a disturbing mask of fear – lay on the floor near Borne's feet. The Arma didn't feel any great desire to move that massive corpse with any dignity, so instead rolled in under the table with one foot, resolving to give his boot a good wash at the first opportunity.

Jacob Carvallen had already started marshalling the newly freed Chapter Guards into some semblance of order. They were now busy rounding up the few Morodai Wordsmiths who hadn't managed to escape in the chaos.

Imelda sat on a pile of rubble with Merelie and Garrowain, who had limped his way up to the Great Hall a few moments ago.

Merelie held the League Book in her hands, willing it to make a sign that Max was coming back.

'He shouldn't have gone like that, not without help,' Imelda said.

'He had no choice. Morodai was getting away,' Merelie argued.

'We must hope Mr Bloom's new found capabilities were enough to save him,' Garrowain said, putting an arm around her.

On cue, the League Book began to glow. Merelie leapt to her feet, put the book on the ground and stepped back.

It flipped open, sent out a pulse of bright blue light and Max Bloom appeared, covered in blood, nursing a broken hand and swearing like a drunk Glaswegian docker. Under his good arm were tucked both the Carvallen and Morodai Cornerstones.

'Max!' Merelie threw her arms round him, eliciting a howl of pain. She noticed his hand and the state of his face.

'Oh my. You're hurt. '

'Yeah, that would be from the torturing,' he told her, swallowing painfully.

Imelda strode over and took one look at his left arm. 'That's going to need splinting, young man. And what do you mean by torture?'

'Your best friend and mine Lucas Morodai thought he'd have some fun snapping bits off me to show how his Wordsmiths are trained to shatter people's bones.' Max sat down with a grateful sigh on a nearby pile of rubble. 'Breaking my wrist was a bit much though, so I decided to pull his house down on top of him. Anybody got an aspirin?'

Garrowain laid a gentle hand on Max's arm, closed his eyes and muttered a few words under his breath. Pleasant warmth flowed over the damaged hand, reducing the pain.

'That should help for the short term,' the old man smiled. 'Our Wordsmiths are trained to heal bones, rather than break them. We'll need to work on it properly before it's fixed, though.'

'Cancel the aspirin,' Max said with a dreamy expression. 'You'll have to teach me how to do that, chief.'

'What happened to Morodai?' Merelie asked, picking up the two Cornerstones.

'A question I'm keen to hear the answer to,' muttered Jacob Carvallen as he joined the group, having left Halia in charge of the clean up operation. He gave Max a sympathetic look when he saw his mangled hand. 'I hope he came off worse than you?'

Max's expression darkened and he told them what had happened, ending with Morodai's escape.

Garrowain took the golden Cornerstone from Merelie. 'This might not be as bad as it seems, Max. Lucas can only return to our world through this book and we will make sure it remains here under careful guard. He's effectively imprisoned himself on the Morodai Earth. By all accounts, it's a miserable place due to his rule, so quite fitting he should be stranded there.'

'Agreed,' Jacob folded his arms. 'The Morodai Cornerstone will stay here and be guarded twenty four hours a day by our most powerful Wordsmiths. If Lucas attempts a return, he will be captured immediately.'

'Was demolishing the entire Library really necessary?' said Imelda, still feeling guilty about what she'd done to the one in Farefield.

'Necessary? No. Fun? You *betcha*,' Max held up his broken hand by way of explanation.

'That's enough questions for the time being,' Merelie announced. 'Max is hurt and needs some medical attention. Father?'

'Yes?'

'Order the Chapter Guards to prepare a litter. I want Max taken to the infirmary as soon as possible.'

Jacob, knowing not to argue when Merelie used such an imperious tone, beckoned over a group of guards and issued them with new orders.

A few minutes later, a bemused Max Bloom - who felt he was quite capable of walking - was being borne aloft by several armoured guards and carried down to the Chapter House infirmary, accompanied by a fussing Merelie Carvallen. Garrowain had also left the clean-up to return to the trashed Library. He took both Cornerstones with him, under strict instructions from Jacob to place them under constant guard.

Merelie's Arma had made off to the barracks to arrange the first watch of Chapter Guards that would take on the job.

This left a rather awkward Jacob Carvallen standing with his estranged sister. They hadn't been alone in the same room for decades and a deathly silence descended. Neither could think of anything constructive to say. Eventually, Imelda felt the need to break the tension.

'Halia seems comfortable in command,' she remarked.

Jacob looked over at where his wife was ordering prisoners escorted to the Chapter cells. 'Yes, she's a fine woman.'

More silence. Jacob kicked a piece of rubble.

'I fancy taxes will have to go up in the short term to pay for repairs to the city,' he forecast.

'Mmmm.'

'The citizens won't be pleased, but they've just been saved from certain death, so shouldn't have grounds to protest too much.'

'Mmmm.'

'You played your part in that, Emerelda… in saving us, I mean.'

'Yes, I know.'

Jacob looked down at his feet. 'I shouldn't have exiled you.'

'No, you shouldn't.'

'It seemed the right thing to do at the time. I was young - father's death still hung heavily on me and you were saying… saying some very controversial things.'

Imelda rolled her eyes. 'Oh for God's sakes, Jacob. I was young and stupid too. We both said and did things we'd later regret.' She patted him on the shoulder.

He gave her a shy smile. 'Will you help me rebuild this place?' Jacob asked.

Emerelda Carvallen sighed. Men could be such little boys sometimes.

Still, she couldn't help but feel a swell of pleasure at the prospect of coming home. She'd miss Earth, but the thrill of being a librarian in an underfunded suburban library had waned in recent years.

Emerelda figured somebody else could be in charge of the overdue fines from now on.

8

Lucas Morodai sighed with relief as his Cornerstone transported him away from Max Bloom and the ruined Library. He wasn't a man that scared easily, but the extent of the boy's power had been colossal.

He'd escaped with his hide more or less intact though, and while there was breath in his body, Lucas Morodai was a threat to anyone, no matter how powerful. He'd lick his wounds and plan a counter-attack - which would begin by dealing with that boy.

Something was wrong.

Morodai had expected to appear in the grand and ostentatious castle he'd built with the sweat and blood of a thousand slaves. Instead, he found himself floating in space - a sickly purple ocean, boiling and churning all around him, punctuated with silver specks of light.

Max would recognise this place. Morodai did too and fear sent a sheet of ice down his spine.

At the periphery of his vision, he saw dark and smoky shapes start to crowd around, examining this new intruder into their cold, dark world. There weren't just hundreds or thousands of them.

There were *millions*.

In his dread, he fancied he could see faces beginning to form - all of them looking extremely angry… and eternally *hungry*.

9

Max Bloom flexed his mended left hand and decided the next time he was a bit under the weather, he'd forego the usual visit to the doctors and pop over here using his new buddy The Cornerstone.

Speaking of which, the book now resided in a stout large chamber in the centre of the Library. Garrowain had given it a rather plush new cushion to sit on, by way of a reward for recent efforts. The Morodai Cornerstone was placed in a box in one alcove of the chamber. Six Carvallen Wordsmiths were stationed outside the chamber, watching for any signs indicating Lucas Morodai's return.

Across The Chapter Lands, some semblance of normality was beginning to reassert itself.

The citizens of all the Houses that came into conflict with Morodai were returning to their homes and beginning the long process of cleaning away the detritus caused by the invasion. Those unlucky enough to have been mind-eaten by the Dwellers were being cared for - though the question of what to do with them in the long run was yet to be answered.

The people who were saved when the Dwellers were ripped out by the Morodai Cornerstone were more fortunate and most were recovering well from their ordeal. None of them were likely to be wearing purple any time soon though. Bethan Falion was one, and after some profuse thanks to Max Bloom, she returned home to oversee the rebuilding of her House. She hadn't mentioned the education of her citizens again, but Emerelda had held a private conversation with the Chapter Lord, sending her away with some hard thinking to do.

All in all, the aftermath was being dealt with as best it could be. The populace could only hope that lessons had been learned and that there wouldn't be a repeat performance of this catastrophic chain of events any time soon. The cleaning bills alone should be enough to put anyone off the idea.

This was all well and good, but Max Bloom couldn't give a monkey's about any of it. He was feeling homesick and anxious to get back as soon as possible. He'd put the finishing touches to an elaborate cover story and was looking forward to giving it an airing with his mother… and the local authorities, if needs be.

Jacob Carvallen and his daughter wanted to stage a meal in his honour. This sounded like a nice idea, but Max was impatient about getting back to his boring little life and persuaded them not to. He knew it would take days to organise it - and he'd have to dress up smart for the bloody thing as well.

Anyway, a great send off didn't seem all that appropriate. He figured he'd probably be back here again sooner or later. Imel - *Emerelda* had made it quite clear he needed some proper tuition in Wordcraft at the Carvallen Academy. He'd started to argue, but stopped when he saw the look on her face. It could have curdled milk.

There was one final problem he had to face before popping off though, in the shape of a pretty sixteen year old girl. Currently, she was holding his hand as they walked through the Library to where Garrowain waited to send him home. Max knew all too well that this was the end of their time together for now, and he was acutely aware it was about the time he should be kissing Merelie goodbye.

She was also aware of this.

Embarrassment levels were at critical mass.

'Will you come back?' she asked, slowing her pace.

'Um... yeah, if that's ok. I wouldn't mind a bit more training in this Wordcraft stuff. I don't want to sneeze one day and blow the top of my head off.'

'I doubt you'd do that,' she smiled. 'But learning how to control it more would be a good idea. I'm sure Garrowain and Emerelda will help.'

Max had said goodbye to the woman who'd retaken her true name some ten minutes earlier. It hadn't been a heartfelt farewell - that just wasn't the nature of their relationship. Instead, she had shaken his hand in a brisk manner and wished him well.

'You're stopping here, then?' he'd asked.

'For the time being. My brother has asked for help in restoring this place and I'd rather avoid any uncomfortable questions from the Farefield police. I'm sure I'll have to come back at some point though, so keep The Cornerstone safe.'

Max had also said goodbye to Borne and the others he'd encountered on this strange and perplexing journey, trying to get it over with as quickly as possible. There was something extremely awkward about saying farewell to people who owed you their lives. The looks of gratitude made him want to curl up and die with embarrassment. He was aware that he'd gained a level of celebrity across The Chapter Lands and wanted to get out of town before people started asking for his autograph.

That just left Merelie and the bloody kiss.

They stopped at the junction leading to The Cornerstone's new home and Max did some feet shuffling.

'I really am grateful for everything you've done, you know,' Merelie said, moving closer and making his beetroot red face go a shade even more scarlet.

'S'not a problem.'

'I'm so glad The Cornerstone chose you,' she said, touching his arm.

'Me too.'

'Come back soon, ok?'

'Will do.'

'Stay safe over there.'

'Okay.'

This wasn't getting her anywhere, so Merelie took control of the situation. She put her hands on both sides of his face and kissed him in such a way that it made all the ridiculous, dangerous and painful stuff he'd been through in the past few weeks *completely* worth it.

- 10 -

Nugget, ever watchful guard dog and farter of epic proportions, sat up on the futon Charlie had dragged down from the spare room and barked. The old man jumped, dropping a garibaldi into his cup of tea.

'Nuggie!' he scolded, trying to fish the biscuit out without burning his fingers.

Nugget barked again and pointed his snout at a place halfway up the bookcase next to Charlie's chair. The Cornerstone was glowing.

'Oh blimey!' Charlie exclaimed and pulled the book out.

He laid it flat on the coffee table just in time for Max Bloom to appear in a blaze of silver light, spilling the plate of biscuits onto the carpet, which had only just been vacuumed. The only one happy about this was Nugget, who knew that anything ending up on the floor was his to eat by default. The black Labrador tucked into the biscuits as Charlie stood up, a huge smile on his face.

'Maxwell!' he cried, putting his arms around his grandson.

'Wotcha, Grandad,' Max replied, beaming back.

'You've been gone for days! Your mother's been having kittens.'

'Really? Crap.'

Max hoped his cover story would hold up under his mother's scrutiny.

'Did the coppers catch up with you?' he asked Charlie.

'They did indeed. I had to do my best doddering old geezer impression. Gas explosions can be quite a handy excuse in the right circumstances. I think they went away happy with the story I regaled them with.'

Nugget, who had wolfed down every garibaldi in sight, now turned his attention to Max, giving him a friendly whack in the testicles.

'I trust everything worked out well?' Charlie asked. 'Order restored, villains vanquished, fair maidens saved and the good folk of The Chapter Lands able to rest easy in their beds once more?'

'Er... yeah, more or less. It was touch and go for a while, but it all got sorted. I pretty much rocked, that was the main thing.'

'Excellent, my boy. I knew you had the wherewithal to rise to the challenge. I expected nothing less of you.' Charlie paused. 'One thing still remains a poser, though.'

'What's that?'

'Yonder strange tome, lying at your feet.'

Max bent down and picked up The Cornerstone. He supposed he should take it back to the library, but without Emerelda there, that probably wouldn't be the best place for it.

'You know what, Grandad?' Max glanced around Charlie's rich collection of books. 'I can't think of a better place for it than right here.'

'Then by all means, young man,' Charlie replied with a flourish, 'place it somewhere appropriate and fetch more biscuits from the pantry, if you'd be so kind!'

Max looked up and saw a space perfect for The Cornerstone. He slid it in next to Jack London's Call of the Wild.

The Cornerstone seemed happy with this, as it glowed softly for a moment, before the light dimmed, and it became just another book in a world of millions.

The End

Max Bloom's story continues in

WORDSMITH: THE CORNERSTONE BOOK 2

About the author:

Nick Spalding is an author who, try as he might, can't seem to write anything serious. He's worked in the communications industry his entire life, mainly in media and marketing. As talking rubbish for a living can get tiresome (for anyone other than a politician), he thought he'd have a crack at writing comedy fiction - with an agreeable level of success so far, it has to be said. Nick lives in the South of England with his fiancée. He is approaching his forties with the kind of dread usually associated with a trip to the gallows, suffers from the occasional bout of insomnia, and still thinks Batman is cool.

Nick Spalding is one of the top ten bestselling authors in eBook format in 2012.

You can find out more about Nick by following him on **Twitter** or by reading his blog **Spalding's Racket**.